P9-DTY-662

KILT AT THE HIGHLAND GAMES

Books by Kaitlyn Dunnett

Kilt Dead

Scone Cold Dead

A Wee Christmas Homicide

The Corpse Wore Tartan

Scotched

Bagpipes, Brides, and Homicides

Vampires, Bones, and Treacle Scones

Ho-Ho-Homicide

The Scottie Barked at Midnight

Kilt at the Highland Games

Published by Kensington Publishing Corporation

KILT AT THE HIGHLAND GAMES

KAITLYN DUNNETT

KENSINGTON BOOKS
www.kensingtonbooks.com

KENSINGTON BOOKS are published by

Kensington Publishing Corp.
119 West 40th Street
New York, NY 10018

All Kensington titles, imprints and distributed lines are available at special quantity discounts for bulk purchases for sales promotion, premiums, fund-raising, educational or institutional use. Special book excerpts or customized printings can also be created to fit specific needs. For details, write or phone the office of the Kensington Special Sales Manager: Kensington Publishing Corp., 119 West 40th Street, New York, NY, 10018. Attn. Special Sales Department. Phone: 1-800-221-2647.

Library of Congress Card Catalogue Number: 2016933894

ISBN-13: 978-0-7582-9291-9
ISBN-10: 0-7582-9291-0
First Kensington Hardcover Edition: August 2016

eISBN-13: 978-0-7582-9292-6
eISBN-10: 0-7582-9292-9
Kensington Electronic Edition: August 2016

10 9 8 7 6 5 4 3 2 1

Printed in the United States of America

KILT AT THE HIGHLAND GAMES

Chapter One

An overweight Maine coon cat dozed in an open bedroom window, his bulk pressed against the screen so that the gentle breeze of the summer night could ruffle his long yellow fur. With a start, he went on alert. A moment later, he leapt from the windowsill to the top of the dresser and from there to the foot of the bed. He landed squarely on Liss MacCrimmon Ruskin's bare legs.

The impact, not to mention the slash of sharp claws, jerked her out of a sound sleep. On autopilot, she rolled over, reared up, and gave Lumpkin a none-too-gentle shove to the floor. She was already sinking back down onto the mattress, this time tugging the top sheet over her, when the insubstantial feeling that something was "not right" stopped her.

She blinked, bleary-eyed, at her surroundings. Shoving a tangled swath of dark brown, shoulder-length hair out of her face, she peered at the illuminated dial of the bedside clock. It was 3:35 in the morning. For some reason, she'd thought it would be later.

Except for the shapes of the windows, backlit by the streetlights that dotted the perimeter of the Moosetookalook town square, Liss could see very little in the darkness of the room she shared with her husband. The two front windows were raised as far as they would go, since Liss had been taught at an early age that fresh air was one of nature's best sleep aids. She had never had any reason to doubt that small bit of folk wisdom.

The side window held an air conditioner. It emitted a low hum when it was running, but there had been no need to turn it on after a day when the temperature never topped seventy-five degrees. Although it was now mid-July, there had been only a handful of nights that required extra cooling. This *was* Maine, after all.

Liss listened hard but heard only the tick of Lumpkin's claws on the hardwood floor and Dan's soft snoring. If a burglar was creeping about downstairs, he was doing so with remarkable stealth.

Cautiously, she sniffed. A tantalizingly familiar smell teased her nostrils. After a second, even in her groggy state, she identified it as wood smoke. Odd, she thought. Lots of people heated with wood or pellet stoves, but not at this time of year. A bonfire? There had been one to celebrate the Fourth of July. This was—she fumbled for a date—the seventeenth of the month.

With an abrupt movement, Liss swung her legs over the side of the bed and stood up. There was something wrong with the streetlights. They were flickering. The most likely explanation had her stumbling toward the windows, her heart in her throat. She almost fell when she tripped over a cat—not Lumpkin this time but Glenora, whose long black fur made her nearly invisible at night. Liss reached her goal just as an antiquated air-raid siren went off at ear-splitting decibels.

Glenora took off like a shot. Liss clapped her hands over her ears. The whistle wound slowly up to full volume and died away again, but it would keep repeating until someone shut off the power. The town of Moosetookalook used this means to signal emergencies of all kinds, but nine times out of ten it meant there was a fire. Dreading what she would see, Liss looked out.

She made an inarticulate sound of distress at the sight that met her eyes. It *was* a fire, and it was the bookstore on the far side of the square that was burning.

For a few crucial seconds, her mind simply refused to accept reality. Gripping the window frame for support, she squeezed her eyes tightly shut and tried to convince herself that she was still asleep, that this was just another nightmare.

Eight months earlier, Liss, Dan, and their friend Sherri Campbell had been, albeit briefly, trapped inside a burning house. That fire, too, had broken out in the middle of the night. It had been weeks afterward before Liss had been able to sleep soundly again.

Her eyes popped open in time to see flames shoot up behind the first-floor windows of Angie's Books. Angie! Where was Angie? Where were her children? The bookstore owner lived in the apartment above her shop with sixteen-year-old Beth and twelve-year-old Bradley.

The Moosetookalook Fire Department was located right next door, housed in part of the town's redbrick municipal building. The overhead door had already been raised. As Liss watched, unable to move, unable to look away, the truck pulled out, maneuvering so that it could get closer to the burning building.

More volunteer firefighters arrived on the scene as the siren continued to wail. Two of them hauled one of the fire hoses into position and aimed a steady stream of water at the blaze. Farther down the street and on the green, ordinary citizens had already begun to gather to watch in horrified fascination as the bookstore was engulfed in flames. There was no hope of saving it. Paperbacks, hardcovers, magazines—they were all extremely flammable.

Liss squinted, searching frantically for Angie and Beth and Bradley. She couldn't spot them anywhere. Her chest rose and fell in time with her agitated breathing. What if they were still inside? What if they were trapped?

Struggling for calm, Liss told herself that they must have escaped. Angie was scrupulous about changing her smoke-alarm batteries. She and her kids would have had plenty of time to get out. Heck, Angie was probably the one who'd alerted the fire department.

But where was she? Where were Beth and Bradley?

An overwhelming need to make certain they were safe broke the spell that had held Liss motionless. She pushed away from the window. On legs that felt like rubber, her brain as sluggish as molasses, she headed for the bedroom door.

"Clothes!"

Dan's shout was accompanied by the sudden flood of light from a bedside lamp. Liss stopped in her tracks to look down at herself. She couldn't go outside dressed as she was. Her lightweight summer nightshirt barely covered the essentials.

Dan, who'd had the good sense to start dressing as soon as he rolled out of bed, reached for the jeans she'd left draped over a chair and tossed them at her. She fumbled the catch and had to stoop to pick them up off the floor.

Although he had to be as shaken as she was, Dan was in better control of himself. Clothing in place, he jammed his feet into running shoes, barely taking time to tie the laces before he moved past her into the hallway.

Liss scrambled into her jeans. Her hands shook so badly

that she had trouble managing the simple task of getting a T-shirt out of a drawer and pulling it over her head. Slipping on sandals nearly defeated her. It seemed to take forever to make herself decent. By the time she reached the foot of the stairs, the front door stood open and Dan was halfway across the town square.

Dan raced past the playground with its jungle gym, slide, merry-go-round, and swings without giving it a second glance. The gazebo-style bandstand and the flower beds weren't on his radar, either. He didn't even stick to the paths. Sighting on the flagpole, he cut across the grass.

The siren, which fell silent just as he reached the municipal building, had done its job, alerting the neighbors. Summoning volunteer firefighters from every corner of the village had been done by pager. Trucks from neighboring towns would be on their way to help, but it would take at least another quarter hour for them to arrive.

A few months earlier, Dan had started the mandatory training required by the state before a person could serve as a volunteer firefighter. He had his CPR certification, but he wasn't even a quarter of the way through the 244 hours of class time, nor had he yet taken the CPAT—the Candidate Physical Ability Test that required him to complete eight components while wearing fifty pounds of equipment and racing the clock. He was confident he would pass every test with flying colors. He'd worked in construction for years and had the muscles to prove it. But the cold, hard truth of the matter was that, even in a pinch, the most he was allowed to do at the moment was work the pump.

Every little bit helps, he told himself as he ducked into the now empty bay and headed for the lockers where spare protective gear and helmets were stored. He'd be freeing someone else to do more complicated tasks. Even so, he berated himself at every step for not having volunteered years ago. He'd be able to do so much more now if he'd only found the time to start his training earlier.

As soon as he was suited up, Dan headed back out. He was just in time to catch sight of two similarly outfitted men, their faces hidden behind self-contained breathing apparatus, making their way back down the stairs at the side of Angie's building. He took it as a good sign that they weren't carrying any unconscious bodies. Then again, if Angie and the kids were already out, why had the firefighters risked going up there at all?

Just to make sure, he shouted a question. "Clear?"

Following much the same route through the town square that her husband had taken, but at a slower pace, Liss changed course only when she reached the flagpole. She veered left at that point, in order to end up directly across from the bookstore. At the narrow strip of sidewalk, Mike Jennings, a part-time Moosetookalook police officer, stepped in front of her.

"Don't come any further, Liss." His words were audible only because the siren had finally been turned off. "You'll just get in the way."

Mike wasn't much taller than Liss. At five-foot-nine, she towered over most of the women and a fair number of the men who populated Moosetookalook. Mike, however, was in uniform. He spoke with authority. More than that, he was right.

"Have you seen the Hogencamps?" she asked. "Did they get out safely?"

"Someone just went up to check the apartment."

He meant his words to be reassuring, but Liss saw the same anxiety in his eyes that she felt in her heart. She had just started to ask another question when his attention shifted to an over-eager civilian trying to cross Main Street to get closer to the blaze.

"Hey! You there! Back off!"

The fire burned hot, forcing Liss to retreat a few more steps and ignore the KEEP OFF THE GRASS signs. Ominous crackling sounds followed her, as did the eerie glow given off by the flames. The building was going to be a total loss.

Eyes swimming with unshed tears, Liss turned away from the appalling sight. She couldn't help fight the fire, but she could offer shelter to the Hogencamp family. She scanned nearby faces, once again searching for Angie and her children in a crowd that grew larger with every passing minute. She recognized most of the people she saw, but nowhere did she spot the familiar features of the three she most wanted to find. Neither could she pick out their voices in the general babble, although she had no difficulty recognizing others.

"Good thing the municipal building is built of brick."

That was Dolores Mayfield, the Moosetookalook librarian, sounding just a tad smug. The municipal building not only housed the fire department and town office, but also the police station and the public library. The latter took up the entire second floor.

Dolores's words forcefully reminded Liss that all the houses around the square, including her own, were white clapboard structures, quaint old Victorians that would be at risk if the fire spread. Most of them had started out as single-family dwellings. Nowadays, the house where Liss and Dan lived still was, but most of the rest had been remodeled to house shops of various sorts downstairs and apartments above.

Liss saw that the firefighters had already begun wetting down the three buildings closest to Angie's Books—the house behind it; Gloria Weir's Ye Olde Hobbie Shoppe on Elm, a street running along one side of the bookstore; and the old funeral parlor, currently the home of the Moosetookalook Historical Society Museum, which sat kitty-corner to the bookstore, facing the west side of the town square.

Above the racket created by dozens of voices, all talking at once, Liss heard someone call her name. She turned to see her aunt, Margaret MacCrimmon Boyd, jogging toward her.

Tufts of silvery-gray hair bouncing, Margaret came from the direction of her apartment above Moosetookalook Scottish Emporium, the gift shop Liss owned and operated on the Pine Street side of the square. Margaret hadn't taken time to dress before she rushed outside. Her bright red velour bathrobe only partially covered the hot pink cotton pajamas beneath.

"Have you seen Angie and the kids?" Fear made Margaret's voice shrill. "Are they safe?"

Liss's lips trembled. "I've been looking. I can't find them."

Margaret leaned forward, hands on her knees. "Give me a second to catch my breath."

She was only sixty-five and in good shape for her age. After a moment, she straightened.

"I was the one who called it in. The dogs woke me. I could see flames behind the bookstore's display window from my place. I'd have been out here sooner but when the siren went off it spooked Dandy and Dondi."

Margaret pronounced it si-reen, as did many of the locals. Ordinarily, that would have made Liss smile. Not this time.

If Margaret had alerted the fire department, did that mean Angie had not done so? Liss looked back at the burning building, her sense of dread deepening as she stared at the flames. Smoke drifted toward them, hanging over the scene like a pall. She bit her lip in a futile effort to hold back tears, wishing that image had not been the first one to spring to mind.

The horrific possibility that her friends might have been trapped inside the burning building had never been far from her thoughts. Liss's stomach twisted into knots. Despite the warmth of the night and the heat of the fire, she shivered.

Stu Burroughs, who owned the ski shop next door to the Emporium, materialized beside them. Significantly more winded than Margaret had been, he had to cough a few times before he could speak. "A couple of the firemen went up the outside stair. Broke down the door. They say there's no one in the apartment."

"Thank God!" Liss's sense of relief was so intense that she threw her arms around Stu and hugged him. It was an awkward embrace. He was a good seven inches shorter than she was and as round as a pumpkin.

Squirming out of her grasp, Stu sputtered in protest. "You don't have to smother me!"

Liss straightened, unrepentant. Stu might be a curmudgeon on the surface, but she'd known him for years. A soft heart beat beneath all that crustiness. Why else would he have gone out of his way to reassure them that no one had been trapped in the Hogencamps' apartment?

Surreptitiously, she wiped the heel of her hand across her wet eyes. Although losing the bookstore was bad, it could be rebuilt. There was no bringing back lost lives.

Margaret's brows pinched together in confusion. "If they

weren't there, then where are they? What if they tried to escape through the shop instead of taking the outside stairs?"

Stu ran his fingers through his salt-and-pepper hair and looked surprised when they came away streaked with soot. "No need to borrow trouble," he said in a gruff voice.

He was reluctant to contemplate new horrors, but Liss heard the worry beneath his words. They all knew that if Angie and her children had gone down into the bookstore, they might have been trapped inside the burning building.

Unbidden, memories of her own recent experience rushed back. Liss pushed the worst of them away, unwilling to relive the terror of those endless minutes when she'd thought they would never be able to escape.

A resounding crash made her jump and drew her attention back to the fire. The structure was now fully engulfed in flames. The streams of water volunteers were directing at the fast-burning blaze didn't appear to be doing any good at all.

Margaret slid one arm around Liss's waist. "I'm sure we'll find them safe and sound. You just wait and see. They'll have taken shelter in the town office or the police station. Or maybe they went to Patsy's."

She gestured toward Patsy's Coffee House, located just beyond the far side of the municipal building. The interior lights were on. Patsy always got up well before daylight. She usually started her daily baking around three o'clock in the morning.

"We could go look," Liss suggested.

Margaret agreed, but reaching the café was easier said than done. The town square was full of people who had come out to watch the fire, making it difficult to move. The crush only got worse when they were ordered to fall back to the other side of the monument to the Civil War dead.

Slowly, Liss and her aunt eased through the crowd, taking a circuitous route that would bring them out on Birch Street, right in front of Liss's house. Patsy's place faced Main Street, looking straight down Birch.

Almost everyone they encountered on their way was a friend, a neighbor, or a casual acquaintance. Liss noticed only two people who were complete strangers. One was a barrel-chested man with bulldog features, the other a tall, dignified-looking older gentleman who sported a neatly trimmed little beard and carried a walking stick.

"Guests at The Spruces?" she asked Margaret. The luxury hotel on the outskirts of Moosetookalook village was owned by Dan's father, Joe Ruskin.

"Probably." Although Margaret was Joe's events coordinator, she didn't come in contact with everyone who booked a room.

Ghouls, Liss thought. The local people were there out of concern for a neighbor and friend. The only reason for anyone else to be at the scene of a fire in the middle of the night was rude curiosity.

At last, they emerged on Birch Street. A sharp crack—far louder than the earlier crash—signaled the collapse of the roof beam. Liss couldn't stop herself from looking back. Sparks flew upward as the walls came down, destroying everything in their path.

After her own narrow escape, when they'd watched the house they'd been staying in burn to the ground, she had been overwhelmed by a sense of relief because she and Dan and Sherri had made it out alive. That had been all that mattered, since she'd had no emotional attachment to the place where they'd been staying. She had lost nothing more than a few insignificant personal possessions to the fire.

For Angie and her children, this would be a thousand

times worse. To watch both home and business go up in flames would send anyone into a state of shock. They were probably sheltering somewhere, dazed and grief-stricken. The last thing on Angie's mind would be reassuring their neighbors that they were safe. It might not occur to her for hours yet that Liss and Margaret and other friends would be worried sick about her.

Liss dragged her gaze away from the fire scene. With Margaret beside her, she took to the middle of Birch Street to walk back to Main. Angie and the kids would be at Patsy's Coffee House, she told herself, but she was already close enough to see through the front windows of the café. There was no one visible, not even Patsy herself.

"Let's try the town office." Margaret caught her arm to pull her in that direction. "There are lights on in there, too."

Since the bay for the fire truck was on the far side of the main entrance to the municipal building, Liss and Margaret could enter without getting in the way of the firefighters. Liss was not unduly surprised to find Moosetookalook's longtime town clerk, Francine Noyes, at her usual post behind a wide wooden counter. Even though it was hours yet until the town office officially opened, she looked crisp and professional . . . and out of sorts.

The reason was obvious. Francine wasn't alone. Leaning across the counter in a manner that could only be characterized as aggressive, was Jason Graye, one of Liss's least favorite people. A few years earlier, shady real-estate dealings had cost him his seat as a town selectman, but he'd somehow managed to reclaim it in the last election.

Graye straightened at the sound of the door opening. His beak of a nose was perfect for looking down, and the thrust of his jaw marked him as pugnacious. Francine's relief at the interruption was obvious.

"Liss. Margaret. Something I can do for you?"

"We're hoping you know where Angie, Beth, and Bradley are," Margaret said.

Francine's face fell. "I haven't heard where they went. Isn't it a shame? That was such a nice old building, and the bookstore was such an asset to the community."

"And now it's just an eyesore," Graye cut in. "I'm going to recommend that the town take the property by eminent domain. It will make a good location for a parking lot."

Graye's callousness both angered and offended Liss. She glared at him. "You'd better watch that sentimental streak. Someone's liable to accuse you of having a heart."

If her insults bothered him, it wasn't apparent. Ignoring her, he barked an order at Francine. "Send that notice out ASAP." Then he brushed past Liss and Margaret and left the building.

Francine sent a mock salute after him. Under other circumstances, Liss would have laughed.

"Has anyone seen them?" she asked the town clerk. "Do we know for certain that they got out safely?"

"I'm so sorry," Francine said. "All I know is that there was no one in the apartment. I just assumed . . ." Her voice trailed off in distress.

"I bet Patsy knows where they are," Margaret said in an overly hearty voice. "She and Angie are good friends."

Francine cheered up at her confident statement, but Liss's sense of foreboding only deepened. She dragged her feet, her heart heavy, as they walked the few dozen feet from the municipal building to the coffee shop.

The heavenly aromas of freshly brewed coffee and baking cinnamon buns rose up to greet Liss as soon as Margaret opened the door, almost canceling out the smell of smoke. Overhead, a bell tinkled, causing Patsy, the tall, cadaverously thin genius-in-the-kitchen who owned the place, to poke her head out from the back to see who had come in.

"Help yourself to coffee," she hollered when she recognized them. She was already ducking back into the kitchen when Liss hailed her.

"Patsy, wait! Have you seen Angie since the fire broke out?"

"No." The answer was short and short-tempered. "No reason I should have, and I haven't got time to chat. I'm busy."

"She doesn't seem worried," Margaret remarked.

Liss had to agree, but she wasn't sure that meant anything. She'd so hoped to find Angie and Beth and Bradley by now. The fact that she hadn't left her feeling frustrated and even more worried than she had been earlier. What if the firemen had missed seeing them? What if—?

"They'll turn up," Margaret said, cutting short Liss's imaginings. She busied herself pouring coffee into two mugs and doctoring it the way they liked it. "They're somewhere safe," she added as she carried their drinks to one of Patsy's small tables and sank gratefully into a chair. "I'm certain of it."

"Of course they are." Liss joined her aunt.

She lifted her mug to her lips and took a long, reviving sip of the fragrant brew. As she did so, she caught sight of her reflection in the window glass. Her hair stood out in all directions. She supposed she looked no more odd than most of the people in the town square. When the fire alarm went off in the middle of the night, good grooming was the least of anyone's worries. Margaret didn't seem at all bothered to still be in her nightclothes, her light gray hair uncombed and her face devoid of makeup.

Could that be why Angie was staying out of sight—

good, old-fashioned embarrassment? If so, then she'd turn up as soon as she'd found something decent to wear.

Liss held to that belief until her mug was empty. Then she convinced herself that Angie just needed some time alone to process the scope of the disaster. That reasoning lasted until the fire had been reduced to a few smoldering hot spots.

She'd run out of excuses by the time the sun came up. The bright morning light revealed the full extent of the devastation. It also exposed the stark reality that Angie Hogencamp and her children were nowhere to be found.

Chapter Two

After staring long and hard at the wreckage of what had once been a friendly, thriving business, Sherri Campbell averted her eyes. She wished she could avoid inhaling the stench that easily, but the smell of smoke hung heavily in the sultry morning air. At Sherri's side, Officer Mike Jennings wrapped up his report.

"This is *so* not good," Sherri muttered.

"Someone from the fire marshal's office should be here soon."

"I'm glad we're not responsible for that part of the investigation."

Even the slight possibility of finding human remains in the ashes sent a shudder through Sherri's petite frame. She was usually the first to appreciate the dark sense of humor that kept cops from making themselves crazy in no-win situations, but today none of the old jokes about "crispy critters" seemed at all funny. At last report, no one had seen Angie, Beth, or Bradley Hogencamp since well before the fire.

Toughen up, she told herself. How would it look if Moosetookalook's duly appointed chief of police tossed her cookies in public? Her looks were enough of a handicap. Even when she was in uniform and wearing a gun, some people still looked first at her blond hair and curves and had trouble taking her seriously as a law-enforcement professional. It didn't help that she barely topped five-foot-two and was the mother of three young children.

"Are you officially back at work?" Mike asked.

"Looks like it. My maternity leave would have run out on Monday anyhow."

Sherri had been looking forward to spending one more obligation-free weekend with Pete and the kids. There was no way she could do that now. She was faced with what she hoped was a missing persons case—the alternative was too awful to contemplate. Add in possible—make that probable—arson and there was no way she could justify staying home while other officers did her job. Time to take charge.

"Can you put in another hour or two, Mike? Someone needs to keep an eye on the place to make sure no one goes in and starts poking around."

"I'm good. I don't go on patrol again until tomorrow."

Sherri studied his face for signs of fatigue. Throughout her maternity leave, Mike Jennings had worked a lot of extra hours for Moosetookalook while also holding down a full-time job with the Carrabassett County Sheriff's Department. Alert green eyes met her baby blues. His were bloodshot from all the smoke, but otherwise he looked no worse for wear. Satisfied, Sherri was prepared to trust her newest hire's word for it when he said that he knew his limits.

He'd been hired by the county on the strength of recommendations by Sherri and her husband, Pete, who was a deputy sheriff for the county. Helping Mike find a new job had only seemed fair, since Sherri had been responsible, albeit indirectly, for the loss of his previous post. She and Pete had also helped him find a place to live. In January, when he'd pulled up stakes and moved to Moosetookalook, he'd taken over the lease on their apartment above Carrabassett County Wood Crafts, Dan Ruskin's storefront on the town square.

"I'll leave you to it," Sherri said, thinking that the fact that newcomers were so readily welcomed into their small, close-knit community made the possibility that the fire had been deliberately set all the more heinous.

She had already sent out a BOLO for Angie, Beth, and Bradley. Her next task was to start canvassing the area. With any luck, she'd find a witness who had seen what happened at Angie's Books right before the fire started. If she was really fortunate, the request to "be on the lookout" for the Hogencamps would also produce results.

They weren't wanted for any crime, but the alert would have fellow police officers keeping their eyes peeled for the three missing persons while they went about their normal day's work. Sherri had supplied detailed descriptions and photographs. She had every reason to be optimistic . . . except that she couldn't think of any good reason why Angie and her kids hadn't already turned up.

The bookstore had faced Main Street, looking out over one corner of the town square. By rights, it should have been located on the corner of Main and Ash, since Ash Street formed the western side of the square, but Moosetookalook had developed without the benefit of a preconceived street plan. Ash stopped where it met Main. Elm began a few yards to the west, just past Angie's Books.

Sherri had intended to start her quest for information

by circling the town square, stopping at each of the buildings that faced it. She changed her mind when she took another look at the smoldering ruin.

The bookstore's nearest neighbor was a light yellow house on Elm Street. Built in the 1920s, it belonged to an elderly couple, the Permutters. Since Moosetookalook's population was just a bit more than a thousand souls, Sherri knew them, if only slightly. She was also well aware that both Kate and Alex Permutter were hard of hearing. Even so, they could scarcely have been unaware of the fire. As she approached the porch, Sherri saw that soot discolored a large section of one side of the house.

It was Kate who answered the door, after Sherri banged on it for several minutes with a knocker shaped like a rose. Once she'd gestured for Sherri to come into the foyer, she made the universal sign for "wait a minute" before disappearing down the hallway. From the living room, a TV blared, the volume turned up to screech.

"There," Kate said as she returned, fluffing her hair. "Sorry for the delay, but I had to put my ears in."

Belatedly, Sheri caught on. Kate meant her hearing aids.

Raising her voice as they entered the living room, Kate addressed her husband. "Alex! Turn that thing down!"

"What?"

Kate rolled her eyes. "Stubborn old fool. He refuses to admit he's going deaf."

While Sherri tried to hide a smile, Kate commandeered the clicker and turned off the television.

"Hey!" Alex yelped. He might have said more had he not caught sight of Sherri. Ever the gentleman, he lowered the footrest of his recliner and tried to stand. "Sorry. I didn't know we had company."

"Please, don't get up. I just have a couple of questions to ask you."

"Say again? You young people are always whispering. It's not natural."

Sherri raised her voice until she was very nearly shouting. "I'd like to ask you some questions about last night."

After that, the interview proceeded smoothly, although Sherri did have to repeat almost every question two or three times for Alex's benefit.

Midway through the interview, they were joined by an elderly striped cat. It ignored both Kate and Sherri and tottered straight to Alex. He picked it up, raised the footrest again, and deposited it in the feline-shaped dent between his knees.

"We were both sound asleep until the fire siren woke us," Kate Permutter recalled. "I was terrified when we realized it was the bookstore that was burning. We were afraid sparks would set our house on fire, too."

"Did you go out into the square?"

"Oh, no. We were too busy. We bundled Hector there into his cat carrier, grabbed a few irreplaceable photo albums and a cookie jar, and took refuge in the car, just in case we had to run for it."

Sherri didn't bother to ask Kate why she had taken the cookie jar. It was a well-documented fact that people would try to save the most unlikely items during an emergency evacuation.

"Did you happen to notice when Angie and her children left? Your side windows had a good view of the back of her building."

Kate looked surprised. "Do you mean to say they weren't at home when the fire started?"

"It doesn't appear so."

"Well, imagine that! I don't know whether to be pleased or saddened. Do they even know about it?"

Sherri hesitated. "It doesn't appear so. Did you see them yesterday?"

Kate shook her head. "Not that I remember, but we wouldn't necessarily have noticed. The view from our kitchen windows is . . . *was* of the side of the garage. Once in a while I'd see one of the kids out in the yard, but it's a pretty small lot, and they never set up a grill or anything."

Sherri had noticed the remains of the garage as she'd walked to the Permutters' house. If Angie's car had been inside, there should have been some sign of it. Metal burned, but not completely. She made a mental note to look up the make, model, and license plate and add that information to the BOLO.

"So," she continued, getting ready to wrap up, "you don't know Angie all that well?"

"Not really," Kate admitted. "The bookstore kept her pretty busy. Oh, she was friendly enough, but she didn't socialize with us. Well, that's only to be expected, really. We're a generation older than she is, and to her children we must seem like a couple of fossils." She chuckled and sent her husband an affectionate look.

When Alex had confirmed everything his wife said, Sherri left, moving on to the next three houses along the east side of Elm Street. No one was home at any of them. That didn't surprise her. Despite all the tumult in the wee hours, this was still a Friday morning. Most people, unless they were retired like the Permutters or lived above their businesses, had jobs to go to elsewhere.

Crossing to the west side of Elm, Sherri didn't bother to

stop at the Congregational church. Next in line as she walked back toward the town square were two newer, one-story buildings. The first was a dentist's office, and the second housed an eye doctor. Even during daylight hours, neither was open every day, and no one occupied either building at night.

Next door to the eye doctor was Ye Olde Hobbie Shoppe, which sold supplies for all kinds of hobbies and crafts. There Sherri did stop. The owner, Gloria Weir, lived upstairs. More importantly, from both her store and her apartment she'd have had an excellent view of Angie's garage.

"This whole place stinks of smoke," Gloria complained the moment Sherri walked into the shop. The wide smile for which she was known was conspicuously absent in the wake of the fire. She looked downright woebegone.

Sherri took a look around. Gloria's stock included embroidery silks and fabrics. She supposed such things did hold onto smells, but surely they could be washed. She wasn't so sure that the paper materials used for scrapbooking could be salvaged.

"Did you see anything last night?" she asked the ginger-haired shopkeeper.

"Oh, gee. Let me think. How about a big honking fire?"

Sherri ignored the sarcasm. "I mean before the fire. Anything suspicious?"

"I was asleep." Gloria's eyes narrowed. "Are you telling me that fire was set?"

"It's too soon to tell, although naturally in a case like this the municipal fire inspector, as directed by the state's attorney general, notified the office of the state fire marshal. An investigator will be here soon to take a look at the scene and make the call."

Gloria's already pale complexion went even whiter. "That's all we need—a firebug."

Sherri tried to think what she could say to reassure Gloria. She wasn't used to seeing her like this. Most of the time, she was a self-assured go-getter, full of inventive ideas and active in the Moosetookalook Small Business Association.

"Chances are it will turn out to have been an accident."

"What does Angie say happened?"

And there it was—the central problem. "We're not quite sure where she and the children are. When is the last time you saw them?"

Gloria's eyes widened. "They weren't . . . please tell me they—" She was visibly shaken by the possibility that her neighbors had perished in the fire.

"No bodies have been found." Sherri refused to add "yet" to that statement. "So? Did you see Angie or Beth or Bradley yesterday?"

"I don't think so. It's been a couple of days at least. I can . . . I *could* see the side of Angie's building through my windows. Their garage faced this way, but most of the time they went in and out through the front of the shop."

Sherri peered out through the windows Gloria indicated, trying to picture the building as it had been. Only a narrow strip of grass, now blackened by smoke and much trampled, flanked the sidewalk on Elm. Angie's driveway had extended for barely a car-length before it reached the overhead door of her garage.

"I wish I could be more help," Gloria said, "but I didn't see all that much of Angie. I'm stuck here at the shop most of the time. She was stuck in the bookstore. Mostly I saw her at MSBA meetings. You know how it is with a one-person business. There's not a lot of time for visiting the neighbors."

Sherri did know. After reminding Gloria to give her a call if she remembered anything that might help the investigation, she left Ye Olde Hobbie Shoppe and crossed Main Street, entering the museum by the side entrance. Once upon a time, when the large house had been a funeral parlor, bodies had been taken in and out through this door.

As she'd expected, no one had been around at three in the morning.

She left through the front door, noticing as she did so that an investigator from the fire marshal's office had arrived and was talking to Mike Jennings. She didn't imagine that they needed her input. If they did, she had her portable radio attached to her belt. Mike could give her a holler.

Three buildings faced the town square on each side. The one in the middle of the Ash Street block was the jewelry store owned by Fred and Nicole Lounsbury. Some years back, they'd retired after successful careers in the big city corporate world to move to Maine and open a small business. They specialized in jewelry made by local artisans from two Maine gemstones, tourmaline and garnet. More significant from Sherri's point of view was that they lived above their shop. She was still hoping to find someone who'd seen something in the wee hours.

Once again, the story was the same. Fred and Nicole had been asleep until the fire alarm went off. Like Kate Permutter, Nicole wore hearing aids. Nothing short of the siren would have awakened her.

"Do you remember when you last saw Angie or her children?" Sherri asked.

Nicole thought it was a week earlier. Fred was sure he'd caught sight of young Bradley on Wednesday, racing across the town square with some of his friends.

"Do you know the friends' names?" Sherri asked, but there the couple could not help her.

She moved on to the corner of Ash and Pine and entered the post office, which occupied the front half of the first floor. In the back was Betsy Twining's Clip and Curl. Sherri herself had once lived in the second-floor apartment, right after she and Pete had first been married and before they'd moved into the apartment Mike now occupied.

Julie Simpson was not much older than Sherri, but she had been Moosetookalook's postmaster for nearly ten years. A sturdily built brunette with a loud, nasal voice, she had come to Maine from New York on vacation, met Will "Simple" Simpson on a nearby ski slope, and never left. She was delighted to see Sherri walk in.

"Finally! Someone who knows what's really going on."

"I only wish that were true." Since she was there, Sherri collected the police department's mail and her own. Moosetookalook was too small a place to rate door-to-door delivery.

"Give me a break," Julie wheedled. "You must know something."

"I know I've got three missing people and a suspicious fire, but that can't be news to you."

Julie gave a raucous laugh. "Hardly."

"I know you weren't here at that hour, Julie, but is there any chance that a mail truck was making a delivery just before three in the morning?"

"The mail comes in early, but not that early."

A witness at the crucial time had been too much to hope for, Sherri supposed, and the apartment upstairs was currently empty again. No joy there, either.

She continued south along Ash, past the end of the town

square, to canvass a few more houses, but her efforts yielded only more of the same—a frustrating dearth of information. Backtracking brought her to the section of Pine Street that paralleled the south side of the square. All three businesses on Pine had apartments upstairs. Mike Jennings lived above Carrabassett County Wood Crafts, Margaret Boyd above Moosetookalook Scottish Emporium, and Stu Burroughs above his ski shop.

Mike had been in the office at the back of the municipal building when Margaret called to report the fire. Sherri made a mental note to ask them both when they'd last seen Angie, Beth, and Bradley, but that could wait. She didn't want to interrupt Mike, and Margaret was at work at The Spruces. That left Stu.

Her feet took her into Moosetookalook Scottish Emporium instead.

Since she had seen no point in sitting around the house and brooding, Liss had gone to work at the usual time. She'd entered by way of the stockroom, made a fresh pot of coffee, and filled her mug before she ventured out onto the sales floor to open her specialty gift shop to the public. When she'd unlocked the door and turned the CLOSED sign around to OPEN, she'd been careful not to look in the direction of the town square. It had been harder to avoid glancing through the plate-glass window at the front of the store. Even with her eyes averted, she'd caught a glimpse of the bright yellow police tape that cordoned off the ruins of Angie's Books. All that remained standing was the brick chimney.

If only to keep both her mind and her gaze fixed elsewhere, she'd decided to start pulling inventory for the Highland Games. She already had a list of the items she wanted to take to stock the booth she'd have there. They just had to be removed from the shelves and boxed for transport. For once they weren't going very far—just up to the castle.

Liss smiled for the first time all day as the old nickname for The Spruces popped into her head. The hotel did look a little like a castle when seen from the village below. It had five octagonal towers, four rising to four stories and one to five . . . with a cupola on top. Of course it wasn't built of stone, like a proper castle, but rather of wood. Its glistening white walls stood out against a backdrop encompassing every shade of green under the sun—the tree-covered mountains of western Maine.

This pleasant image shattered at the sound of the bell over the door. Liss started, then relaxed when she saw that it was Sherri Campbell who'd entered the shop.

"Any news?" Liss asked.

As Sherri headed for the stockroom, she shook her head. Liss could hear her friend filling a mug with coffee and adding sugar and creamer. When she emerged again, she homed in on the Emporium's "cozy corner," an area designed with both book browsers and bored spouses in mind. Shelves within easy reach of two comfortable chairs held books about Scotland's history and scenic beauty, biographies of Scottish people, and a selection of novels set in Scotland. A few large coffee-table books were, appropriately, displayed on the coffee table Liss had placed between the chairs.

She retrieved her own mug, nearly full and still hot enough to be drinkable, before threading her way through racks of kilts and tartan skirts and shelves loaded with Scottish-themed knickknacks to join her friend. She sank down into the second chair and took a swallow of the coffee before she burst out with the question that had been plaguing her ever since she'd realized that Angie and her children were nowhere to be found.

"How can three people just vanish into thin air?"

"I wish I had an answer to give you, but at this point you probably know more than I do."

"How do you figure that?"

"I wasn't here during the fire. I didn't make it to the scene until a couple of hours ago."

"Be grateful you didn't have to watch the bookstore burn to the ground." To quell the lump in her throat, Liss hastily took another sip of her coffee.

"I should have been here."

"It was ghastly."

"I know. That's probably why I convinced myself that I should stay at home. I didn't have anyone to stay with the kids, but Adam's fourteen. I could have left him in charge of Amber and Christina."

"Adam is a good kid, as responsible as any young teenager I know, but Christina isn't even three months old, and Amber is only four. You have no reason to feel guilty about being a good mom."

"The siren woke us. Then we could see the flames and smell the smoke from the house. I felt so helpless." Sherri stared into her coffee, as if the answers she was seeking were hidden in the bottom of the ceramic mug.

"So did everyone who was here. Be glad you were a few blocks away."

"Mike Jennings is the new guy. What if he—?"

"New here, but not inexperienced," Liss reminded her.

She was unaccustomed to seeing Sherri like this—insecure and in need of reassurance. She wondered if it was a form of postpartum depression. If it was, she was doubly glad she and Dan had decided not to have children.

"Still—"

"Cut yourself some slack, Sherri."

Hearing the sharpness in her voice, Liss instantly regretted snapping at her friend, but maybe firmness was called for.

"You're supposed to be on maternity leave," she continued. "In fact, if I remember right, you weren't planning to return to work until next week."

Liss directed a pointed look at the uniform Sherri wore. It was obvious she'd gone back on the job ahead of schedule.

A little silence fell between them as Sherri polished off her coffee.

Liss absently rubbed the side of her calf through her lightweight cotton slacks. Lumpkin's claws had left a deep, two-inch long scratch. She hadn't felt it until she returned home to take a shower and dress for the day. Then it had stung like the dickens, and the tape she'd used to cover it with a gauze pad made her skin itch.

"Thank you," Sherri said.

"For what?"

"Listening. I couldn't unload on just anyone, you know. I'm supposed to be the boss—in charge and in control."

"You were right to stay with your children. They must have been scared, what with the siren wailing and all. They needed their mom nearby to reassure them everything was okay. Pete was working. I saw him on the far side of the town square, directing traffic. That left you."

"And Mike handled things at the scene just fine without me." The side of Sherri's mouth quirked into a wry half smile. "You might as well say it—I wasn't needed at the scene at all."

Liss rolled her eyes. "Feel sorry for yourself some other time. You're obviously running the show now. What happens next?"

"We wait for Angie to turn up."

"That's it?" Liss frowned. "What's wrong with that picture?"

"A lot," Sherri admitted.

"Angie would never take Beth and Bradley and disappear, no matter how shook up she was by the fire, not without telling someone where she was going. She'd know how worried everyone would be."

"And yet it appears that's just what she did do. Her car is missing."

Liss didn't like the sound of that.

"I've been talking to neighbors this morning, hoping someone noticed them leaving. So far my inquiries have yielded zip. No one saw anything. When was the last time you saw Angie?"

Liss had to stop and think. "The fire broke out around three-thirty this morning—Friday. Wednesday, maybe? I'm not sure. But I'm certain I'd have noticed if the bookstore was closed on Thursday. Even if I didn't, someone would have mentioned it to me. That means Angie was open yesterday. She can't have disappeared into thin air between one day and the next."

"Not unless she wanted to."

"What are you saying?" Liss didn't wait for an answer. Sherri's suspicions weren't hard for her to read. "No! You can't believe *Angie* set that fire."

"I don't know what to believe, but there is definitely a

strong suspicion of arson. The state fire marshal's office has already sent someone to investigate."

Liss racked her brain to come up with another explanation. "Maybe they were kidnapped."

A faint smile touched Sherri's lips. "You know that theory doesn't make a lick of sense." Her hand was unsteady as she placed her empty mug on the coffee table. Ceramic and wood collided with an audible thunk.

"It makes more sense than thinking that Angie set the fire and then ran away. I mean, think about it. If you're going to torch your own business, it's usually so you can collect the insurance. That means you have to stick around for the payoff."

They sat in glum silence for a few minutes more. Realizing that her coffee had gone cold, Liss abandoned her mug next to Sherri's. She ought to get up and take them both back to the stockroom to be washed, but these depressing speculations had drained the energy out of her. So much for the reviving power of caffeine!

"I've got to get going," Sherri said, although she made no move to rise.

"Wait. You said you've been talking to Angie's neighbors?" That was a sensible thing to do. "Have you questioned everyone around the square?"

"Not yet. Still working on it."

"Who's left?"

"Stu Burroughs here on Pine. Then around the corner on Birch Street there are your neighbors on either side, Dance Central and the Farleys."

"Stu was the one who told us—Margaret and me—that there was no one in Angie's apartment."

"How did he know that?"

"I assume one of the firemen told him."

"Did Stu say anything else?"

Liss shook her head. "And I'd be astonished if Sandy or Zara saw anything. They live above the dance studio, but Sandy would have been busy fighting the fire, and I didn't see Zara at all."

That didn't surprise her, now that she thought about it. Zara's priority, like Sherri's, would have been keeping her children calm. With all the smoke in the air, she'd have made sure that her two little carrottops stayed inside the apartment.

Liss and Dan's neighbor on the other side was John Farley, an accountant. He used his living room as an office in tax season, but during the rest of the year it was just part of the family's home.

"The Farleys have gone to visit her sister in Boothbay Harbor for a week," she said aloud, belatedly remembering that she'd seen them load up their station wagon and head out on Thursday morning.

"One less place to stop," Sherri said. "Although I suppose I should add the antiques shop on Birch to my list. They must have been able to see Angie's Books from their place."

The antiques shop didn't face the town square, but it did have a diagonal line of sight that went straight to the corner of Main and Elm. Liss considered for a moment before shaking her head. "The trees would have been in the way."

Flowers were more prevalent along the walkways within the town square, but two apple trees flanked the gazebo that doubled as a bandstand. Another grew next to the merry-go-round, while a small stand of birches had been planted by the monument to the Civil War dead. Near the center of the square grew a tall, nicely shaped blue spruce, the tree that the town decorated at Christmas. Until today, Liss had always been glad that none of them blocked her view through the Emporium's front window.

"I'd better talk to them anyway." Heaving herself out of the chair, Sherri adjusted her utility belt, plunked her uniform hat back onto her head, and fixed a determined expression on her face. "Keep your fingers crossed that I get lucky . . . but don't hold your breath."

After she left, Liss had a difficult time keeping a sense of doom and gloom at bay. The steady trickle of customers should have helped, but she soon realized that none of them were particularly interested in buying Scottish knickknacks.

Locals wanted to know if she'd heard anything from Angie or to speculate about whether or not the fire had been set. Folks from away came inside to gawk at the dismal scene in air-conditioned comfort.

In late morning, a familiar-looking, barrel-shaped man entered the shop. Liss recognized him at once as one of the two strangers she had noticed at the fire. At the time, she'd suspected he was a guest at The Spruces. That he was still around made that seem even more likely.

The tourist clothes he sported backed up her assumption. He was dressed in shorts that showed off stumpy, stocky, hairy legs. A snug T-shirt revealed that his torso was muscular rather than flabby but did little to enhance his overall appearance. He was, Liss decided, shaped not so much like a barrel as a beer keg.

The woman who came in with him had a long-suffering

look on her face. Liss pegged her as the walking beer keg's wife. She was not surprised when they separated to explore the contents of the shop. The woman headed straight for the cozy corner and, after a few minutes of browsing, settled into one of the chairs with a biography of Mary, Queen of Scots.

Liss shifted her attention back to the man. He was examining shelves stocked with imported Scottish foodstuffs, everything from shortbread to canned haggis. That made her wonder if he had a genuine interest in things Scottish. It was possible. The Western Maine Highland Games were still a week away, but someone planning to attend might have decided to come to town early.

The man moved on to the Emporium's selection of tartan skirts and ready-made kilts. Liss saw his lips compress into a thin line as he pawed through them. She tensed even before he swung his massive, balding head in her direction, revealing an unlovely face dominated by hooded eyes and sagging jowls. When he frowned, his eyebrows all but knit together.

"This is an abomination," he announced in ringing tones. "You must not sell kilts to *women*!"

Bracing herself to endure a tirade, Liss held her ground. Over the years, she had encountered a few other Scottish Americans like this one. Pasting a the-customer-is-always-right expression on her face, she waited for the next salvo.

He marched right up to the sales counter, hands curled into fists at his sides. He was no taller than Liss was, but that didn't stop him from trying to look down his nose at her. "Only men are permitted to wear the kilt."

"That was true at one time," Liss said in the mildest tone

she could manage. Her jaw already ached from forcing her muscles to hold a "shopkeeper" smile. "These days, however, when both men and women play in bagpipe bands, things have become a bit more flexible, especially here in Maine."

"It's *wrong,*" he insisted. "If you were a true daughter of Scotland, you would insist on maintaining tradition."

That this criticism was delivered in the nasal accent of a New Jersey native only made it more grating. After a brief struggle with her better self, Liss gave up and rose to the bait.

"I am a MacCrimmon," she informed him. "You may recognize the name. The MacCrimmons produced some of the finest pipers in Scottish history."

"And all of them were men," he shot back. "I am a Grant myself. Angus Grant. No doubt you are familiar with the famous painting of the Grant piper."

"I am." Liss had to bite her lip to keep from adding that she'd always thought it was an extremely ugly and poorly executed portrait.

"Well, then?"

A soft, pleasant voice insinuated itself into this awkward exchange. "Angus dear, come and look at this thistle pin. I've never seen one quite like it. The card says the stone is a tourmaline."

Liss glanced over the man's shoulder to send a grateful smile in his wife's direction. She was quiet and colorless in comparison to her husband, but a dimple flashed in her cheek when she smiled back. Then she winked.

With one final scowl for Liss, "Angus dear" obeyed his better half. They spoke together in low voices for a few minutes. Then he left Moosetookalook Scottish Emporium to stand staring at the ruin on the far side of the town square. Mrs. Grant—Janine, according to her credit card—purchased the pin.

In a way, Liss was sorry when they'd gone. Angus Grant's diatribe had been annoying, but at least it had distracted her from wondering what had happened to Angie, Beth, and Bradley.

Chapter Three

As Dan Ruskin worked, he listened to music on a sound system he'd installed when he converted the one-time carriage house into a workshop for his custom woodworking business. He'd been in the mood for folk songs that morning and cued up a selection that dated from his parents' childhood—Peter, Paul, and Mary, Simon and Garfunkel, Gordon Lightfoot, and others. He was applying a coat of polyurethane to a jigsaw-puzzle table and humming along with "Bridge Over Troubled Water" when the door opened and his next-door neighbor, Sandy Kalishnakof, walked in.

"Talk to you a minute?" Sandy had to raise his voice to be heard.

"Sure thing." Dan kept up the steady strokes necessary to ensure a smooth finish. "Go ahead and kill the music. I don't want to stop in the middle of this."

Like Dan, Sandy was self-employed. He owned Dance Central in partnership with his wife, Zara. Years ago they'd both been members of the same touring dance company Liss belonged to, before a knee injury ended her career as a professional Scottish dancer. Later, when the company disbanded, Sandy and Zara had decided that Moosetookalook would be a good place to settle down and raise a family.

Dan laughed about it now, but when he'd first met Sandy, he'd been jealous of Liss's former dance partner. Sandy was a bit shorter than Dan's 6'2" and a couple of years older, but his jet black hair and dark blue eyes and the fact that he looked good in a kilt always made women give him a second glance. Although Dan wasn't exactly Frankenstein's monster, he knew his own looks to be ordinary—light brown hair, brown eyes, and regular features. Fortunately for everyone, Sandy had been head over heels in love with the woman who was now his wife. In the years since, Dan had become good friends with Liss's "best pal."

Sandy had been in the shop often enough to know where the controls for the sound system were located. With the music off, he eased himself onto a high stool to one side of Dan's oversized work table. "Zara's been after me to buy her one of your puzzle tables."

"You'll get the neighbor discount, but you'll still have to wait a couple of months for me to make you one."

"Doing that well, are you?"

"Can't complain."

Dan usually had seven or eight orders backed up, and it took about a week to complete each jigsaw-puzzle table. He wasn't making a fortune by any means, but he liked working with his hands, and he liked being his own boss. The trade-off was worthwhile.

"Greg's called a meeting for tonight," Sandy said.

Dan wasn't surprised. Like a coach following a game, Greg Holstein, Moosetookalook's fire chief, liked to gather all the town's volunteer firefighters together after a fire to discuss what had gone right and where they needed to improve.

"He wants you there," Sandy said.

"Issue me a pager and he won't have to send a messenger."

Dan continued applying polyurethane, but he no longer found the repetitive motion soothing. The frustration he'd felt the night before came rushing back. He hadn't contributed much, and that nagged at him.

Sandy stopped toying with a small piece of discarded wood to send a questioning look his way.

"Sorry. It's my own fault. I haven't made time to finish the classroom stuff and pass the CPAT. I should have started the whole process a long time ago."

"Greg's talking about setting up a training session, making the equipment available so everyone can practice carrying the hose and raising the ladder."

"I'll be there."

"It'll be fun at this time of year. Ninety degrees in the broiling sun, suited up and lugging fifty pounds of equipment."

Dan shot him a disgruntled look. "I can manage."

"Uh-huh. Then there's the stair climb. You'll have to wear additional weights—two of them at twelve and a half pounds apiece."

Dan managed to suppress a groan. "What about the other CPAT components? Any chance of practicing things like forcible entry and the ceiling breach and pull?"

Sandy shrugged. "Maybe. Greg's hoping to get permission to set fire to an old barn in Little Moose. The roof collapsed last winter under the weight of the snow. It's going to fall down on its own, so we might as well have the good of it."

Little Moose was one of the four villages that made up the town of Moosetookalook. Moosetookalook village, with its town square and municipal building, was the largest of the four. They didn't have the tax base to support more than one fire truck and had to rely on an outfit in Fallstown, where the closest hospital was also located, for ambulance service. Since it took at least twenty minutes for those folks to respond to a call, Moosetookalook's lone fire truck was loaded with supplies for medical emergencies, as well as for search-and-rescue missions and equipment for fighting fires, but only a few of the volunteers were qualified as EMTs.

Sandy was one of them.

"Were you one of the ones who checked out Angie's apartment?" Dan asked.

He glanced up in time to catch Sandy's nod and the bleak expression on his face. "We should have gone on down into the bookstore. Just to be sure."

Dan's movements stilled. "They haven't—?"

"No." Sandy huffed out a breath. "No sign that anyone was in the building. Thank God. But early this morning, when I heard that Angie and her kids hadn't been seen anywhere . . ." He let his voice trail off, reluctant to utter aloud the paralyzing fear he must have felt until it was confirmed that no bodies had been found.

"No one in their right mind would have tried to get out through the shop."

Sandy gave a snort of laughter. "Since when do fire victims think straight? But the door to the stairs was closed. Hell, it was locked. I tried it myself. And I know I did everything by the book. Checked the bedrooms, the closets, even pulled back the shower curtain to make sure no one was hiding in the bathtub." He shook his head. "But the place was already full of smoke. It would have been easy to miss something in the rush to get back outside and help put out the fire."

"But you didn't miss anything. There was nothing to miss."

A furrow appeared in Sandy's forehead. "Nothing to miss, but there *was* something missing."

Dan cocked a brow at him. "What?"

"No idea. I'd forgotten till now, but there was something odd in one of the bedrooms—a couple of shelves on one wall."

"What about them?"

"They were empty." He shook his head. "I don't suppose it's important. Maybe Angie had been cleaning house. Or she was getting ready to redecorate. Hardly matters now. Those shelves are nothing but ash."

"I can't believe how fast the whole place went up. If we'd had more men, we might have saved the building."

"We need more volunteers. No question there. Especially younger guys."

Dan just looked at him. Neither of them were exactly over the hill.

"You want to help recruit? Talk to anyone over eighteen who has a high school diploma and a driver's license."

"I couldn't have started that young," Dan admitted, "but I should have volunteered when I first came back to Moosetookalook after college." The application of polyurethane finished, Dan turned his back on Sandy to clean the brush he'd been using.

"And when, exactly, would you have scraped out time for training? Until the last year or so, you were working three jobs."

"There weren't so many requirements back in the old days."

It seemed to Dan that the state added more rules and regulations every year. Even when he qualified to fight fires, his training wouldn't be finished. There were required meetings, like the one tonight. Even without the hours spent fighting fires and cleaning up after them, volunteering required a huge commitment, and if he ever opted to go to the Maine Fire Academy, at his own expense, he'd have to be away from home for the duration.

Dan put the can of polyurethane on its shelf with a little more force than necessary. Other people managed to find time to take the training. Ninety percent of the firefighters in the state were volunteers.

Sandy eased himself off the stool. "I've got to get going. See you tonight."

He winced as he stood, making Dan wonder if he'd hurt himself fighting the fire at Angie's Books. That was yet another obstacle in the recruitment of volunteers. There were no benefits, and if a volunteer firefighter was paid at all for his services, it was at a rate of no more than eight dollars a call. Dan shook his head as he watched his neighbor walk gingerly toward the door.

What a deal, he thought. *Risk your life and pay for the privilege of doing it.*

The quiet of Liss's house acted like a balm after a day that had, at times, seemed endless. The latest news from the fire scene was mixed. Good because no human remains had been found. Bad because arson was looking even more likely, and the Hogencamps were still among the missing.

Liss wanted nothing more than to collapse on the comfy sofa in the living room, put her feet up, and use the landline on the end table to call Graziano's and order a pizza with everything. No way was she cooking supper. She felt as if it would use up her last reserves of energy just to lift the phone off the hook.

The cats, of course, had other ideas.

No sooner did Liss apply backside to cushion than Glenora appeared. She had stayed out of sight earlier in the day. She'd been taking no chances. What with Liss tripping over her and that godawful wailing siren, who could blame her? But cats had short memories, and bottomless pits where their stomachs should be. Staring hard at Liss, she let out a plaintive meow, cocking her head as if to ask, "Aren't I just the cutest little thing you ever saw? Why aren't you feeding me already?"

Liss sighed. "Give me a break, okay? I'm too pooped to pop."

Glenora leapt into her lap and began to knead. Needle-sharp claws easily penetrated Liss's cotton slacks to make contact with bare skin. Biting back a yelp of pain, Liss came to her feet, dumping the little black cat onto the floor. She could swear Glenora smirked at her.

"All right. All right. You win." Brushing cat hair off her slacks, Liss followed the feline through the arch between the living room and dining room and headed toward the kitchen. She was not at all surprised to find Lumpkin waiting for them. "What are you? Backup?"

The big yellow Maine coon cat was almost twice Glenora's size. He had already opened the door of the kitchen cabinet where his food was stored. He had not yet figured out how to pop the top on a cat food can, and since he'd once chewed his way into a bag of dry food, Liss had taken to storing kibble in a large plastic container with a secure lid.

By the time she'd dished out equal portions and refilled the cats' water bowls, Dan had come in from his workshop. His custom jigsaw-puzzle tables were even more of a niche market than selling Scottish-themed knickknacks. It had only been in the last few years that profits had been high enough for him to stop working part-time in the family business, Ruskin Construction, with the occasional weekend filling in at The Spruces. Together, Dan and Liss managed to make ends meet and then some, and they'd long since agreed that being happy in their work was more important than earning a lot of money.

Dan greeted her with a kiss, which instantly made her feel better. She was about to broach the subject of pizza and suggest they make it an early night when a quick, one-two rap on the front door was immediately followed by the sound of footsteps in the hallway. A moment later, Margaret Boyd walked into the kitchen.

"Oh, good. You're here. We need to talk."

Liss and Dan exchanged a worried look. That was a phrase that never preceded *good* news.

"What's wrong?" Liss gestured for her aunt to take a chair at the kitchen table and sank into one herself. She was not at all sure she wanted to hear what Margaret had to say.

"Do you need me?" Dan asked.

Margaret shook her head. "It's Highland Games business."

With a wave, he went off to take a shower.

Liss sent her aunt a narrow-eyed look. "I thought everything was set."

As events coordinator at The Spruces, Margaret had been responsible for bringing the annual Western Maine Highland Games back to the grounds of The Spruces. For many years, the venue had been the county fairgrounds in

Fallstown, but the one year they'd held the festivities at the hotel, The Spruces and several other businesses in Moosetookalook had seen a healthy profit.

"So did I," Margaret said, "but what sealed the deal for us was our promise to augment the games with a parade and fireworks."

Liss's heart sank. She'd been so distraught by the fire and the disappearance of three people she cared about that she hadn't twigged to the wider ramifications. "The parade route isn't going to work, is it?"

"You can see the problem. The parade was supposed to start at the hotel, wind its way through town, and end up in the town square for the opening ceremonies. All the village shops were planning to stay open—if not to sell things on the spot, then at least to show attendees what they had to offer in the hope they'd come back during the weekend. We were planning to trade on our image as a quaint New England village, picture-postcard perfect and all that."

No wonder she looked glum. "I don't suppose there's any way to get the fire site cleaned up before next Friday?"

"Not a prayer. Worse, according to Francine, the board of selectmen has what they're calling a work session scheduled for this evening. She tells me Jason Graye wants to cancel the parade entirely."

"Damn. That's a little extreme. Surely we can find a new route."

"I need you to come to this work session with me. Help me convince them that it isn't necessary to throw in the towel."

"Moosetookalook isn't all that big," Liss said, beginning to have doubts of her own. "Most of it is pretty ordinary-looking." The stores a block away were typical—a laundromat, Graziano's Pizza, High Street Market, and, in back of that, a hardware store. "But I suppose the parade could finish up at the athletic field at the school instead of in the town square."

"I knew you'd think of something."

"They may not go for the idea," Liss warned her.

Margaret was undaunted. "We have nearly a week to figure something out. The important thing is to stop them from canceling the parade."

"I'll back you up," Liss promised, "but you may have to pinch me to keep me awake. I can't remember the last time I felt this bushed."

"You'll be fine." Margaret patted her hand. Then she sighed. "Now if I could just figure out what to do about Boxer."

Liss sat up straighter, appalled to realize that she hadn't given a thought to how upset her young cousin must be. Boxer, whose real name was Edward, had been friends with Beth Hogencamp for years, and at some point during the last six months the relationship had blossomed into romance.

"You know where he lives, out on Owl Road. That's beyond the range of the siren. He didn't even hear about the fire until after he got to work this morning at that big box store down to Fallstown. I managed to calm him down when he phoned me, and convinced him to stay on the job until his regular quitting time, but he's terribly worried about Beth."

"He doesn't have any idea where she is?"

"He says he doesn't. You know my grandson—he may be seventeen, but he's not one of those kids who has to be texting and sending selfies every five minutes. It's not unusual for the two of them to be out of touch with one another for a day or two at a time."

Liss did know Boxer. Her cousin was mature for his age, even if he was something of a wiseass. "Did he come by to see you at the hotel after he got off work?"

Margaret shook her head. "That's what worries me. I don't know where he's gotten to. His mother hasn't seen him, either. I called her again just before I came here."

"Maybe we should hope he *does* know where to look for Beth. Even now, he could be bringing the whole family back to Moosetookalook."

"From your mouth to God's ear." Margaret glanced at the wall clock and sighed. "I'd better get a move on. I don't want to face the board of selectmen on an empty stomach. I'll collect you on my way there. According to Francine, they plan to meet in the municipal building at seven."

Sherri Campbell jumped when someone banged on the locked outer door of Moosetookalook's police station. Officially, she wasn't on duty. The officer who was had been sent to stand guard over the scene of the fire. In an emergency, he'd be the obvious choice to approach. As for Sherri, she'd only stayed late to catch up on paperwork. She'd been about to call it a day.

Two battered, army-surplus-style desks, two swivel chairs, an antiquated metal file cabinet, a side table holding a coffeepot and all the fixings, and a couple of plastic chairs for visitors had been crammed into the tiny office. Weaving her way through this obstacle course, she passed the door to the closet-sized holding cell, currently unoccupied, moved at a more rapid pace through what passed for a waiting area, and unlocked the door.

Liss MacCrimmon's cousin Boxer stood in the hallway

on the other side, his fist raised to pound again. "Where is she?" he demanded. "Where's Beth?"

Hearing the anguish in his voice, Sherri took his arm and pulled him inside. Poor kid. At his age, every little set-back was a crisis. When a real disaster came along, it must seem like the end of the world.

"No one was caught in the fire." She eased him into one of the red plastic chairs in the outer room and swung a second one around so she could sit facing him. "Wherever Beth is, she's safe."

He turned his head away from her, raking one hand through a mop of unruly reddish brown hair. His choked voice hinted at barely repressed tears. "You can't be sure of that."

Sherri's heart went out to him. She had to fight an urge to take him in her arms and give him a comforting hug. That would have been a bad idea even if he was still the skinny preteen he'd been when she first met him. Back then he'd been all awkward angles and seething rebellion. These days he was a good eight or nine inches taller than she was. His summer job as a stock boy had honed ropey muscles and given him a new maturity. There might even be the tiniest hint of a mustache on his upper lip.

"Boxer, when did you last see Beth?"

Again he raked his fingers through his hair. His plain, square face was a mask of misery. "We went to a movie the middle of last week on my day off. Then Sunday we sat to-gether in church and hung out afterward."

"Not since then?"

He shook his head. "I know Fallstown is only a twenty-minute drive, but I'm usually pretty beat by the time I get home, and Beth works hard, too."

"In the bookstore?"

He nodded. "For her mother. We don't often have the same days off, and both of us work a lot of weekends."

"So you haven't crossed paths since Sunday?"

He shook his head.

"What about talking on the phone? Do you e-mail or text each other?"

Boxer didn't answer at once. His emotions were so raw that it hurt Sherri to watch him. Even the simplest, most routine question was a painful reminder that Beth had vanished into thin air.

"Phone?" she prompted. "I thought most young people your age were glued to their smartphones?"

"All I have is a 'stupid' phone. It's good for calling for help in an emergency and not much else."

"Liss said you were saving for college." Since Boxer would have to pay most of his own bills, he was pinching every penny.

"I called Beth on my mom's landline on Wednesday. She didn't say anything about going away." Boxer leaned toward her. "What do *you* know?"

"Not much," Sherri admitted. "Only that no one has seen Beth or her mother or her brother since well before the fire. Is it possible they were called out of town and don't yet know they've been burned out?"

"That doesn't make any sense." Frustration had Boxer clenching and unclenching his fists. "Where would they go? And why wouldn't Beth tell me they were leaving? And even if they did go somewhere, how could they not hear about the fire and come back?"

That was exactly what Sherri wanted to know. She tried a different tack. "Has anything been worrying Beth lately?"

Boxer shook his head. "I don't think so. She's not crazy about me commuting to Fallstown when I could have worked at The Spruces, but it's not like I took a job on the coast for the summer."

Sherri placed one hand on his forearm and gave it a squeeze. "We'll find them."

"How?"

"Well, for one thing, you probably know more about Beth than you think you do. Can you give me a list of her closest friends?"

For the first time, she saw a glimmer of hope in his dark brown eyes. "Yeah. Okay. I can do that."

"What about Beth's father? Is he still alive?" No one Sherri had spoken to seemed to know anything about Angie Hogencamp's husband.

Boxer looked blank. "She's never mentioned him. I guess he must be dead. I never gave it much thought. I mean, I don't have a father either."

Margaret Boyd's son, Ned, had died several years earlier. Since he'd never bothered to marry Boxer's mother, Sherri could understand why the subject of fathers hadn't come up.

After Boxer wrote down the names of a half dozen of Beth's friends and promised to contact the police department if he heard from her or thought of anything that might help, Sherri sent him on his way. It took her only a few more minutes to put away the paperwork scattered across her desk. More than ready to head home, she stepped out into the hall.

The parking lot where she'd left her car was just through the door to her immediate right. She'd almost made good on her escape when the sound of loud, angry voices stopped her in her tracks. Tempting as it was to ignore the ruckus taking place in the suite of rooms that comprised Moosetookalook's town office, Sherri's sense of duty wouldn't let her leave without investigating.

Heaving a resigned sigh, she headed for the front of the municipal building.

Chapter Four

Selectman Jason Graye stopped in mid-bellow when the door to the meeting room opened and Sherri Campbell walked in. At the sight of her uniform, his eyes lit up. "Chief Campbell, your timing is impeccable. Please remove these unauthorized persons from the premises at once!"

"I have a right to be here," Margaret insisted. "By law, selectmen's meetings must be open to the public."

"This is a work session. It is closed to the public."

"Don't play games with me. Not when it was the hard work done by my committee that brought the Highland Games back to Moosetookalook in the first place."

Liss said nothing. It wouldn't bother her to be thrown out of the municipal building. She and Margaret hadn't accomplished anything by coming here. The moment they'd shown up, Graye had started shouting at them to get out. Margaret, most uncharacteristically, had lost her temper and yelled back at him.

The other two members of the board of selectmen had kept their mouths shut. It was Sherri's arrival that prompted one of them, Thea Campbell, to break her silence. Pete's mother, and therefore Sherri's mother-in-law, was a woman known for her forceful personality. Tact was not one of her strong suits.

"We've already decided to cancel the parade and the opening ceremonies, Margaret. Treating visitors to the sight of a burned-out shell would not be in keeping with our claim to be a scenic Maine village."

Hands on her hips, Margaret turned her back on Jason Graye in order to face this new opposition. "Then demolish it. Bring in a bulldozer to fill in the cellar hole. We have until Friday. Let's make the best possible use of the next few days."

Three voices spoke at once.

Sherri said, "The arson investigation isn't complete."

"It would cost a fortune!" Graye's objection came out as a bleat of protest.

Thea's was the voice of reason. "The town can't do a thing until Angie Hogencamp shows up. It's her property. Much as we might like to, we can't just rush in and take the land by eminent domain, not without jumping through all kinds of legal hoops. And that, Margaret, takes much more time than we have."

"Then erect a tent over the site." Margaret's voice rose along with her desperation. "Build a fence around it. Anything is better at this late date than ruining all our plans."

"I'm sorry, Margaret," Thea said. "We've made the decision to cut our losses."

Tired as she was, longing for home and her bed, Liss felt obliged to offer the suggestion Margaret had intended to make to the board of selectmen. "What about an alternate parade route, one that avoids the town square?"

"What would be the point?" Thea asked. "The businesses that anticipated making a profit from the spectators would still be bypassed."

"They could set up under awnings along the new parade route," Margaret shot back.

"Why be fancy? Just have them sell out of the back of their trucks." Graye's sarcasm went over like a lead balloon.

Thea sent a narrow-eyed look in his direction, but she didn't change her mind. "If they want to take their stock to the crowd, then they can set up booths at the Highland Games. That would be much more appropriate anyway."

Margaret was shaking her head even before Thea finished speaking. "I can't add vendors to the games. The organizers control that. The Spruces just provides the venue."

"Then have our people hawk their wares in the lobby." Graye made a production of dusting his hands together. "There. Problem solved. You two can leave now."

Sputtering with indignation, Margaret clearly had more to say, but Liss knew when they were licked. She slung an arm around her aunt's shoulders and steered her toward the exit.

"I'll walk you out," Sherri said. Suiting action to words, she left last and closed the door behind her.

The three women passed in somber silence through the darkened section of the town office where, in daylight hours, Francine Noyes held sway. By the time they stepped outside, into a mild July evening, Margaret's shoulders slumped and her head drooped.

Liss hated seeing her aunt so dispirited. "We still have the fireworks."

"Things will look brighter in the morning," Sherri added.

When Margaret made no response to either comment,

Sherri's worried gaze momentarily locked with Liss's. There was nothing more she could say. With a shrug and a wave, she left them, following the walkway between the municipal building and Patsy's Coffee House that led to the parking lot.

"Do you want to come in?" Liss asked her aunt when they reached the sidewalk that led up to Liss's front porch.

Margaret glanced at the house and frowned, as if she didn't quite know how she'd gotten there. Then she literally shook herself, dislodging Liss's arm as she squared her shoulders and stiffened her spine. "We're not dead yet," she announced, misquoting one of Dan's favorite lines from *Monty Python and the Holy Grail*.

Liss felt a grin spread across her face. Margaret had recovered her fighting spirit.

"I've been events coordinator at The Spruces long enough to have plenty of tricks up my sleeve," the older woman announced. "The original plan was to kick off the Highland Games with a parade, an opening ceremony in the town square, and fireworks that would be set off on that hill behind the hotel. We'll just have to have a procession around the hotel grounds instead. The opening ceremonies can take place in one of the fields where the competitions will be held. Thank goodness Joe bought that adjoining land two years ago. We have plenty of room."

"What about the town square merchants?" Liss asked. "I'm okay, since I already have a booth at the Highland Games, but what you told Thea is true. The organizers won't allow you to add vendors. Could her suggestion about the lobby work?"

Margaret shook her head. "I can offer limited display space in the hotel gift shop, but even that would take some doing." Her expression turned rueful. "I'm in for a busy couple of days!"

"I'll help all I can."

"I know you will, dear. We'll talk more tomorrow." With that, she walked on toward her apartment.

Liss sighed. Her impulsive offer to help was likely to come back and bite her in the butt. By morning, Margaret would have produced a to-do list that was the proverbial mile long, one that would have them both running right out straight until the Highland Games opened.

Liss let herself into the house, scooping up the black cat waiting just inside the door. At least there would be one bright side to staying so busy. Juggling a thousand and one details would distract her from constant worry about Angie and the kids. As it was, questions about what had happened to them crept into her thoughts at every opportunity. Despite her exhaustion, sleep that night was a long time coming.

Two hours after Liss opened Moosetookalook Scottish Emporium on Saturday morning, Sherri turned up wearing her uniform and a worried frown. Liss froze in the act of cleaning a shelf full of china figurines—pipers, dancers, drummers, and a few Scottish lions.

"Any news?"

Sherri glanced around, as if to make certain they were alone before she said anything.

"Relax. Business has slowed to its normal crawl. You want coffee?"

"No time."

"If it's bad news, just spit it out."

"Not bad. Not anything. That's the problem. If there weren't children involved, we wouldn't even be able to call

Angie a missing person yet. Not officially. It's been less than forty-eight hours since the fire."

Liss made a spiraling motion with one hand, urging her friend to get to the point.

"Okay, here's the thing. A logical step in the attempt to locate Angie and the kids was to look into Angie's background." Sherri didn't seem to be able to stand still. She prowled toward the area of the shop where a set of bagpipes (not for sale), drumsticks, penny whistles, and practice chanters were displayed on a wall.

"Makes sense." Liss abandoned her can of lemon-scented furniture polish and dust rag to trail after her friend. When Sherri made an abrupt about-face, it caught her by surprise. The two women came within an inch of colliding.

"Sorry."

"Why don't you sit down and tell me what this is all about?" Liss headed for the cozy corner.

Grumbling under her breath, Sherri threw herself into a chair and stretched her legs out in front of her. "I am *so* frustrated!"

"Welcome to the club. Now tell me what in particular has you so het up."

"Angie Hogencamp doesn't exist."

Liss sat up straighter in her armchair and stared at her friend. "How is that possible?"

"I have no idea, but as far as anyone has been able to discover, there is no record of her before she arrived in Moosetookalook."

"You're saying there are no records of anyone by that name?"

"Not exactly." Sherri shifted into a more upright position. "There are a couple of Angie Hogencamps around. One of them is even kind of famous in a weird sort of way. She attends a lot of those mystery fan conventions, like the First Annual Maine-ly Cozy Con that met at The Spruces that one year. It seems that most of them hold charity auctions where they sell mystery-related items. This real Angie Hogencamp likes to bid on the right to have a character named after herself in an author's next mystery novel. Her name has ended up in at least a half dozen of them over the years."

Liss was only half listening. "Angie *has* to exist," she insisted. "We've known her for ages."

"Not very well, apparently." Sherri let that sink in before she continued. "Neither of us had yet returned to Moosetookalook to live when she appeared out of the blue and opened the bookstore. That was twelve years ago. Everyone took her at face value and assumed she was either widowed or divorced, since there was no Mr. Hogencamp in the picture."

"What about the children? Wouldn't they know if they had another name before they came here? That would be a pretty big secret to keep, and Beth has always been an outgoing girl."

"Think about it. Twelve years ago, Beth would have been about four years old. Bradley is twelve now, so he was only an infant, maybe even a newborn."

Liss had a hard time accepting what Sherri was saying. Angie was as honest as the day was long . . . wasn't she? "Maybe she just decided to change her name. People do. And you can call yourself anything you like. Plenty of people use pseudonyms."

"Angie is a bookseller, not an author. Besides, this isn't just a case of calling herself something else part of the time. She created an identity for herself under what has to

be an assumed name. If she changed it legally, there would be a record somewhere. So far, nothing has turned up. I hate to say it, Liss, but this development makes both the fire and Angie's disappearance look very suspicious."

Liss leaned back, feeling gobsmacked. She didn't like any of the possibilities that sprang to mind. Picking the least alarming of the lot, she said, "Maybe she's in the witness protection program."

"Maybe." Sherri looked doubtful. "But I think information can be shared with local law enforcement in a case like this one where the fire is likely to have been set."

"Even if the arson is somehow connected to Angie's past and she and the kids have already been given a new set of identities?"

"It's not like they'd have to tell me where they are."

Liss sent her a skeptical look. She'd never had the impression that federal agencies played well with others.

"It's not a subject I know a lot about," Sherri admitted, "and there are other, more likely possibilities. What if Angie changed her name to hide a criminal background? Or she could be running away from an abusive husband."

Liss frowned. "She mentioned a sister-in-law once."

Sherri went on alert, reaching for the small spiral notebook and pen she kept in her breast pocket. "Did she give you a name?"

"I don't think so." Liss racked her brain, trying to remember exactly what Angie had said. It had been a casual remark made several years earlier. "Angie just said her sister-in-law was taking care of the shop and babysitting Bradley so Angie wouldn't have to be in two places at once. It was the weekend of that mystery convention you just mentioned. Angie was at the hotel, set up to sell books in the dealer

room. The Moosetookalook Scottish Emporium's tables were right next to hers, and we were spelling each other for bathroom breaks. She took over so I could attend a couple of the panels, too, and I held the fort while she went back to the bookstore to host a signing by the guest of honor."

"You never met the sister-in-law?"

Liss shook her head. "Never even caught a glimpse of her, but someone must have been working at Angie's Books that weekend, as well as keeping an eye on young Bradley."

"I'll check into it, but knowing what we do now, it wouldn't surprise me to find out that Angie invented her."

"What would be the point of leading me to believe she had family?"

"What was the point in creating a new identity for herself?"

"I suppose," Liss mused, "that the bookstore might have been closed. I'd have had no way of knowing, since I was at The Spruces. But someone still had to look after Angie's son."

"Beth?"

"Beth was in the dealer room with us, helping her mother."

"Bradley could have been at a friend's house," Sherri suggested. "Maybe Angie asked Patsy to look after him. Or Gloria Weir. I'll ask around."

"I hate this!" Liss exclaimed. "This suspicion. I like Angie."

"Cheer up. Maybe the sister-in-law will turn out to be real, after all. If so, she'll know where to find Angie and the children. You're certain Angie didn't mention a name?"

"Positive." She sent Sherri a rueful look. "And the more

I think about it, the more I realize that Angie never talked about her past."

Sherri heaved herself to her feet. "I've got to get going. Now that it's almost certain we're dealing with a case of arson, I need to talk to everyone who showed up to watch the bookstore burn. Some sickos who set fires for kicks like to witness the results of their handiwork. With luck, I may be able to locate a witness who saw someone acting suspiciously *during* the fire."

"Everyone I noticed looked appalled." Liss rose to follow her friend to the door.

"Did you spot anyone you didn't know?"

Liss frowned. "There were a couple of men I had never seen before, but one of them turned out to be a guest at the hotel. He came into the Emporium yesterday with his wife." She shrugged. "You can hear the fire siren as far away as The Spruces. I wouldn't be surprised if several guests decided to come down and take a look at the action."

"I've never understood why people do that," Sherri grumbled as she opened the door, setting the bells above it jangling. "They're a damned nuisance. If they're in cars, they slow down to gawk at traffic accidents. On foot, they crowd in at fires and crime scenes. Sometimes they even try to sneak in past the police tape to get a closer look."

"There was one of those."

Sherri swung around in the doorway. "One what?"

"A gawker trying to get closer. Ask Mike Jennings. He yelled at the guy."

"Thanks," Sherri said as she finally made it onto the Emporium's front porch. "I'll do that. It probably won't amount to anything, but at this stage I can't leave any stone unturned.

* * *

"Just who do you think you are?" Dolores Mayfield shouted.

The librarian's loud, strident voice reached Liss when she was halfway up the wide flight of stairs that led to the second floor of the municipal building. Like most small town libraries, the one that served Moosetookalook had a limited budget. It was only open three afternoons and one evening a week. A few minutes earlier, Liss had put the BACK IN FIFTEEN MINUTES sign on the door of the Emporium and scurried across the town square, anxious to pick Dolores's brain. The librarian was the most inquisitive woman in the entire county, and Liss hoped she would have some notion of where Angie and her children had gone.

The voice yelling back at Dolores belonged, unmistakably, to Jason Graye. "Who am I? I'm one of your duly elected selectmen, that's who!"

Liss hesitated only a moment before she pushed open the glass door with the library's hours etched on the outside and went in. The combatants were so intent on their quarrel that neither of them noticed her arrival. She'd planned to interrupt, but one look at their faces changed her mind. She decided it would be better to stay off their radar until she figured out what was going on, or until Graye finished venting his spleen and left.

Taking advantage of their intense concentration on each other, she ducked into a convenient row of floor-to-ceiling bookshelves. This gave her a prime view of the action—all she had to do was peer through the space between the books at eye level and the underside of the shelf above.

Graye barely topped five-foot-ten and was, if not overweight, at least badly out of shape. He compensated by pushing into Dolores's personal space, his thin lips pursed and jaw outthrust. Red-faced and seething, he looked ready to explode. "I'm doing you a big favor to warn you ahead of time!"

"Some warning!" Dolores didn't back up. Instead she leaned toward him until they were nearly nose to nose. Hers was needle-thin. His resembled the beak of a hawk. "You've already decided to close the library."

Liss's gasp of surprise and dismay gave away her presence.

"Who's there?" The small, rimless spectacles Dolores wore improved her vision to 20/20. She had no difficulty spotting Liss's hiding place. "Come out of there, Liss Ruskin. What do you mean sneaking around in my library?"

Liss felt heat rush into her face as she emerged from the shelter of the shelves. Dolores could give a school marm lessons when it came to putting miscreants in their place. "I, uh, didn't want to disturb your, uh, discussion."

Dolores snorted, but her attitude softened. "How much did you hear? Do you know what this moron wants to do?"

She did, and the very thought appalled her. She forgot her embarrassment at being caught eavesdropping and rounded on Jason Graye. "How can you even think of closing the library?"

"This is none of your business, Liss." He was at his huffy, arrogant best. "Stay out of it."

"It certainly is my business," she shot back. "It's the business of everyone who uses this library. This *public* library," she added for emphasis.

"Exactly. The word public in public library means it's run with public funds, which we can no longer afford to throw away on such trivialities."

"Trivialities? Would that be just the books?" Liss asked in acid tones. "Or do you mean the computers, too?"

The library provided two computer workstations at no cost to library patrons. For many in this rural area, the library computers were their only access to the Internet. They came in to send and receive e-mail and do research, to look for jobs and apply for them, to file income taxes, and to put ads on *Uncle Henry's* to sell the things they no longer used.

The terminals weren't the only amenities tucked in among the heavily laden bookshelves in two large rooms that took up almost all the space on the municipal building's second floor. There were microform readers, too, and a large vertical file cabinet where Dolores hoarded her collection of newspaper clippings on subjects of interest to residents of the town.

Graye was still on his high horse. "We have to make up for lost revenue somehow, especially now that the parade has been canceled."

Liss's jaw dropped. "*You're* the ones who canceled it."

A wave of one hand dismissed that quibble. "The fact remains that the town is strapped for money. After you and your aunt were evicted from our work session, we came up with several new plans to make up the deficit. My only regret is that we didn't think to close the library in time to implement that action in the current fiscal year. As things stand now, this waste of space is fully funded until the end of December."

"Merry Christmas and Happy New Year," Dolores muttered under her breath.

Graye turned away from Liss to glower at the librarian. At his most brusque and condescending, he added, "I don't know what you're complaining about, Dolores. You're plenty old enough to retire."

The look she leveled at him should have turned him to stone. Color high, hands on narrow hips, she answered him in a voice dripping with contempt. "You are lower than pond scum, Mr. Selectman. It is a great pity that you were not drowned at birth."

Jason Graye laughed.

Liss could have told him that was not a smart thing to do.

Dolores had always been a prima donna, presiding over her domain with the air of a queen holding court, albeit one who was always willing to help a library patron find what he needed. She prided herself on being in control of both her environment and herself. Until today, Liss had never thought to see the other woman give way to rage. She stepped quickly out of the way as Dolores advanced on the man who dared suggest closing *her* library.

Lifting one hand, she jabbed the brightly painted nail on her index finger in Graye's direction. Had it been a knife and she'd thrown it, it would have penetrated what passed for his heart. "You will regret this action, Jason. You think I'm powerless to stop you, but I'm not."

"Ooh! I'm *so* scared." He held both hands in front of him in mock terror. Then he straightened to his full height and glared at her. "It's a done deal, Dolores. Accept it."

With that parting shot, he turned on his heel and stalked out of the library.

"You don't deserve to live!" Dolores shouted at his back.

Liss said nothing until the sound of Jason Graye's descending footsteps faded away. "I'm sure there's something we can do to stop him, Dolores. The library is too important to the town to let the board of selectmen close it down." To Liss's mind, it was irreplaceable.

"Not as important as money." Dolores let her bitterness show. "Do you know what they want to do with this space?"

"I can guess."

"Yes, I suppose that much is obvious. Graye is in real estate, after all. It's no surprise that he wants to rent out these rooms to bring in revenue. Well, he won't succeed. I mean to stop him."

"Good for you. We can pack the next town meeting and convince the board of selectmen to reverse their decision. Closing the library might have financial advantages for the town, but access to a public library should be a basic human right."

"The others will give up on the idea once Graye is out of the picture," Dolores muttered, more to herself than to Liss. "Cut off the head and the body dies."

The bloodthirsty image momentarily startled Liss, but she could understand Dolores's anger. She was glad she was not in Jason Graye's shoes. He'd misjudged Dolores badly if he'd thought she'd take a blow like this lying down. Any minute now, she'd be on the phone, rallying public support. Before she could get started, Liss needed to ask her the question that had brought her to the library in the first place.

"Do you have a minute, Dolores? I could use your help."

It seemed to take the librarian a long time to shift focus. Liss sympathized with that reaction, too. In Dolores's place, she'd still be thinking up inventive ways to rain down pain and suffering on Jason Graye's thick head.

Abruptly, Dolores jerked out of her reverie. "Yes, of course. What can I do for you, Liss?"

"I just have a quick question. Do you have any idea where Angie could have gone?"

"Not a clue." Dolores pursed her lips. "It was most inconsiderate of her to run off like that."

"You think she ran?"

"Well, she's not here, is she?"

"When did you last see her?"

"Wednesday." The answer came promptly, making Liss suspect that Dolores had been pondering the mystery of Angie's disappearance all along. Either that, or Sherri had already been by to ask her the same question.

"Was she here? If Angie consulted a travel guide or used one of the computers—"

"She passed by twice, once going to and once coming from Patsy's Coffee House."

Although the library was open fewer than twenty hours a week, Dolores was on the premises almost every day and some evenings, too, working without pay to keep everything running smoothly. That was not to say she reaped no benefits from her selfless devotion to her job. Dolores was Moosetookalook's resident snoop. She didn't miss much that went on in their quiet little village. From the library windows, even though they'd been made smaller some years back to conserve energy, she had a bird's-eye view of all the buildings around the town square. Liss knew for a fact that she also kept a pair of high-end binoculars in the drawer of the checkout desk.

"It's a pity you didn't see them drive away."

"Angie's garage faces Elm. Besides, there are trees in the way." Dolores's disgruntled voice told Liss that she'd tried more than once to spy on that particular neighbor and been frustrated in her attempts.

"I don't suppose you know where Angie lived before she came here?"

Dolores gave her a sharp look. "I can find out."

Apparently, Dolores did not know everything. Liss debated with herself for less than thirty seconds before sharing what Sherri had told her. "The police haven't been able to find any trace of her before she moved to Moosetookalook. It's as if she didn't exist until twelve years ago."

Dolores took this as a challenge. "They have their sources. I have mine."

"You'll tell me what you find?"

The librarian's eyes narrowed. "I'll tell both you and Sherri. Now if that's all, I have a great deal to do besides digging into Angie Hogencamp's past."

She started toward her large, old-fashioned desk, its highly polished surface piled high with the books she'd removed from the night drop. Abruptly, she stopped and glanced back, an enigmatic expression on her long, thin face.

"There's something very odd going on here. I'd never have pegged Angie as the flighty type. She's not one for strange or irrational behavior, unlike some people I could mention. She's a good businesswoman and a good mother."

"She's a good woman, period." Liss truly believed that.

"That remains to be seen, given the current situation. You never really know about the quiet ones, do you?" Dolores started to say more, then abruptly fell silent, her brow creasing in thought.

"Dolores? Have you remembered something?"

"What? No. And now I really must get to work." Her tone

turned to acid. "If you recall, I have more on my plate just now than figuring out what Angie Hogencamp is up to."

"So do I," Liss said.

It had been considerably more than fifteen minutes since she'd left the Emporium.

Chapter Five

By the time Sherri arrived at Margaret Boyd's office at The Spruces at one on Sunday afternoon, Margaret, Liss, and Joe Ruskin were already there. Margaret had called this strategy session to plan new events to replace those the town had canceled.

The tea service on the glass-topped coffee table was already in use. Green tea was Sherri's bet, to keep them alert and energized. Margaret offered chamomile when she thought her guests needed to stay calm.

Liss looked as if she could use the caffeine. Since Sherri had her own bad memories of being trapped in a fire, she suspected her friend hadn't managed to get much sleep since Friday. Even if Liss had succeeded in avoiding nightmares, she'd probably stayed awake worrying about Angie and the kids and wondering where they were.

Joe sat on the love seat at Liss's side. He was an older version of his son—a little over six feet tall with the same well-muscled build. He had more laugh lines around his mouth and eyes than Dan did, and more gray at the temples, but if Dan took after his father as he aged, Liss would be a lucky woman.

Sherri knew the story behind Joe's ownership of the

hotel well. He had worked at The Spruces over forty years earlier, when old-fashioned "grand hotels" had still been popular tourist destinations and had fallen in love with the place. When it went bankrupt and was slated for demolition, he'd bought it, renovated it, and reopened it to the benefit of the entire town. Things had been touch and go for the first few years, but now The Spruces had earned a solid reputation as a vacation spot, and the future looked rosy, especially if the hotel made a success of staging special events like the Western Maine Highland Games.

"Oh, good," Margaret said, catching sight of her. "Come in and sit. Tea?"

"I'll pass."

Sherri perched on the edge of an armless chair to the right of the love seat. Both faced Margaret's desk and had a good view of the three pen-and-ink drawings of Carrabassett County landscapes by local artists that hung on the pale green wall behind it. Margaret herself occupied the desk chair.

Margaret was a cheerful person by nature, and an active one. When she was enthusiastic about something, she talked a mile a minute, carrying others along on a wave of energy. She left nothing to chance if she could help it, and Sherri was not surprised to see her consult a handwritten agenda.

"First up," Margaret said, directing her gaze toward Sherri, "is there any news about Angie and her children?"

"No luck finding them so far." Sherri tried not to let her discouragement show. "Strictly speaking, it hasn't been that long. There could still be a simple explanation for everything."

"What?" Liss's teacup landed in its saucer with a clatter. "That they were called away on some sort of emergency and left without telling anyone? That Beth wouldn't call

Boxer? That they wouldn't have heard about the fire by now and come back?"

"Stranger things have happened. Turns out neither Angie nor Beth owns a cell phone." She shrugged at Joe's look of surprise. "Not everyone sees the need."

Everything possible was being done to find them. All the usual stones had been turned over, but, to mix her metaphors, they'd revealed nothing but dead ends.

"It looks as though Angie produced some very convincing documents twelve years ago—phony birth certificates for her children and a phony driver's license from New York State for herself. Don't get excited. Since it was fake, it's doubtful that's where she came from. Still, it was good enough for the state of Maine to issue her a driver's license with no questions asked. She hasn't needed much else in the way of paperwork. There's no requirement to have a business license to open a bookstore."

"What about taxes?"

"She paid state sales tax and income taxes as Angie. Her social security number didn't trigger any red flags. Don't ask me how that works. I have no idea."

"You're sure witness protection isn't involved?"

"I'd have been warned off by now if they were. Meanwhile, the next step is to have all the local news stations show Angie's picture on the air, together with a description of her car."

Liss's eyes widened. "Won't that make her look like a criminal?"

"The announcement will clearly state that there is no warrant for her arrest. We just want to make sure she's safe." Since Liss would leap to Angie's defense, pointing out that there was no proof of any wrongdoing, Sherri kept to herself the increasingly likely possibility that the bookseller did, in fact, have something to hide.

To break the tension, Joe picked up the plate of chocolate chip cookies Margaret had set out and passed it first to Sherri and then to Liss before taking one himself. They had come from Patsy's and smelled wonderful. "I attended church services this morning," he said before taking his first bite.

Sherri frowned over her cookie, uncertain why he'd bring that up. She had no idea if Joe was a regular churchgoer or not. "And?"

He chewed and swallowed. "And during the socializing afterward, there was a lot of chatter. No one had anything useful to suggest about where Angie might have taken Beth and Bradley, but there were plenty of people up in arms about recent events. Everyone seems to know the fire was set, even without an official announcement."

"No surprise there." Sherri bit down hard, taking what comfort she could from the explosion of chocolate as the cookie melted in her mouth.

"There wasn't a lot of talk about the parade being canceled," Joe went on. "Seemed to me that most of the residents of Moosetookalook, as opposed to the downtown merchants, are ambivalent about the Highland Games."

"People truly don't object to the change in plans?" Margaret's brow puckered, as if such a possibility had never occurred to her.

"Seems not." A twinkle appeared in Joe's eyes. "Now, if we'd had to ditch the fireworks, that would be another story."

Margaret sighed and scratched something off her list.

"What had folks up in arms was this plan by the board of selectmen to close the library."

"Such a stupid idea," Margaret said.

Sherri could tell that she was itching to move on to the next item on her agenda, but Joe wasn't done with his report.

"Dolores Mayfield has started a petition to remove Jason Graye from office."

"Good for her," Liss said. "I'll be happy to sign it."

"And she asked for volunteers to come to her house this evening to form a committee to save the library. Funny thing—she seemed to think Liss here has already agreed to be on it."

Liss groaned. "Just what I need—another committee!"

"We should all lend a hand," Margaret said, "but not until after next weekend. Now then, we still need to schedule an event to replace the parade. Here's what I have in mind."

Dan Ruskin reluctantly followed his wife up the steps to Dolores Mayfield's front porch. She lived on Upper Lowe Street, just three houses away from his father's place, the house where he and his brother, Sam, and his sister, Mary, had grown up. They'd learned at an early age not to bother Mrs. Mayfield at home, whether it was Mary trying to sell her Girl Scout cookies or Dan wanting to retrieve a baseball that had accidentally ended up in her backyard. Her drunk of a husband, universally known as Moose, had frightened small children even when he was sober. He wore his long hair shaggy around an oversized head that was home to a brain the size of a pea.

Dan glanced at Liss as she rang the bell. Coming here as a guest must feel strange to her, too. The ghost of a smile flitted across his face. The one and only time she'd previously set foot on the Mayfields' property, she'd been sixteen and bent on "borrowing" Moose's truck. The memory of her one and only foray into grand theft auto embarrassed her now, but Dan thought the whole escapade was pretty funny.

The way Liss told it, she'd been in desperate need of transportation to get to a Scottish dance competition. Since everybody in town knew that Moose had a habit of leaving his truck parked in the driveway with the keys in the ignition, she'd had the bright idea to take advantage of that fact. It had been sheer luck that she hadn't been caught and arrested, but as things turned out, Moose had been so drunk that day that he'd never even noticed that his truck had gone missing.

Liss had won her competition.

When Dolores opened the door and invited them in, she was smiling. "We're in the living room," she announced.

"We" turned out to be most of the members of the Moosetookalook Small Business Association, together with many of the library's regular patrons. It was standing room only. Dan and Liss threaded their way through the crowd to squeeze in next to Stu Burroughs in the corner by the fireplace. Only then did Dan get a good look at the room's décor.

"Holy crap," he whispered.

Liss's eyes widened as she followed the direction of his gaze. "Oh, my."

Weapons were displayed on every wall. Crossed swords hung above the fireplace with a shield showing a family crest between them. On the opposite side of the room were two glass-fronted cabinets. One contained an assortment of hunting rifles. The other held a collection of knives, most of them with wicked-looking blades. A bow and a quiver of arrows, the kind used in competition, not the Renaissance Faire–Robin Hood variety, occupied a place of honor atop an upright piano, while a blunderbuss, the style of gun used in colonial days, rested on a shelf three-quarters of the way up the wall behind the sofa.

"You didn't know about Dolores's little hobby?" Stu's lips twitched. "She's quite the expert. Moose likes things that go bang. Dolores prefers stuff that stabs."

Dolores clapped her hands together. "All right, people. Listen up. We're here for two reasons. First, we need to rally support to remove Jason Graye from office. Then we must convince the other selectmen to change their minds about closing the library. One way to do that is to come up with alternative sources of funding."

"Hey, Dolores," Stu called out. "I've got one. Why don't you give a lecture on 'Curious Weapons of the Past' and charge admission."

Dolores looked as if she might consider it, although there was a marked lack of enthusiasm from the rest of those present.

The warped sense of humor for which Stu was famous had him throwing out another suggestion. "Or you could give a fencing demonstration."

Belatedly, Dolores caught on to the fact that he was mocking her. Her mouth tightened into a thin, hard line before she forced herself to smile and wag a finger at him. "I was a champion fencer in college. You'd best remember that."

If she meant to look playful and sound good-natured, she missed by a mile. Dan doubted she'd ever been able to laugh at herself.

Chuckling, Stu was quick with a comeback. "Here's a thought: challenge Graye to a duel. Now *that* I'd pay money to see."

"If you're through making ridiculous suggestions," Gloria Weir cut in, "I have a serious proposal to offer. The library can host a craft fair."

"I see how that would benefit you and your shop, but how does it help the library?" Thanks to Stu's needling, Dolores sounded testy.

"The library would get a percentage of the proceeds."

"We could organize a bottle drive," Betsy Twining suggested. The proprietor of the Clip and Curl, Moosetookalook's combination beauty parlor and barber shop, didn't hesitate to jump in with her idea. She did everything the way she cut hair—boldly and with no excuses. If you hadn't expected your hair to end up quite as short as she cut it, Betsy would assure you that you'd love the new style when you got used to it.

Dan went out of town when he needed a trim, rather than turn Betsy loose with scissors and razor blade.

"Never work," Moose Mayfield muttered from the depths of his recliner.

"Sure it will," Betsy insisted. "Collect returnable cans and bottles and put all the money we get from the local bottle redemption center into a special library account."

"Anyone who bothers to save up all them cans and bottles," Moose shot back, "is gonna want to keep the nickel apiece for himself and buy more beer."

Betsy glared at him. "I'll have you know that the animal shelter down to Fallstown does very well with a similar deal. The woman who runs the place told me all about it when we went there to adopt Skippy."

"Is it still bringing in money?" Dan asked. If he remembered right, it had been four or five years since the Twinings agreed to take in the two-year-old fox terrier. When Lenny Peet, Skippy's previous owner, had died of old age, Liss had made it one of her causes to find him a new family. She'd even made a speech about it at Lenny's funeral. Right after that, Betsy had come forward to volunteer.

"I can find out," Betsy answered.

"You do that." Dolores's terse comment served to put her back in control of the meeting. "If it looks feasible," she added, "go ahead and start negotiations with the local redemption center on behalf of the library."

Dan had to smile. The grimace on Betsy's face made it clear she hadn't intended to offer to do quite that much for the cause. He was well aware that, with the notable exception of Jason Graye, people didn't often say no to Dolores Mayfield and resolved to keep his own mouth firmly shut for the rest of the meeting. Like most bossy women, Dolores was good at delegating time-consuming tasks to others.

Kate Permutter spoke up next. "The other day, I read a blog written by the librarian in Hartland. It was all about selling donated and discarded books online to raise money. He claimed to have made $4,500 for his library in just one year."

Dolores promptly assigned her to e-mail the Hartland Library for additional details.

Hesitantly, Liss raised her hand. "What about contacting the *Daily Scoop*?" When several people looked blank, she clarified. "That's our local online newspaper. It isn't exactly the *Washington Post*, but a lot of people do read it."

"Do you want them to interview Dolores?" Stu asked. "Or to skewer Jason Graye?"

"Why not both?" Dan spoke before he could stop himself.

"I could give them an earful," Dolores muttered.

"You need to be careful what you say if it's going to appear in print," Liss warned. "None of the accusations against Graye over crooked real estate deals ever held up in court."

"How about this?" Dolores made air quotes to indicate a newspaper headline. "Local librarian vows Jason Graye will be first against the wall when the revolution comes!"

An appalled silence fell over the room.

"Oh, for heaven's sake!" Dolores rolled her eyes. "That was a joke, people!"

Maud Dennison, a retired school teacher who worked full-time as the manager of Dan's shop, reprimanded her in a prim voice. "You shouldn't kid around about shooting people, Dolores."

"That was a *quote,* Maud."

"Yes, I know. From *A Hitchhiker's Guide to the Galaxy*, I believe. That's not the point."

"The point," Dolores declared, "is that nobody in this room would be the least bit upset if someone did shoot Jason Graye."

Before the argument could become any more heated, a hulking figure erupted from his chair. "Hell of an idea," Moose Mayfield mumbled. "Shoot the bastard."

He staggered slightly as he crossed the room, his inebriated condition so obvious that Dan was embarrassed to witness it. He suspected that everyone else in the crowded living room felt the same way. No one said a word as Moose made his way to the antique oak lowboy the Mayfields used as a TV stand and fell to his knees in front of it.

He jerked open the bottom drawer and reached inside. When his hand reappeared, it held a gun.

"Holy shit!" Stu hit the floor.

Seeing that Liss seemed frozen in place, staring in disbelief at the weapon, Dan thrust her behind him. He took a step toward the lowboy, then stopped as Moose rose to his feet. What did he think he was going to do? Even if Moose had been unarmed, he outweighed Dan by a good fifty pounds.

"Is that thing loaded?" Gloria's question came out as a squeak.

"'Course it's loaded." Moose gestured with the gun as he spoke. "Wouldn't be much use against a burglar if it wasn't."

Everyone ducked as he swung the weapon in a wide arc.

Moose laughed. "Got robbed once. Some lowlife stole my truck and went joyriding. Filled the tank up again and thought I wouldn't notice. If I ever find out who that sumbitch was, I'll teach him not to mess with Moose Mayfield!"

"Oh, God," Liss whispered.

Dan felt her shift so that his body completely hid her from Moose's view.

"For God's sake, Roger. That was more than a decade ago." Dolores sounded thoroughly disgusted with her alcoholic husband. "Stop obsessing about it."

Moose shifted his big, awkward body toward his wife, but as he turned, his already precarious balance deserted him entirely. In a last-ditch effort to stay upright, he flailed both arms. The hand holding the gun flew upward. A split second later, the weapon discharged with a deafening roar.

Dan turned, wrapped Liss in his arms, and dragged both of them to the floor. Plaster rained down on their heads. Shrieks and curses rose up all around them, but Dolores's outraged bellow drowned out everyone else.

"Roger Mayfield, you put that gun down this instant!"

Dan lifted his head far enough to see what was going on. Moose was still on his feet, staring at his gun as if he couldn't figure out how it had come to be in his hand. "Aw, geez, Dolly," he whined, "I was just trying to help."

Dolores marched right up to him, eyes blazing. "If anyone's going to shoot Jason Graye, it's going to be me. Give me that gun, you moron."

Meek as could be, he handed it over. As soon as she grabbed hold of it, he winced and shrank back, almost as if he expected her to strike him.

Dan's mind boggled. Moose Mayfield was scared to death of his wife.

"Dolly?" Liss whispered.

Was anything as it seemed?

Liss did not sleep well. On Monday morning, she detoured to Patsy's on her way to open Moosetookalook Scottish Emporium. She was not in the mood for her own coffee, or for her own company.

As usual, Patsy was doing a brisk morning business. Those who didn't come for the coffee showed up for the baked goods. The good smells alone would add inches to her waistline, but for once Liss didn't care. She ordered two sticky buns to balance out the infusion of caffeine and hoped the combination would distract her from increasingly dismal thoughts.

She'd dreamed of Angie, Beth, and Bradley. They'd been running across an open field. She'd been trying to catch up with them, but she kept stumbling and falling. Their lead had increased with every tumble until she could no longer see them at all.

Order in hand, she looked around for a place to sit. Both tables were occupied. So were the five stools at the counter. Two of the three booths were also taken, one by a family of four and the other by a man sitting alone.

She stared at him, taking in an average build, a snub nose, and long, thin fingers wrapped around the coffee mug he was just lifting to his lips. He wore his hair in a buzz cut so short it was impossible to tell its color. He was no one she recognized—probably another hotel guest who'd wandered into the village on an early-morning constitutional.

Liss had been hoping he'd turn out to be one of the regular fixtures of the place, like Alex Permutter. Then she could have asked to join him and left the remaining booth free for the next customer. Instead, she headed for the empty booth, the one between the other two.

The first sticky bun went down easy. The second turned to cardboard when the woman in the adjoining booth spoke in a voice loud enough for everyone in the café to overhear.

"Such a shame the bookstore burned down," she said. "Now I suppose I'll have to drive all the way to Fallstown just to buy a birthday card for Aunt Prunella."

A tear dripped into Liss's breakfast blend. She swiped at her eyes, but it was too late. She couldn't stem the flow no matter how hard she tried. It was all she could do not to sob out loud. She was fumbling in her pocket for a tissue when an oversized napkin appeared in front of her nose.

Liss grabbed it and dabbed at her damp cheeks. Her vision blurry, she looked up into Patsy's sympathetic face.

Without asking if she wanted more, the coffee shop owner refilled Liss's mug. Then she slid onto the bench seat opposite Liss, set the carafe on the table, and reached across the wooden surface to squeeze her friend's forearm. "Do you want to talk about it?"

"It's stupid. Such a little thing."

"Sometimes that's all it takes."

"I was thinking about Angie."

"Figured that. Go on. What set off the waterworks?"

Liss lowered her voice. "The woman in the next booth." She gestured toward the one behind Patsy. "She said she used to buy cards from Angie's Books. Angie stocked the best cards."

Patsy's eyebrows lifted. "*That's* what made you cry?"

"Not exactly." Liss managed a watery smile. "It was that Angie always sends us anniversary cards. Every year. Silly ones that make you laugh out loud. Except for Aunt Margaret, she's the only one who always remembers the date we got married. Even my parents forget, and you know how involved my mother was in planning the wedding."

"Violet did get a bit carried away." Patsy chuckled, remembering. "But whose fault was that? You were the one who agreed to tie the knot at that year's Western Maine Highland Games."

"You'd think that would make the date easier to remember, wouldn't you?" Maybe it would, this time around. Just as it had then, the date would fall on the Saturday of the games.

"Which anniversary is it?" Patsy asked. "Seems like just yesterday that you came back home to Moosetookalook."

"It's our sixth." And Liss had suffered a career-ending knee injury just over eight years ago. She'd returned to Maine to recuperate, never intending to stay longer than a few months.

Funny how life worked out.

"Sixth. Let me see." Patsy's brow creased in thought. "That would be the candy anniversary. That's the traditional gift, anyway. I'm not in favor of that new list someone or other came up with."

"Why? What does the updated version say people should give on the sixth anniversary?"

"Wood." Patsy made a face. "Boring."

Liss had to agree, although given that she was married to a professional custom woodworker, she wouldn't mind if Dan was even now making her a new bookcase or a magazine rack or even a set of TV tables.

"Feeling better?" Patsy asked.

"Yes, thank you. Although I still wish I knew where Angie and her children are."

Patsy's voice sounded a tad too hearty when she replied. "Maybe you'll hear from her this year, too. Nothing to stop her from putting a card in the mail, is there? Wherever she is, there's got to be a post office."

Liss brightened a bit at the thought. "You're right. Why, I might have a card from her as early as today or tomorrow. She always sends them well ahead of time. I kidded her about that once—told her it must be because she didn't *really* remember the exact date. She said *she* knew what it was, all right. She figured she was doing me a favor by sending her card early, as a reminder so that *Dan* wouldn't forget."

"That sounds like her." Patsy chuckled.

"I wonder . . . do you think Angie's husband used to forget their anniversary?"

"No idea, hon. She's never talked about him, has she?"

"Not to you, either?"

"Never, although I've got to say she does have strong opinions on what makes a marriage work." Patsy shook her head. "Wasted on me, of course, since I never saw the sense in being saddled with a husband in the first place."

Now that Liss thought about it, she realized that Angie had always been after her to make more time for herself and Dan, even when that meant neglecting their businesses for a day or two. What kind of marriage *had* Angie had?

Liss swallowed hard to rid herself of a new lump in her throat.

"I thought Angie and I were friends," she whispered. "I don't understand how she could just take off like that, or how she can stay away when she must know we're all worried about her and the kids."

"I'm sure she has her reasons." Patsy administered a brisk pat to Liss's shoulder as she rose to tend to a new customer waiting at the counter. "And I'll bet good money she sends you that anniversary card. Likely it's already in the mail."

"Thanks, Patsy."

Patsy shrugged her bony shoulders. "She's my friend, too."

Chapter Six

Tuesday started out as an ordinary day. Liss left the Emporium at ten to walk the short distance along Pine Street to the post office on the corner of Pine and Ash. There was no door-to-door delivery in Moosetookalook. Collecting the mail from her post office box was a daily ritual six mornings a week.

Her mind on other things, Liss tugged on the post office door. When it wouldn't open, she was momentarily stymied. Only belatedly did she notice the handwritten sign taped to the other side of the glass.

CLOSED TODAY. BROKEN WINDOW. SORRY.

"Broken—?" Her gaze darted to the expanse of glass to the right of the door, but it appeared to be intact. It had even been washed in the not-too-distant past.

Puzzled, Liss circled to her left. She found the explanation along the side of the post office, where a second large window faced the section of Pine Street that ran west from the town square. It had been blocked off with a large sheet of plywood, but Liss could imagine the mess shattered glass must have made inside. If the window had been broken with any amount of force, shards of glass would have sprayed directly into dozens of post office boxes. They had little doors that unlocked by keys at the front, but in back they were open so that Julie Simpson, Moosetookalook's postmaster, could fill them with letters, postcards, advertising flyers, and package slips.

Liss was about to turn away and return to Moosetookalook Scottish Emporium when Betsy Twining stepped out of Clip and Curl. While the post office, at the front of the building, opened onto Ash Street and the town square, the entrance to Betsy's business was on Pine.

"Awful, isn't it?" Betsy asked. "What some people get up to!"

"Did they catch whoever did it?" Liss asked.

"Not so far." She made a face. "I don't think much of that new part-timer Sherri's got working nights. He's supposed to patrol. Do door checks. He never even noticed the broken window."

"It's pretty dark on this side, away from the lights in the town square." Liss knew and liked Mike Jennings, but to Betsy he still carried the taint of being "from away."

"Be that as it may, it was left to Julie to spot the damage when she came in this morning. By the time I got here for my first appointment, a couple of men were already putting up that hunk of plywood."

Julie Simpson was not only Moosetookalook's postmaster, she was the only United States Postal Service employee to work at Moosetookalook's tiny post office. Most days she came in at half past six and had the mail sorted and slotted by eight, at which point she opened the lobby to customers.

"Is Julie still in there?" Liss asked.

"Went home a half hour ago, and not in the best of moods, either." Betsy chuckled. "It wasn't just the vandalism that had her riled. It was the attitude of the higher-ups in the postal service. I don't know who she reports to, but she phoned him right after she called the cops. I think she was hoping he'd come give her a hand, or at least send someone to help out, but he just told her to close the facility. Facility! Then he told her to make sure none of her customers got cut on broken glass because it was embedded in their mail."

Not a pretty picture, Liss thought.

"Poor Julie had to pull everything out of every box to make sure nothing had glass stuck to it. Then she had to vacuum the boxes before she could put the mail back in. And that's not all. She had to clean everything—the floor, the sorting tables, even the bins."

Liss could sympathize. Glass had a tendency to fly in all directions and end up in the most unlikely locations.

"Then, on top of all that," Betsy continued, clearly relishing the chance to regale someone with the details, "Julie still had to put out the new mail that came in this morning."

"Who put up the plywood?" Liss asked.

"Well, that's another story. It was the glass company. You'd think they'd just come out and replace the glass, wouldn't you? But no. Seems that high-mucky-muck post office guy called that outfit down to Fallstown and instead of just ordering a new window, he insisted that this one be replaced with safety glass."

"And this created a problem?" Liss didn't try to hurry Betsy along. She was in no rush to get back to the Emporium, and she was curious to hear all the details.

"Well, yes," Betsy said, as if that should have been obvious. "That made it a special order, and that meant the glass people couldn't replace it right away because they don't keep that kind of glass in stock. Not the size needed to replace that window, anyway."

Liss wasn't surprised. Fallstown might be considerably larger than Moosetookalook, but it was far from being a big city. No sensible business kept an expensive product in stock when there wasn't much call for it.

"Lot of nonsense, if you ask me," Betsy went on. "What's wrong with plain old window glass?"

"It shatters," Liss said.

"Well, yes. But how often do you think anyone's going to throw a rock through the post office window?"

Betsy might have continued in this vein indefinitely, had it not been for the arrival of her next customer. Liss returned to the Emporium in a thoughtful frame of mind. First the fire. Now this. What was happening to their peaceful little village?

She hesitated all of five minutes before picking up the phone and calling the police department.

On her way to Moosetookalook Scottish Emporium, Sherri Campbell stopped in at Patsy's Coffee House to pick up four sticky buns, knowing full well that they were Liss's favorite treat. The topping was even gooier by the time she crossed the town square. The day was going to be a scorcher. It was already getting hot, and far more humid that any native Mainer liked.

Fifteen minutes after she answered Liss's phone call, Sherri was ensconced in one of the chairs in the cozy corner, nibbling on a bun. Liss joined her, for once bringing ice water instead of coffee.

"Anything new on the fire?" she asked.

Sherri shook her head. "And before you ask, no sign yet of Angie, Beth, or Bradley, either." She was beginning to wonder if they'd ever turn up.

"And now we have a vandal on the loose."

Sherri could understand why she was concerned. If someone was into breaking windows, that nice big plate-glass one up front was a natural target. "Looks that way."

"Kids, do you think?"

"Probably, but it's hard to say for sure. The thing is, who-ever broke the window at the post office went in through it. Once inside, he, she, or they tossed the mail around and in general made a mess of the whole place."

"Did they take anything?" Liss polished off her first sticky bun and reached for a second.

"Julie says nothing seems to be missing, but I don't know how she can be sure. There were hundreds of pieces of mail, both sorted and unsorted. No way can she re-member each and every one of them."

"Betsy Twining didn't pass along that tidbit."

Sherri grinned, but it faded fast. "I'm pretty sure Julie didn't tell her. Think of the uproar if even a fraction of the townspeople thought their mail might have been stolen."

There was one sticky bun left in the bakery box. Sherri eyed it, sorely tempted, and kept both hands wrapped around her glass to prevent herself from reaching for it. It would go straight to her hips, and she didn't need any more padding.

"Maybe someone had a grudge against the post office," Liss suggested. "I suppose they call it 'going postal' for a reason."

"I hate crimes like this—the ones with no apparent rhyme or reason. We dusted for fingerprints, but I doubt it will do much good. These days, even kids know to wear gloves when they're committing a crime."

"So when does the FBI show up?" Liss asked. "Or do you actually have to have proof that someone has stolen mail for the crime to qualify as a federal offense?"

Sherri hated to shatter illusions, especially one she'd believed in herself until a few hours earlier. "I don't know how to break this to you, Liss, but that's yet another myth perpetrated by television crime dramas. In real life, even though stealing the mail is a federal crime, it doesn't rate much of a response."

"Seriously?" In her astonishment, Liss picked up the remaining sticky bun and chowed down on it.

"No lie. And when I told Pete that, he just laughed and said it figured. Seems back when he first started out as a patrol deputy for the sheriff's department, he arrested a guy who got drunk, stole a mail truck full of mail, and crashed it into a tree. He was sure the drunk would end up in Leavenworth. You know what happened instead? Two postal inspectors showed up. All they were interested in was reclaiming the mail truck. They left prosecution to the Carrabassett County DA. Then the drunk got himself a good lawyer, and aside from the few hours he spent in the county jail before he made bail, he didn't serve any time at all. He ended up with what amounted to a slap on the wrist—a hundred hours of community service."

"That's . . . words fail me." Having devoured the third sticky bun, Liss polished off the last of the ice water in her glass and lifted it by way of asking if Sherri wanted a refill.

"I'm good." She took a long swallow and sighed.

"So, asking as a local business owner, what are you going to do to protect the shops around the square?"

"There isn't all that much we can do except keep a close eye on the storefronts for the next little while."

"Better check the sides, too."

Sherri acknowledged the jibe with a roll of her eyes. "You know how small my department is. No way can we be everywhere at once. To tell you the truth, I'm hoping the post office break-in *was* just kids on a spree. I'd hate to think someone has it in for downtown Moosetookalook."

Sherri's words stuck with Liss the rest of the day. The thought of someone holding a grudge against their little town was sobering. She couldn't completely discount it, but neither could she think of anyone who'd be out to get all of the town square merchants. And why target the post office? That made no sense at all.

An even less palatable theory sprang to mind as she packed items for the coming weekend at the Highland Games. What if there weren't two separate villains, an arsonist and a vandal, but only one? The very thought made her shudder, and she quickly talked herself out of the notion. She had an active imagination, but even she had trouble believing in the existence of an unknown madman intent on random destruction.

It was late in the afternoon when two men entered Moosetookalook Scottish Emporium. One was Angus Grant, the hotel guest who had taken her to task for selling kilts to women. His companion was the other stranger Liss had noticed on the night of the fire.

Close up, the second man's snowy white hair and short, precisely trimmed beard looked as if they'd never dare look mussed. At a guess, he was in his seventies. He carried a silver-headed cane but didn't seem to need it. She saw no hint of a limp as he crossed the sales floor to where she stood behind the counter.

"Good afternoon, miss," he said in a cultured voice.

"Good afternoon. How may I help you?"

"You can explain to me why your post office is closed. I walked into town specifically to purchase stamps, and now I find I cannot do so." Although he didn't look angry, there was something in his voice that made Liss think he was more than a little annoyed.

"There was an incident earlier today. Vandals broke a window. For the moment, the post office is a crime scene, and no one is allowed in, not even the postmaster."

Liss had made up that last part. Only now did it occur to her to wonder why Julie hadn't been ordered to open the post office as soon as she'd cleaned up the mess. Could it be that the postal service really was going to send someone to investigate?

"Is there somewhere else I can buy stamps?" the man asked.

"Are you staying at The Spruces, Mister . . . ?"

"Eldridge. Martin Eldridge. Yes, I am."

"Then I think you'll find that the hotel concierge has stamps."

Eldridge's lips lifted in a pleasant enough smile, but it didn't reach his eyes. "Of course. I should have thought of the concierge myself. Are you ready to go back, Grant, or shall I return without you?"

Having made a circuit of the Emporium, Angus Grant was now glowering at one of Liss's locked display cases, the one that contained an assortment of the small knives men in Scottish dress wore tucked into the top of their hose. The blades were all similar, and not sharp enough to do much damage, but the hilts were uniquely decorated. Some sported clan crests. Others were ornately carved. A small, hand-lettered sign inside the case identified them as *skean dhus*.

"Wrong. Wrong. Wrong," Grant muttered.

Liss repressed a sigh. "What is, Mr. Grant?"

"Look at that spelling!" He indicated the *skean dhus* sign. "You need an adviser to help you with your Gaelic, my good woman. For one thing there is no letter K in Gaelic. For another, *dhu* is a non-word. If there were such a word, it wouldn't be pronounced correctly for the second word in the Scottish term for a stocking knife. The correct nomenclature is *sgian dubh*."

To Liss's secret amusement, Grant butchered the Gaelic pronunciation, although he followed that up by spelling the words correctly.

"You have a point, of course." *The customer is always right,* she reminded herself, *no matter how obnoxious he is.* Clearly, this issue was important to him. "The thing is, Mr. Grant, we are not in Scotland. My customers are Americans and Canadians, many of whom do not have a drop of Scots blood in their veins. The Anglicized version of the term—"

"One should always stick to the spelling of the relevant language." Leaving the display case, he stomped over to the sales counter to glare at her.

Liss knew it was futile to argue, since nothing she said would change his mind, but hasty words popped out of her mouth before she could stop them: "The relevant language is American English."

Grant's piggy little eyes narrowed. The term "hot under the collar" took on new meaning as a dull red color crept upward into his face. Liss had no intention of changing her sign, but since he looked as if he might be about to explode, she rushed into a partial apology.

"I realize that the spelling I chose must be annoying to someone as familiar with Gaelic as you are. Shall we agree to disagree?"

Grant clearly did not find any kind of compromise acceptable. He started to sputter, so riled up that his words were incomprehensible.

Martin Eldridge cleared his throat.

Grant, belatedly remembering that they had an audience, closed his mouth and turned toward the other man.

Eldridge said, "Perhaps you might continue this another time, my dear fellow? It's past time we were heading back to the hotel." Before Grant could spit out any more venom, he added, "Didn't you say your wife has plans for this afternoon?"

Liss sent the older man a grateful smile. "Are you here for the Highland Games, Mr. Eldridge?"

"My stay is indefinite at this point." With a slight nod of farewell to Liss, he steered Grant toward the exit.

"That's another thing," Grant complained to his companion. "She's one of the people behind bringing Highland games to this backwater."

Liss bit back a retort. She'd been on the committee, but it had been her aunt, as the hotel's events coordinator, who had done, and was still doing, most of the work. Best not to antagonize him further, she decided, and he didn't need to know that she and Margaret were related.

"I do not have high hopes for the event." With that final condemnation, Grant left the Emporium.

Shaking her head, Liss watched the two men walk past

her window. She was just about to turn away when a flash of bright yellow caught her attention—a loose section of the police barrier on the far side of the square.

The diversion over, she was plunged back into wondering and worrying.

"Where are you, Angie?" she whispered.

Liss had racked her brain to think of where a woman, a teenaged girl, and a young boy might have gone. She came up blank every time. She had no idea where to begin to look for them. For all Liss knew, they might have run off to Canada, or California, or the moon!

Frustration had her reaching for one of the college-ruled yellow legal pads she kept on the shelf beneath the sales counter. Felt-tip pen in hand, she stared at the blank spaces on the top sheet.

What did she really know about Angie? She had birthdays, or at least she had the dates Angie, Beth, and Bradley had been celebrating. She wrote them down, together with the years in which Beth and Bradley had been born. She wasn't sure how old Angie was.

What else? Angie collected designer teddy bears. Had she done so before she came to Moosetookalook? Was there any way to trace them if she had?

Not when they had burned up along with the rest of Angie's possessions! Liss sighed.

Angie had a sister-in-law. Maybe. Liss tapped the pen on the pad. Had Sherri followed up on that? She hadn't said. Maybe Liss should ask around. Someone must have gone into the bookstore that day, when Angie was selling books at the hotel. But would anyone remember details more than six years later?

She made a sound of frustration. If the police couldn't

pin down Angie's real name, what hope did an amateur have of finding even more elusive information?

It was then that a possible course of action occurred to her. When you needed specialized knowledge it made sense to consult an expert. Before she could talk herself out of the idea, she reached for the phone.

Chapter Seven

Early the next day, shortly after Liss opened the Emporium, the bell over the door jangled. She looked up in time to see a man come into the shop. His dark brown hair was on the short side but not especially neat. His face was unlined, making it impossible to guess his age. He was about her height, but somehow managed to look shorter. The only distinctive thing about him was the steady movement of his jaw. He was chewing industriously on a wad of gum. As she watched with reluctant fascination, he blew an enormous pink bubble.

Inevitably, it popped, leaving gooey residue on his chin and upper lip. In a nonchalant manner, he sucked it in before tipping an imaginary hat in her direction.

"You're looking good, sweetheart," said Jake Murch, Private Investigator.

"Liar," Liss retorted, but she couldn't stop a smile from spreading over her face. "How have you been, Jake?"

"Same old, same old." His broad, friendly grin faded as he approached the sales counter. "But it looks like you got trouble. That's a heck of a mess out there. Arson, huh?"

"That's the general consensus."

Shaking his head, Jake extracted a small, dog-eared notebook and a stub of a pencil from his shirt pocket. "The way I hear it, it's officially arson."

"Then you know more than I do."

Liss decided to take this as an encouraging sign. Jake Murch might strike some as a caricature of a private eye, but he had the kind of street smarts she lacked, not to mention the contacts. She had a sneaking suspicion he could tap into more sources than the police could, maybe even more than Dolores had access to as a librarian. She had done the right thing by contacting him.

"I did some checking after your phone call," Jake said. "I'll level with you. I'm not sure I can do any more to find your friends than the police have."

"Please don't say that!"

"I don't mislead clients, Liss. There have been no sightings of Angie Hogencamp's car. There have been a few reports of seeing one or the other of the children, but none of them panned out. Did you come up with any more photos? The ones the cops are circulating aren't the best. Driver's license for the mom. School pictures for the kids."

Liss produced a folder she'd left on the shelf beneath the counter and pulled out an 8½ by 11 print of a snapshot she'd taken with her cell phone a few months earlier. It showed all three of the Hogencamps.

"Bradley's grown some since then." She pointed to a twelve-year-old with an infectious grin. "Add at least another inch in height."

She hoped nothing had happened to dim that smile.

The photo had been taken inside Angie's Books during Moosetookalook's annual March Madness Mud-Season Sale. Back then, there had been no hint of trouble on the horizon. Angie's business had been booming, and as far as Liss had been able to tell, the bookseller hadn't a care in the world.

"It's a good clear shot of Angie and Beth. Unless they've deliberately changed their appearance, this is what they looked like when they disappeared."

Angie was an ordinary-looking woman in her mid-forties with dark, wavy hair, worn short, and big brown eyes that always, now that Liss thought about it, seemed a little sad. She was a few pounds overweight, but in good physical shape. She had to be to haul cartons of books around.

Her daughter favored her, having inherited the same coloring, but her hair was shoulder-length and her build was slighter. Beth had taken up Scottish dancing for a while—first with Liss as her teacher, and later, after Dance Central opened, with Zara—but over the last couple of years she'd given it up in favor of various extracurricular activities with her friends in high school. Even though Moosetookalook's children were bussed to the consolidated school in Fallstown after eighth grade, a good twenty minutes away by car, most of them managed to bum rides back and forth when they needed them, just as Liss and her friends had done back in the day.

"Who's the other boy?" Murch asked, pointing to a young man who had an arm slung around Beth's shoulders.

"That's my cousin Edward. His mother calls him Teddy, but he prefers the nickname Boxer. He's Beth's boyfriend."

Liss perched on the stool behind the counter while Jake studied the photograph. She didn't need to look at it to call Boxer's appearance to mind. He had his father's plain, square face, but he had inherited his reddish brown hair from his grandmother, Liss's Aunt Margaret. In the picture he was a few inches taller than Beth, but he was still growing.

Murch studied the smiling group for a long moment before returning the photo to the folder and setting it atop the counter. "I assume Boxer doesn't know anything either?"

Liss shook her head. "Believe me, he'd have said if he did. He's crazy about her. I haven't seen him myself, but I know he's talked to Sherri and to Margaret."

She felt certain Murch remembered both women from the time, six years back, when he'd been hired to investigate another crime with ties to Moosetookalook. Despite an uncanny ability to give the impression that he couldn't keep two facts straight at the same time, the PI had a mind like a steel trap.

"Did you talk to all the neighbors?" he asked.

"Not all of them, but Sherri Campbell did. She says no one saw them leave, and no one noticed any unusual activity around the bookstore before the fire started. Of course, it broke out around three-thirty in the morning, so everyone was asleep."

"And no one has any idea where the Hogencamps would go?"

Liss shook her head. "Believe me, I've asked everyone I thought might know. And Sherri has made it clear how important it is to find them. I can't imagine anyone in town holding back information, not in a situation like this one."

Murch looked skeptical. "Someone knows, sweetheart. Okay, we'll start with Angie's closest friends. Who did she hang out with in her free time?"

Liss had already opened her mouth to rattle off a list of names when she realized she didn't know the answer. Frowning, she closed it again. What free time? You didn't have much when you ran a one-person business, and Angie had also had what amounted to a second full-time job taking care of her two children.

"I don't think she had much leisure for socializing."

"No girls' nights out? No bridge club? No choir practice?"

Liss rolled her eyes. "No martial arts classes and no early morning jogs to get in shape for the Beach-to-Beacon Road Race, either. She worked long hours in the bookstore, made sure Beth and Bradley got three squares and did their homework, and turned in early. As far as I know, the only organization she was active in was the Moosetookalook Small Business Association."

"Don't know her as well as you thought, do you?"

"I guess not," Liss admitted. If she did, surely she'd have a clue where Angie and her children had gone.

Murch turned so he could look out through the plate-glass display window at the front of the shop. He leaned back, resting his elbows on the sales counter as he studied the view. "This is a self-contained little community you've got here, and yet no one saw anything," he mused. "Nope, I don't buy it. Someone got up to take a leak and looked out his window. Or a restless sleeper heard a car engine and glanced at the bedside clock. And I'm betting someone's lying to the cops when they say they don't know anything."

"Then maybe duplicating what the police have already done isn't such a bad idea after all." Liss started to feel a bit more optimistic.

Still regarding the view through her window, Murch asked, "Who's the local nosy parker?"

His use of the old-fashioned term for snoop surprised Liss into a laugh. "Who isn't?"

Turning around to pick up the notebook he'd left on the counter, Murch flipped to a blank page. "Names, please, sweetheart."

Liss gave the question a bit of thought before answering. There was more than one likely possibility. After a moment, she rattled off the first four that sprang to mind—Julie Simpson, Betsy Twining, Dolores Mayfield, and Francine Noyes. "Start with Dolores Mayfield at the library on the second floor of the municipal building," she suggested, "but expect to have to fend off her recruitment efforts."

As succinctly as possible, she explained about Dolores's campaign to overturn the board of selectmen's decision. She did not give him details of the meeting at the Mayfield house. They weren't relevant to the case she'd asked him to investigate. More importantly, as far as Liss knew, no one had reported the incident to the police. There was an unspoken agreement among those who had been there to spare Moose any trouble with the law. It wasn't as if he'd hurt anyone.

When she'd finished her account, Murch gave a low whistle. "She sounds like a formidable woman, and a bad enemy. I'd watch my back if I were this Graye fella. Okay, which one of these others should I talk to after the librarian?"

"Since you'll be right there in the municipal building, try Francine Noyes, the town clerk. The police department is in the same building, by the way. You should probably touch base with Sherri Campbell."

"Already talked to her." His fleeting grin was impish. "She never did know what to make of me, but she can't stop me from making inquiries."

"She knows you've helped me before. That ought to be enough."

"Okey-dokey. If you say so."

"Julie Simpson is our postmaster, and Betsy Twining owns and operates the Clip and Curl, which is in the back half of the same building."

"I noticed the plywood over the window," Murch said.

Of course he would. Liss repeated what little she knew about the incident.

"Huh," he said. "Okay. Anyone else who keeps an eagle eye out on this backwater burg?"

"Do *not* insult my hometown," Liss warned him, even though she knew he was kidding.

"Just answer the question, sweetheart. Time's a wasting."

"The only other person I can think of is Patsy at Patsy's Coffee House, but I doubt she'll tell you anything useful. There isn't much that goes on in this town that she doesn't know about, but unlike the others, she's not the gossipy sort. She just . . . hears things."

"I like a challenge," Murch said. "I'll just have to sweet-talk her into confiding in me."

"Good luck with that," Liss said with a laugh. Patsy would make mincemeat of him.

"Anyone else who knows all the players?"

"Not that I can think of."

"Okey-dokey." He closed the notebook and tucked it back into his pocket, then picked up the folder with the photograph. "I'm off to take a preliminary look around." The impish grin reappeared. "You'll have noticed that I parked the truck a couple of blocks away. I'm practically incognito."

"Uh-huh. Are you sure that piece of junk didn't just die on you?" As far as Liss knew, he was still driving a dilapidated red pickup. Looks, however, could be deceiving. The interior was outfitted with all the latest gadgets and amenities.

He pulled a face, somehow managing an expression of deep regret. "There are times when it's just not a good idea to advertise."

Liss needed a moment to understand what he meant. Then she remembered. The truck sported a vanity plate that read MURCH PI.

He was halfway to the door when he turned back, doing a good imitation of that classic TV detective, Columbo. "Just one more question. Are there any strangers in town?"

"I'm afraid so. And more coming. The Western Maine Highland Games take place at The Spruces this coming weekend. They get under way on Friday with fireworks and an opening ceremony." Margaret, regretfully, had abandoned her more elaborate plans in favor of an audience-participation talent show.

Murch paused to consider this. "The fire was in the wee hours of last Friday. You notice any new faces on either Thursday or Friday?"

She told him about Angus Grant and answered his laugh with a rueful smile. "Grant is definitely here for the Highland Games. There was a second hotel guest watching the fire, too. His name is Martin Eldridge. He came into town to buy stamps and stopped in here to ask why the post office was closed. I think he's still around, too. He told me his stay was indefinite."

"What's he look like?"

Liss had already started to describe Martin Eldridge when she glanced through her front window. She broke off. "Serendipity is at work. He's right over there, near the gazebo in the town square. See? The white-haired gentleman carrying the walking stick."

"Who's the other guy?" Murch, who had been hovering by the door, about to make his exit, leaned closer to the glass, his face scrunching up as he squinted to see better.

"No idea. He's too far away for me to see him clearly. If it wasn't for Eldridge's distinctive bearing and that shock of white hair and his cane, I wouldn't be certain I was identifying him correctly."

"It's not Angus Grant?"

"Definitely not. Grant is shorter and wider. I can tell that much, even from here." Liss joined Murch in front of the display window.

"Back in a minute," he said.

Liss watched, intrigued, as he slipped outside, sauntered across the street, and walked across the square. With the casualness of a man out enjoying the beauty of the morning, he made his way closer to the two men, managing to pass within a foot of them without appearing to take any interest in their conversation. When he stopped, close enough to eavesdrop but ostensibly watching Zara and Sandy Kalishnakof's two red-haired rug rats play on the monkey bars, neither man paid him the slightest bit of attention.

Ten minutes later, after the two strangers had gone their separate ways, Murch returned to the Emporium.

"Well?" Liss asked.

"Sorry, boss. Nobody confessed to setting the fire."

Liss rolled her eyes. Nobody outside of badly written detective novels ever got lucky enough to overhear something like that.

"But it's funny," Murch said. "The guy your man Eldridge was talking to looks familiar to me. Can't place him, though." He shrugged. "It'll come to me."

"What *were* they talking about?"

He chuckled. "You'll get a kick out of this. Real high-brow discussion those two were having. Talking about Shakespeare, no less."

"Really?" That was the last thing Liss had expected him to report.

"No joke. The guy I can't place mentioned *Much Ado About Nothing*. That's one of Shakespeare's comedies, right?" At Liss's nod, he went on. "Then the other guy, Eldridge, he said something about Elizabethan tragedy, and then I missed a bit because a car went by and the engine noise drowned out their words. The next bit I caught was about Caesar, and even I know that *Julius Caesar* is another of Shakespeare's plays."

"What an odd conversation to be having in the middle of the town square."

"It would be even odder if they were talking about fires and missing persons. Maybe this Eldridge guy just likes to attend festivals and some Shakespeare event is next on his agenda. Looked to me like he's old enough to be retired and have lots of time on his hands. From the way he dresses, he's not hurting for money, so he can probably afford to indulge whatever whim strikes his fancy."

Liss supposed Murch's reasoning made sense, and it was always good to eliminate a suspect. "I guess I can check him off the list then, not that I had any particular reason to think Martin Eldridge was involved in the fire or Angie's disappearance in the first place."

"Right," Murch agreed. "I'll get on with my sleuthing, then. You said the library's upstairs in the municipal building, right?"

Belatedly, Liss remembered something that would put a hitch in his plans. "It is, but even if Dolores is there this early, she won't let you in until she opens up at one. She's very strict about that."

"Then I'll start asking my questions at the post office instead, and stop for lunch at Patsy's Coffee House." He waggled his eyebrows, à la Magnum, P.I. "We'll see if I can work my wiles on the charming proprietor." With another tip of his imaginary hat, Murch toddled off to tap into the village grapevine.

Dan Ruskin spent his day in the workshop behind the house. He was covered with sawdust when he finally quit. He'd been milling, preparing the pieces that would eventually be assembled to form the jigsaw-puzzle tables that were his primary source of income.

It still astounded him that anyone would pay over a thousand dollars for a piece of custom-made wooden furniture that could only be used for one purpose. He liked to do the occasional jigsaw puzzle himself, but he'd always made do with a card table . . . until Lumpkin and Glenora came into his life. There was something about puzzle pieces that was irresistible to cats. They—the pieces, not the cats—ended up scattered all over the house, most of them the worse for having been chewed.

Dan's tables were designed with a cover to keep both cats and small children from messing with a partially completed puzzle. There were drawers for sorting the pieces, too—drawers that closed to protect those pieces when they weren't needed. So far, he was still enjoying the process of putting the tables together and shipping them off to customers all over the country. Only once in a blue moon did UPS screw up and damage a shipment.

He could have lived without that hassle, but to counter it there had been plenty of satisfied customers. Some sent him words of praise. Liss put those up on his Web site.

Then there had been the guy who just happened to own

his own plane. He'd decided that since he'd never been to Maine, he might as well fly up from his home in Florida and collect the table in person. He'd been startled to discover he couldn't rent a car at the nearest airport, a tiny one-runway operation that catered to skiers, hunters, and sport fishermen.

Still smiling at the memory, Dan left his workshop to walk the few yards to the back door of the house. He stopped just short of the stoop to dust off most of the sawdust that still clung to his clothing. There was no way to get rid of it all. He was thinking he should probably just strip down in the combination pantry/utility room and stick every stitch he was wearing into the washer before going upstairs to shower, when he noticed the corner of a pink envelope poking out of the side of the screen door.

Gingerly, in case his hands were still dirty enough to leave smudges, he caught hold of it and tugged. There was no return address, but across the front someone had printed "Mr. and Mrs. Daniel Ruskin."

Dan cursed softly under his breath. An anniversary card. It had to be. It was also a reminder that he hadn't yet bought a present for his wife. There was still time, he told himself. This was only Wednesday. Their anniversary wasn't until Saturday. Of course, that didn't help much when he had no idea what he was going to get for Liss. She wasn't the easiest person to shop for, and she'd once told him straight out that she thought it was a waste of money to buy flowers or fancy candies. Fine heck of a note, when this was supposed to be the candy anniversary!

He waited until he was inside and had downed a glass of ice water before he opened the envelope. It was, as he'd expected, an anniversary card. What he wasn't expecting was the signature. It read "Best to you both. Angie, Beth, and Bradley."

This time Dan's cussing was more creative. He knew his wife well and could predict the effect this message would have on her. Liss would be convinced that the appearance of this hand-delivered card must mean Angie was still close by. That would make her all the more determined to find her friend. Given that someone had burned down Angie's Books, Dan thought that was a very bad idea.

He considered tossing the card and pretending he'd never seen it, but he rejected that thought almost as soon as it crossed his mind. He and Liss didn't hide things from each other. Not anymore. They'd learned that lesson the hard way.

Tapping the envelope against his hand, he considered alternatives. Maybe he could convince Liss that Angie had given the card to someone before she left town. Yeah, that made sense. Someone else had delivered it. Someone who wanted to remain anonymous. Someone who probably didn't have any more idea where Angie and the kids were now than Liss did.

Late on Thursday morning, Liss stopped by the café for a much-needed break.

"Who is that odd little man who was in here yesterday?" Patsy asked. "He came in for lunch, and then he was back again later in the afternoon. He sat in that booth over there for hours, nursing a cup of coffee and a toasted bagel, but I could tell he had his ears perked."

"Can you keep a secret?" Liss lowered her voice, even though Patsy's only other customer was Alex Permutter. Everyone in Moosetookalook knew how deaf he was, and that he was too stubborn to acknowledge his disability. He refused to have his hearing tested, let alone wear a hearing aid.

"Did you ever know me *not* to be able to?" Patsy slid her tall, scrawny frame onto the bench seat opposite Liss.

Déjà vu, Liss thought as Patsy set down the carafe she'd been carrying. She almost smiled. At least today she wasn't dissolving into tears in front of the café's owner. In fact, she was feeling downright chipper.

"His name is Jake Murch. He's the private detective I hired to look for Angie and Beth and Bradley."

Startled, Patsy sat up straighter. "No! Really?"

"I didn't think it could hurt. I'm really worried about them. I've racked my brain for places they might have gone, but I keep coming up empty." It had been sobering to realize how little she knew about a woman she considered a friend. "The thing is, Patsy, I'm sure they can't have gone far. Yesterday, Dan found an anniversary card from Angie tucked into our back door."

For just a second, she felt teary-eyed again.

"Huh," said Patsy. She didn't look surprised, but neither did she seem impressed by Liss's logic.

"I know. I know. Dan says Angie must have asked someone else to leave it there, back before she left town. But whoever that was must know where she went. It's only logical."

"Did you hire this Murch guy before or after you found the card?" Patsy asked.

"Before. In fact, he may well have been in here drinking coffee at the very moment someone dropped off that card." She felt her lips twist into a rueful expression. "Dan was right there in the workshop, but he was concentrating on what he was doing and didn't notice a thing."

Abruptly, Patsy stood. "I don't see how it will do any good, but I don't suppose this Murch fella can do any harm, either. Just don't get your hopes up, Liss. He may not be any better than the police are at tracking down somebody who doesn't want to be found."

With that pessimistic assessment, she topped off Liss's coffee and sailed off to ask old Mr. Permutter if he had everything he needed.

Liss stared after her, surprised by Patsy's pessimism.

She nibbled on a blueberry muffin—she'd overdosed on sticky buns lately—and sipped her coffee. Patsy's brew was *so* much better than what she made at home. All the while, she pondered the fact that quite a few people in Moosetookalook had been behaving oddly since the fire.

Stu Burroughs had installed three additional smoke alarms in Stu's Ski Shop and two in the apartment above. He was said to be contemplating getting a guard dog.

The Lounsburys had a new deadbolt on the front door of their jewelry store.

Julie Simpson had turned surly and uncommunicative, a far cry from her usual loud and talkative self. Betsy Twining said it was because the glass company wanted to be paid in advance and was refusing to install the new window until the US Postal Service showed them the money. Liss could understand why that would be galling—more red tape for the local postmaster to wade through.

As for Murch, PI, his first report had been a tad discouraging. As promised, he'd approached all the sources Liss had suggested to him. His attempts to worm information out of them had met with varying degrees of success. Dolores had apparently been taken with him, but she'd had her own agenda. She'd managed to recruit him to help with her "save the library" campaign.

To keep a possible source sweet, Murch had promised

to dig up dirt for Dolores to use to discredit Jason Graye. Liss didn't imagine he'd have much trouble finding something. Graye walked a fine line between ethical and unethical in his real estate dealings. He had always been out for the fast buck and never seemed to care who got hurt in the process.

Chapter Eight

Liss was lost in thought, remembering some of the shady deals Jason Graye had allegedly been involved in over the years, when something on the far side of the town square caught her attention through the window next to her booth at Patsy's. From that vantage point, her view of Moosetookalook Scottish Emporium was partially obscured by the merry-go-round, but she could see enough to tell that two people were standing in front of her shop, staring at the BACK IN FIFTEEN MINUTES sign she'd left on the door.

That she couldn't tell who they were hardly mattered. As long as there was a possibility that they were potential customers, she had to get over there before they disappeared. Surging to her feet, she polished off her muffin, downed the last of her coffee, and tossed enough money on the table to cover the cost of her snack plus a generous tip. She crossed the square at a trot, catching the pair, a young couple, just as they were starting to turn away.

Walk-in traffic was rarely steady. Liss made most of her money on Internet and mail-order sales. Now, with the Highland Games about to start, she had already packed up most of the merchandise she'd be taking with her to stock her booth on the grounds of The Spruces. Her usually orderly shelves showed all too plainly where she'd removed items. While the young couple browsed, she surreptitiously rearranged what was left to fill some of the gaps.

Liss looked up with a welcoming smile when the bell over the door sounded to warn her of the arrival of another customer. This might just turn out to be a better day than she'd expected.

The pleasant expression froze on her face when she recognized Angus Grant.

This time he was alone, without the moderating influence of either wife or fellow hotel guest. He made a beeline for the young couple, although it was obvious they didn't know him from Adam.

"You mustn't buy a kilt for yourself, young lady," he reprimanded her.

Startled, she nearly dropped the garment she'd been holding against herself. "Why not?"

"Women do not wear kilts. And unless you are a member of Clan MacDonald, you cannot wear that tartan."

Intimidated, the woman hastily shoved the kilt back onto the rack.

"What do they wear?" her male companion asked.

"Long skirts with a sash in their clan's tartan."

"But I don't *want* a long skirt and a sash." The young woman sounded as if she might burst into tears at any moment. "That would make me feel like I was in a beauty pageant."

"Nevertheless, rules are rules."

In the face of Grant's obvious disapproval, the couple beat a hasty retreat without buying anything. Liss glared at the back of the older man's head as he bent to examine the items on a low shelf. She had no doubt that he would find some fault with the cute little stuffed animals she sold.

They were meant to represent Nessie, the Loch Ness Monster.

Fists clenched at her sides, Liss came out from behind the sales counter. This had to stop. It was one thing to have opinions and quite another to drive away paying customers. She meant to give Grant a piece of her mind, but he straightened and made another of his proclamations before she could say a single word.

"I did some research on you, Ms. MacCrimmon-Ruskin."

Taken aback, Liss stopped short and frowned at him. What the heck was he going on about now?

"Your ancestors weren't Scots."

"I beg your pardon?"

"The MacCrimmons came to Scotland from *Italy*." He grimaced as he spoke the name of that country, as if just mentioning it left a bad taste in his mouth.

Liss blinked at him and regrouped. She knew the legends. After all, they concerned her ancestors. "That's one theory."

"Cremona." There wasn't an ounce of doubt in Grant's voice. He crossed his arms over his barrel of a chest as if daring her to contradict him.

"Even if it's true that the first members of the family arrived in Scotland from elsewhere, that all happened a long, long time ago. Centuries. The early middle ages, to be precise."

"Your lack of knowledge about all things Scottish is appalling, but given your heritage, I suppose you can't help it." The smug expression on Angus Grant's face made Liss want to smack him.

"My heritage is not in question! And that's beside the point. I'm trying to run a legitimate business here. What you said to that woman may well have cost me a three-hundred-dollar sale."

Offended, Grant sent her a contemptuous look. "Most people would appreciate a bit of constructive criticism," he snarled as he headed for the door.

Liss didn't know whether to laugh or cry as she watched him leave. She had a feeling she hadn't seen the last of him. After all, he'd come to Moosetookalook to attend the Highland Games. It would be next to impossible to avoid running into him during the weekend ahead.

Sherri Campbell had a raging headache. She was supposed to enforce the law in their tiny community, and here she sat, almost a week after the fire, totally stumped. No arsonist had been arrested. No trace had been found of the three missing persons. No one had any idea who had vandalized the post office. And now she had a pile of complaints on her desk about strangers asking impertinent questions.

It was only natural, she supposed, that unsolved cases would attract outside interest. They weren't exactly paparazzi-worthy, but the curiosity of at least a few people from away had been aroused.

Two were easy enough to identify. One was a private investigator named Jake Murch. Sherri already knew who had brought him into the picture. The second was a reporter from Portland on the scent of a story.

It was the third man who was giving her trouble. He appeared to be a guest at the hotel, one Eliot Underhill. At first, she'd thought he was annoying the locals out of simple curiosity, but when she did a standard background check, nothing popped up. Not just no criminal record. Not just no traffic tickets. Nothing at all.

In this day and age, it was unusual for anyone to be off the grid. Now Sherri had encountered two such individuals. She still had no explanation for Angie's lack of a past. That another person should turn up in Moosetookalook, apparently using an assumed name, bothered her a great deal. If he was pulling some kind of a con, she wanted to know what it was.

She reached for the phone.

Liss answered on the first ring.

"Busy?" Sherri tipped back in her chair, resting her feet on top of the partially open bottom drawer of her desk.

"If you mean do I have customers in the Emporium, the answer is no. The only prospects I did have were driven away by a troll."

Sherri waited a beat, her tension already beginning to ease. Talking to Liss was always good therapy. "Has Jake Murch found anything I should know about?"

"He'll tell you if he does. That was the deal."

"Okay. Good." She drew in a breath. "I'm glad you hired him. I can use all the help I can get."

"Some help! So far he hasn't had any better luck than you have, unless you count the fact that he's made Dolores very happy by agreeing to help her with her recall petition. She recruited him when he tried to question her."

The mental image of Dolores Mayfield and Jake Murch working together brought a smile to Sherri's face. It faded at Liss's next words.

"I understand she's also organizing a demonstration. A picket line and everything. Murch persuaded her to hold off until after this weekend, but he says she's determined to bring down Jason Graye."

"Oh, goodie. Something to look forward to." Sherri didn't hold back on the sarcasm.

It had been a mistake to relax, even for a couple of minutes. She shifted in the chair, placing both feet firmly on the floor. Her headache had returned with a vengeance.

"I need to get back to packing the car with the stuff I'm taking to the Highland Games tomorrow," Liss said. "Was there something else you wanted?"

Sherri hesitated, then figured she might as well ask. "Does the name Eliot Underhill mean anything to you?"

"Nope. Who is he?"

"Well, that's the question." She told Liss what she'd discovered—or, rather, what she hadn't found.

"He must have used a credit card if he's registered at The Spruces."

"Liss, you're a genius!"

But a short time later, after Sherri had talked to Joe Ruskin at the hotel, she was no further ahead. The man calling himself Eliot Underhill had paid cash for his room—in advance. The only bright spot was that she now knew that he was booked through the weekend. Just as soon as she could shake her headache, she'd go out there and have a word with him.

Friday arrived without further incident. No fires. No broken windows. Liss spent most of the day setting up display tables and racks in the Moosetookalook Scottish Emporium booth on the grounds of the hotel. It was actually an awning with sides that could be rolled down for protection against the elements. By early evening, everything was in place and ready to go.

The opening ceremonies were scheduled to start in an hour, after which, as soon as it was dark enough, there would be a spectacular fireworks display. Liss had already decided to take a pass on the first event. As much as Dan loved her, he would never learn to enjoy the skirling of the pipes. He'd have endured the bagpipe bands and the pipers playing for the country dancing for her sake, but there was no need. Since he'd end up listening to more than enough piping on Saturday and Sunday, she had decided to spare him this evening's offerings.

Skipping out would also give her a chance to go home, change her clothes, and enjoy a quiet supper with her husband and cats. Afterward, she and Dan would return to the grounds of The Spruces, the best spot from which to watch the display of pyrotechnics.

The first stage of Liss's plan worked beautifully. She and Dan were just about to leave the house for the hotel when the phone rang.

"I hate to bother you, Liss," her aunt said, "but I need a favor."

"No problem." A glance at her watch told her there was still plenty of time to get back to The Spruces before the fireworks started. It took less than ten minutes to drive there from the town square. "What is it you want me to do?"

"After the way they reacted to the fire alarm, I'm worried that Dandy and Dondi may be frightened by the noise of the fireworks. I know they're inside the apartment, but if they panic, there's no telling what they might do. I don't mean to be a nervous Nellie, but someone was just telling me a truly terrifying story about a dog who got into such a state when fireworks went off that he jumped right through a second-floor window and was horribly injured."

Liss didn't hesitate. She knew how she'd feel if they were talking about Lumpkin and Glenora rather than Dandy and Dondi. Margaret adored her two Scottish terriers, and she hadn't owned them long enough to know for sure that they would take a barrage of loud explosions in stride.

"Don't worry," she assured her aunt. "I'll head over to your place right now. If the fireworks upset them, I'll stay with them until the end of the show."

"I feel terrible asking you to do this. I know you and Dan were planning to come back here to watch the display."

"Think positive. Maybe the noise won't bother the Scotties in the least. If that's the case, we'll only miss the very beginning."

"My fingers are crossed." Margaret sounded much more upbeat.

"Margaret needs us to check on the pups," Liss told Dan when she got off the phone. "We may not make it to The Spruces for the fireworks after all."

"If you want to get back there, I can stay here and look after Dandy and Dondi."

Liss shook her head. "I'd rather spend the evening together, wherever we end up. If worse comes to worst, we should be able to see the fireworks pretty well from the windows in Margaret's bedroom." She took another peek at her watch, calculating. The fireworks were scheduled to start in a half hour. The show would last about that long, too. "If I go over to her place now, I can take the dogs for walkies beforehand. That might be a wise precaution in case they do get upset."

Dan answered her wry smile with one of his own. "Why don't I bring the car over? Once the fireworks start, if it looks like Dandy and Dondi are going to be okay on their own, you can come down and we'll head over there. If you don't show, I'll come up and help you keep them calm."

"Sounds like a plan." Liss delayed long enough to claim a kiss and then took herself off to Margaret's apartment above Moosetookalook Scottish Emporium.

When Liss's aunt had acquired her two Scottish terriers a few months earlier, she'd installed a fenced-in dog run in the building's small backyard. Liss had taken on the responsibility of letting them out several times a day. It was no bother. She was right there in the building and, in the normal way of things, not exactly overwhelmed with walk-in customers in her shop.

Naturally, since the fireworks display was about to begin, Dandy and Dondi, five-year-old, jet-black Scotties who weighed about twenty pounds apiece, took their time doing their business. Liss waited impatiently until her watch told her they had only five minutes left before the first bang. The last of the twilight was already gone.

After a fast game of catch-me-if-you can, Liss attached their leads and headed for the door to the stockroom. She kept the leashes on to take the dogs from the stockroom into the shop. She didn't bother turning on a light. She could find her way through the shelves and racks even in the dark, but as it happened, there was light shining into the shop from the street lamps around the town square.

She glanced out through the plate-glass front window as she crossed the sales floor. There were still a few people out and about on this mild July evening. They were only dark shapes, but she could tell that a couple sat on the adult-size swings in the playground. Their heads were close together, as if they were exchanging secrets. She'd bet money they were teenagers. Anyone older than that had better options for privacy when they were courting. A solitary figure—she couldn't tell if it was a man or a woman—passed them on one of the paths that crossed the square.

Farther away, Liss saw Patsy stick her head out of the door to her place and look all around before ducking back inside. Liss supposed she was getting ready to close up for the night. Patsy owned a lakeside camp not too far out of town and spent some of her time there in the summer months. Liss wondered if she'd choose peace and quiet tonight. It was a toss-up, she decided. Patsy had to be up at three to start baking. It would probably make more sense for her to spend the night in her apartment above the café, her year-round home.

Reminded of the imminent fireworks display—the reason she was in the darkened Emporium at this odd hour in the first place—Liss hurried to the stairwell door behind the sales counter and hauled the dogs after her up the steep flight of steps. She had just unhooked their leashes and handed over the promised treats when the first explosion filled the night sky with pinwheels of color.

Dandy cocked her head, but didn't seem at all disturbed by the sudden loud noise. Dondi never even looked up from his dog yummies. After checking to be sure the Scotties had kibble and fresh water, Liss left the apartment and scurried back downstairs. Dan was just pulling in at the curb in front of the Emporium as she stepped off the porch.

"Need a lift, lady?"

"I don't know, mister. My mother always told me never to get into a car with a strange man."

"Strange, am I?"

"Delightfully so." She settled herself in the passenger seat, leaning over to give him a kiss on the cheek before she buckled up.

With the windows open wide to the soft night air, Dan drove west along Pine Street. The hotel was situated on a height of land off to their right. It was just a couple of miles distant, but the only way to get there was via a twisting roller coaster of a road.

They had barely passed the post office when the next round of fireworks went off. Liss stuck her head out of her window in time to catch a breathtaking glimpse of the five white-walled towers at The Spruces, bathed in red and blue and green light.

She felt a little thrill of excitement course through her. She'd always liked fireworks, and this particular display kicked off this year's Western Maine Highland Games, an annual event that had always been important to her and her family. Every year, the occasion marked a celebration of their Scottish American heritage.

Italians from Cremona indeed!

As a girl, she'd attended the games as a competitor. Now she went as a vendor. And, of course, six years ago tomorrow, she had been married in the midst of the festivities. Liss was already smiling when another boom and another burst of color turned her expression into a grin.

Dan drove slowly, so they could see the fireworks display through the windshield. He applied the brakes as they approached the four-way stop at the corner of Pine and Lowe, even though there was no sign of any other traffic on either street. He was about to hang a right when Liss heard another bang, followed seconds later by more fireworks.

She frowned. There had been something off about that first sound. She twisted around in her seat so she could look behind them.

"Dan?"

"I know. That wasn't all pyrotechnics." He had already turned the corner onto Lowe, but instead of continuing on, he pulled up to the right-hand curb.

"Car backfiring?" She didn't hold out much hope for such a mundane explanation.

The idling engine sounded loud in the silence. Dan turned it off just as the next set of fireworks went off. "You *know* what it sounded like."

As one, they turned to stare at the darkened house on the corner of Pine and Lowe.

It belonged to Jason Graye.

The front porch faced Lowe Street, but there was another entrance on Pine. Out of the corner of her eye, Liss caught a flicker of movement in that direction. She squinted to see better, but all she could make out was a dark shape crossing the open space between Graye's house and that of one of his neighbors. A moment later, the shadowy form had vanished into the neighbor's backyard.

"Did you see—?"

But Dan was already out of the car and heading for Graye's front porch. Liss fumbled with her seat belt, which at first refused to cooperate. She was several yards behind her husband by the time he reached the house.

"Stay back," he cautioned, his voice grim.

"In your dreams."

"The door is open."

That announcement only spurred Liss on. It was barely ajar. That inch or two somehow seemed even more ominous.

As soon as Liss came up beside Dan on the porch, he gave the heavy wooden door a push. Slowly, the gap widened until there was room for him to step inside. Liss was right on his heels. When he stopped, she clutched his upper arm and peered around it.

The only illumination in the foyer came from a night-light plugged into the baseboard. It was more than sufficient to confirm what Liss had dreaded to find.

That lone explosion had not been part of the fireworks display.

It had been a gunshot.

Chapter Nine

Outside, more fireworks lit the night sky, adding eerie flashes of color to the scene. The erratic lighting gave Liss the sense that she was looking at a series of freeze-frame images. The body. The blood. The startled expression on Jason Graye's face, as if he couldn't believe someone had just killed him.

Swallowing convulsively to keep nausea at bay, she watched Dan kneel beside the still form on the carpet and touch his fingers to Graye's neck in search of a pulse. After a moment, he looked up, met Liss's eyes, and shook his head. There was nothing he or anyone else could do to bring the realtor back to life.

Silence descended following the latest series of fire-works. It was suddenly so quiet that Liss could hear the brush of Dan's hand against the inside of his pocket as he pulled out his cell phone.

She wanted more than anything to retreat onto the porch and escape the sight of their horrific discovery. Her feet refused to cooperate. She stood there, paralyzed, as in-capable of closing her eyes or looking away as she was of moving. Only with a tremendous effort did she finally force her body into motion. She staggered a little as she backed up, inching out of the house with excruciating slowness. She supposed only a few seconds had passed, but that little bit of time had seemed like an eternity.

Dan followed her onto the porch, leaving the door open behind him. He looked as rattled as she felt, but he still had sense enough to phone Sherri Campbell directly instead of going through the dispatch center that took over emergency calls to the Moosetookalook Police Department at night. This was not the first time that his ability to remember phone numbers had come in handy. If he hadn't reached Sherri on her cell, he'd have been able to try Pete's or their landline in less time than it would have taken the 9-1-1 dispatcher to notify the proper authorities.

"Sherri, it's Dan," he said when she answered. "We've got a situation here."

As he described what they'd found, he slung an arm around Liss's shoulders and tugged her close against his side. He gave her a reassuring squeeze when he ended the call.

"Sherri's on her way. We lucked out. She was still in her office. Shouldn't take her more than a few minutes to get here."

Feeling too numb to do anything else, Liss nodded to show she understood. Slowly, his words sank in. Her mind began to function again.

This wouldn't be Sherri's case. The state police took over when the crime was murder.

The fireworks continued, filling the night with sound and color, but Liss barely noticed. She fished in a pocket for her own cell phone and speed-dialed her aunt.

Margaret answered on the first ring. "Are the dogs okay?"

For a moment, Liss went blank. Dogs? It seemed eons ago that soothing scared Scotties had been her most pressing concern. She had to swallow convulsively before she could answer.

"Dandy and Dondi are fine, but Dan and I won't be coming back to the hotel after all."

"Liss? What's wrong?"

"Nothing. I just didn't want you to be looking for us."

"There's something the matter. I can hear it in your voice."

Margaret fell silent as the next salvo exploded. It was the beginning of the finale, to judge by the number and size of the pinwheels. By the time the noise quieted enough to hear someone speak, Liss had spotted Sherri coming toward them at a dead run. It would have taken longer to get the police cruiser out of the parking lot behind the municipal building and drive over.

"Margaret, I have to go now. I'll talk to you later." She disconnected abruptly.

"Stay outside," Sherri ordered as soon as she arrived on the scene.

She entered the house to confirm what Dan had told her on the phone. She was back outside in time to see the very last of the fireworks fade way. She ignored the display, using her portable radio to call for reinforcements. That done, she looked first at Liss and then at Dan.

"Why are you two here?"

Dan gave her a terse account of the reason they'd stopped to investigate and what they'd found.

"Liss? Anything to add?"

"I thought I saw someone on the Pine Street side of the house. A person running away."

"Don't move."

Although it was clearly too late to catch anyone, Sherri circled the building to check on the other entrance. Moments later, she returned. "The kitchen door is standing wide open. It looks like Graye's killer left that way just as you were pulling up to the curb. You're lucky you didn't walk in on him."

Liss knew she ought to be horrified by the very idea. Instead she had to fight an insane urge to giggle as the images from a movie chase scene, with comic characters dashing in one door and out another, popped into her head.

"Liss?" Sherri asked. "You okay?"

She didn't dare answer until she had herself under control. Then she said, in a dry voice, "I think I finally get the concept of cop humor."

When things were truly awful, making bad, often tasteless jokes, allowed emergency workers to keep doing their jobs. They knew, as Liss did, that death wasn't anything to laugh about, but there was still something to be said for comic relief. It was a lot healthier to crack wise than to dissolve into tears or have hysterics.

"This person you saw," Sherri said. "Was it a man or a woman?"

"I couldn't tell."

"Headed which direction?"

"Through the backyards toward the town square." The corner of Pine and Lowe was only one block away.

"He probably took the same shortcut you used to get here," Dan said.

"That would be my guess," Sherri agreed. "In that case, he's long gone."

"There was a couple in the square just a little bit ago," Liss offered. "On the swings. If they're still there, maybe they got a look at him."

"Do you know who they were?"

Liss shook her head. "I wasn't close enough to see faces, but they looked like they were really into each other."

"Like most couples who sit on those swings after dark," Dan said.

"If that's so, chances are slim that they noticed anyone else, but I'd better see if they're still there. The only problem is that I can't leave this place unsecured."

Liss grabbed her friend's arm, struck by a sudden thought. "What if the killer saw that couple? He wouldn't want any witnesses."

Sherri swore softly.

"We're stuck here anyway," Dan said. "Liss and I can guard your crime scene while you go check on them."

Sherri didn't argue. She was running again even before Dan finished making the offer.

By the time Sherri reached the playground in the town square, she was out of breath.

There was no one on the swings.

There was no one anywhere in sight.

The powerful beam of her Maglite confirmed that there were no new bodies, either. The courting couple had watched the fireworks, swinging gently side by side, and then gone on their way. She breathed a sigh of relief. Tomorrow would be soon enough to track them down and interview them.

At an only slightly slower pace, she headed back to Jason Graye's house. She wanted to be there before officers from the sheriff's department and the state police arrived and wondered where she was. She popped out onto Lowe Street just as a half dozen vehicles, blue lights flashing, converged on the scene of the crime.

Sherri made her report to Gordon Tandy, the state police detective who had been assigned to Carrabassett County for the last six years. Since he was nearly a foot taller than she was, she had to crane her neck to meet his eyes.

Gordon spared a glance for Liss and Dan, still standing off to one side, but did not try to speak to them. Not just yet. Sherri knew from past experience that he liked to take a look at the scene before he heard what witnesses had to say.

"It might be a good idea to have Dan move his car," Sherri said.

Gordon nodded, but there wasn't sufficient light to read the expression in his dark eyes. He had a history with both Liss and Dan. "Ruskin may as well drive it over to their place."

"Do you want to interview them here or at the house?"

"Tell him to walk back. I'd like them to stick around for a bit." He hesitated, then asked, "How's she doing?"

"Shaky." While Sherri had gone to look for the couple on the swings, Dan had stood guard over the side door, leaving Liss alone at the front. She'd looked a little green around the gills by the time Sherri returned.

"Stay with her," Gordon ordered as he started up the steps to the porch.

Sherri resisted the urge to salute.

She relayed his instructions to Dan and Liss and stuck close to her friend after Dan drove away. Liss heaved a deep sigh as she watched the taillights disappear.

"How did Gordon take it when you said I was the one who found the body?"

"I couldn't tell. He had his cop face on."

"He doesn't like it when I meddle in murder, but it isn't as if I've ever had any choice. I never *mean* to get involved."

"Not your fault," Sherri agreed.

It was just plain bad luck that Liss had encountered more than her fair share of murder victims. Gordon Tandy knew that perfectly well. Besides, he and Liss were friends, after a fashion. They'd even dated for a short while, back before she married Dan. Now that he had also taken a wife—the sheriff of Carrabassett County, no less—there was no reason for any animosity between them.

Liss's face was dimly illuminated by the pool of light from a nearby street lamp. That was more than enough to show Sherri how exhausted she was. Standing around doing nothing after the adrenaline-producing trauma of finding a murder victim was hard on the nerves. Sherri felt the strain herself, although to a lesser degree.

"This time I'm determined to stay out of it," Liss said. "I'll give my statement, and that will be that."

"Good idea," Sherri said.

As for herself, she couldn't help but feel a pang of regret. She would not be part of the investigation. As the local chief of police, she would be kept in the loop as a courtesy, but her role would probably be limited to crowd control. Even that small contribution would not last long. Once the body had been taken to Augusta for autopsy and the crime scene unit was finished with the house, there would be nothing for gawkers to see and thus no need for an officer to stand guard.

Neither Sherri nor Liss felt much like talking as they waited for Dan to return and Gordon to reappear. Sherri watched neighbors begin to drift home from The Spruces, where they'd gone to watch the fireworks display. They weren't happy about being questioned before they were allowed to enter their own houses. Anyone else who showed up was kept at a distance.

When Dan rejoined them, he didn't have anything to say, either. Hands in his pockets, his expression wary, he stared at the yellow crime scene tape that had been strung around Graye's house.

After a television news van from one of the Portland stations showed up, Sherri herded her friends into deeper shadow. The last thing any of them wanted was to see their faces splashed across every wide-screen TV in the state.

A cute and perky-looking reporter, a regular on the evening news, hopped out of the van. She had a reputation as a real barracuda when it came to getting information out of a source. More often than not, people she interviewed came off sounding like babbling idiots.

In less time than Sherri expected, Gordon and a uniformed state trooper emerged from Jason Graye's house. Gordon took one look at the reporter and her cameraman and dispatched the trooper to escort Sherri, Liss, and Dan to a secure spot that was not only behind the crime scene tape but also shielded by a large spruce.

He addressed Sherri first. "Can your department keep an eye on the house for the rest of the night?"

"No problem."

Sherri intended to take on the job herself. The other Moosetookalook officers—two full-timers and three part-timers—were either at The Spruces already or off duty, getting a good night's sleep in preparation for working at the Highland Games in the morning.

Gordon delegated the other officer to question Dan, although the two of them didn't go very far. Then he tugged a small, spiral-bound notebook and a pencil out of his inside jacket pocket. His pointed look at Sherri told her more clearly than any words that he did not intend to conduct his interview with Liss until she'd moved on.

Reluctantly, she stepped away.

She felt much better after she'd sent the news crew packing.

"We have to stop meeting like this," Liss said in a futile attempt to lighten the mood.

"You want to tell me what you and Dan were doing here?"

"We weren't *here,* exactly. We were driving past on our way to the hotel. The car windows were open. We heard what sounded like a gunshot."

A look of surprise flickered across Gordon's face so quickly that she wondered if she'd imagined it.

"What time was that?" he asked.

Chagrined, Liss had to admit that she hadn't thought to look at the dashboard clock. "The fireworks had only just started." She tried to remember how many explosions there had been, but she hadn't been paying close attention. "If you want, I'll clock myself running downstairs from Margaret's apartment and driving from the Emporium to here."

"Why were you at your aunt's place?"

"To check on the dogs. You remember Dandy and Dondi?"

"Oh, yeah." For just a second, he was Gordon instead of Detective Tandy. There might even have been a twinkle in his eyes, although it was too dark to tell. Then he was all business again. "How long were you there?"

"Only long enough to make sure sudden loud noises weren't going to bother them. Then I met Dan, who was waiting in the car in front of the Emporium, and we headed for the hotel."

"Along Pine Street to Lowe? Why didn't you take Ash to get to Main?"

"Have you *seen* what's left of Angie's store?"

Clearly he had not and therefore couldn't possibly understand how much the sight of that burned-out shell upset her. It was bad enough that she could see it from both her shop and her house. She tried to avoid confronting the ruins head on, as they would have if Dan had turned right at the post office and driven along Ash Street. Considerate, as always, he'd chosen an alternate route.

Gordon returned to the sound Liss had heard. "You were sure it was a gunshot?"

"I knew it wasn't part of the fireworks display."

"So you stopped?"

Liss nodded. "Dan heard it, too."

"You didn't think that might be dangerous?"

"I . . . I don't know what we thought. And then I saw someone moving away from the side of Graye's house."

"Moving? Not running?"

Liss frowned. "I only saw it for a second. A shape." She didn't think she'd imagined it.

"And then?"

"We found the front door open and went in and found Jason Graye's body." All of a sudden, Liss started to shake. The delayed reaction took her by surprise and left Gordon at a momentary loss for words.

He flipped his notebook closed and pocketed it and the pencil, then seized her by the elbow to propel her toward his cruiser. He was just stuffing her into the passenger seat when Dan rushed over, closely followed by the uniformed trooper.

"What the hell do you think you're doing, Tandy? You can't arrest my wife."

"I'm not arresting her. I'm taking her home and pouring her a stiff drink. You can meet us there as soon as you've finished giving your statement."

Liss squeezed her eyes tightly shut when they passed Angie's Books. The burned-out building was on Gordon's side of the cruiser. She assumed that he got a good look at it.

Moments later, he stopped in front of her house.

Nothing was very far away from anything else in Moosetookalook.

By the time Gordon had her settled on the living room sofa with both cats in her lap, Dan caught up with them. There was no sign of the uniformed state trooper.

"I'm okay," Liss insisted when he started to fuss over her. "I just got the shakes for a minute there. I do *not* want a glass of medicinal brandy."

"Hot chocolate, then?"

When she nodded, Dan headed for the kitchen to make a cup of her preferred restorative. He was back in less than five minutes with her drink. Glowering at Gordon, he handed it over and plunked himself down next to her on the sofa. He had to take Glenora onto his lap to make room.

Gordon ignored him and resumed his interrogation. "Can you describe the person you saw leaving the scene?"

"Not really. All I saw was a dark shape."

Liss took a sip of her drink, burned her tongue, and grimaced. At least chocolate tasted better than brandy. She'd never been able to understand why so many people tried to push alcohol on someone who'd had a shock. Something sweet, with a hint of caffeine, worked much better as a pick-me-up.

"A man?" Gordon asked.

"It could have been either a man or a woman."

"Size?" Gordon asked.

"Not obese, but beyond that I can't really say." She stroked Lumpkin's soft, thick coat with her free hand. The deep rumble of his purr was wonderfully soothing. "I wouldn't want to make a guess as to age, either."

"Is there anything you can remember about the way the figure moved?"

Liss shook her head.

"As I recall," Gordon said slowly, "you never much liked Jason Graye."

"Very few people did, but if you're asking if I shot him, the answer is no."

This time she couldn't mistake the oddness of the expression that crossed his face. With exaggerated care, she set her mug on the end table and leaned toward him.

"What? He *was* shot, wasn't he?"

"It wasn't a bullet that killed him." Cop face firmly in place, he didn't say anything more.

Frustrated, Liss glared at him.

"Don't stop there, Tandy," Dan said. "It's not like we're going to blab to the press."

"And if you don't explain, we're liable to let slip what we *thought* happened." Liss sent Gordon her sweetest and most insincere smile. "I know you don't want us to do that."

"The medical examiner is the one who rules on cause of death."

Liss waited.

"It looked to me as if he was stabbed through the heart with a blade of some kind."

Startled, Liss sat up straighter. Her hand clenched in Lumpkin's fur, causing him to dig his claws into her leg. "Stabbed? Not shot?"

"Stabbed. Not shot. I take it neither of you saw a knife?"

"No knife," Liss confirmed.

"No gun, either," Dan said, "but the more I think about it, the more certain I am that what we heard was a gunshot."

Gordon's cell phone buzzed before he could either explain or ask more questions. He answered, listened, and ended the call abruptly. "Looks like we're both right. They've just found a bullet in the wall opposite where Graye fell."

"Graye shot at someone and missed, and then whoever it was stabbed him?" Just imagining that scenario made Liss queasy.

"Looks that way." Gordon sent her a stern look. "That information goes no farther than this room. Understood?"

Liss nodded. Beside her, she felt Dan do the same.

"The autopsy results will be made public when we have them. Until then, you don't answer questions from anyone but me or another detective working on the case."

"Fine," Dan said. "Are we done here?"

"Not quite. You said the front door was open when you got there?"

Liss nodded. "That must mean it was someone he knew," she whispered. "Why else would he let them in?"

"Maybe. Maybe not." Gordon shrugged. "I never had any dealings with Graye myself, but I've heard plenty about him over the years. He made enemies. Is there anyone just lately with whom he had a run in?"

Liss's expression gave her away before she said a word.

Gordon leaned toward her. "Liss? Do you know someone who had a bone to pick with Jason Graye?"

Liss felt her tension ratchet up a notch.

Dan left off stroking Glenora to catch her hand in his and give it a squeeze. "He's going to find out anyway, Liss. You may as well be the one to tell him."

He was right. Liss cleared her throat. "There *has* been a bit of controversy this past week," she said, "concerning the Moosetookalook Public Library."

Chapter Ten

Gordon Tandy left soon after Liss filled him in on the conflict between Jason Graye and Dolores Mayfield and gave him her account of the events that had taken place at the meeting at the Mayfield house. Standing by her front window, she watched him drive away. She was relieved to see him go, but she was far from happy that she'd had to rat out Dolores and Moose.

A little sigh escaped her, loud enough for Dan to hear. He came up beside her and took her hands in his. "I know what you're thinking, Liss, but you didn't have any choice. Besides, there are plenty of other people who would have told the police about Moose Mayfield shooting off his mouth, and his gun, if you hadn't."

"I still feel guilty. Because of what I just told him, Gordon must think he's found a likely pair of suspects. Not just Moose, but Dolores, too."

"If Graye *had* been shot, then maybe. But—"

She freed one hand and smacked him on the upper arm. "Did you not *see* the collection of weapons Dolores had on display in her living room? Swords. Knives. Heck, she probably has a pair of fencing foils tucked away somewhere. And I know Stu was just trying to get her goat when he was ribbing her about giving a talk and charging admission, but it sounded to me as if she's been interested in bladed weapons for a long, long time."

"You couldn't prove it by me. That was the first time I was ever inside the Mayfield house."

"Same here. Dolores's wall decorations came as a bit of a shock." She managed a weak smile. "I always thought there were no secrets in a small town, but I'd never have guessed that one."

"And I'd never have pegged Moose as a henpecked husband. Let's look on the bright side. At least you and I aren't on Tandy's short list."

"Don't kid yourself. The person who discovers the body is always a suspect."

Rather than try to cheer her up with words, Dan simply took her in his arms and held her. That might have led to further cuddling, had someone not chosen that moment to rap on their front door.

Liss peeked through the curtains just as Margaret Boyd called her name.

"I know you're in there," she added. "I want to know what's going on!"

Dan muttered something indistinct and probably profane.

"She's only here because she cares," Liss whispered. In a louder voice, she called, "Coming, Margaret!"

Once the door was open, Margaret paused on the threshold long enough to take a good long look at her niece. Seeing no bruises, blood, or bandages, she bustled through to the living room and plunked herself down on the sofa. She patted the cushion beside her.

"Sit down here and explain yourself. Why couldn't you

tell me what was happening when we spoke on phone? Why didn't you come back to The Spruces for the fireworks? And what on earth is going on over on Lowe Street?"

Liss took the seat Margaret indicated. Dan had already disappeared. She could hear him rattling around in the kitchen and hoped he was making another batch of hot chocolate.

"There's not much to tell." She hesitated, remembering Gordon's warning against sharing information that hadn't yet been made public. Still, there was nothing to stop her from revealing the two most important facts. "Jason Graye is dead. Dan and I found his body."

For a moment, Margaret's expression went entirely blank. Then she blinked and gave a low whistle. Liss could almost hear the gears turning as Margaret thought over what Liss had said and what she herself had seen on her way home from the hotel.

"I thought I saw state police cruisers. Graye isn't just dead, is he? He was murdered."

So much for Gordon's attempt to keep the news under wraps. "Yes, he was murdered."

"Well, if that don't beat all! Oh, thank you, my dear." Margaret accepted the mug of hot chocolate Dan handed her and cradled it in both hands.

He passed Liss her refill and, carrying a third mug, retreated to the recliner. Glenora, perched on the back, didn't move when Dan settled in and put the footrest up. Lumpkin was nowhere in sight.

Margaret blew on the hot liquid and took a tentative sip. "Lovely. But how on earth did you two end up being first on the scene of a crime? You didn't kill him, did you?" A twitch of Margaret's lips assured Liss that this wasn't a serious suggestion.

"It was pure chance and an unfortunate series of events," Dan said from his chair. "If we hadn't decided to come home for supper, we wouldn't have been involved at all."

Margaret frowned. "Oh, dear. That means I'm partly to blame. If I hadn't asked you to check on the dogs—"

"No! You mustn't think that."

"You'd have been safely back at The Spruces if not for me. Unless he was killed much earlier?"

Liss shook her head, but did not elaborate. "Go ahead and feel guilty, Margaret. There's plenty to go around. I was the one who wanted to eat supper at home. Dan is the one who chose that route back to the hotel instead of the more usual one."

How long, she wondered, would Graye's body have gone undiscovered if they hadn't happened by?

Then another thought struck her, this one even more unsettling. Dolores Mayfield wasn't the only one who'd been at odds with Jason Graye. Only a week ago, Graye and Margaret had gone at it at the selectmen's work session because Graye had canceled the parade. As a motive for murder, it was pretty thin, but that did not excuse Liss's failure to mention her aunt to Gordon as a possible suspect. She'd been willing to throw Dolores to the wolves. What had stopped her from remembering to add Margaret to Graye's list of enemies?

She told herself that the answer was simple enough. Margaret was obviously innocent, since she'd been at the hotel at the time of the murder. There must be a hundred people who could vouch for that. The same could not be said for Dolores or Moose. Even so, the lie by omission troubled Liss's conscience.

Unaware of her niece's thoughts, Margaret sipped hot

chocolate and contemplated what she'd been told. "Was he killed outside his house?"

Liss shook her head. Margaret's question was taking them close to forbidden territory, not that she supposed any of the details of the murder would stay secret much longer.

"Inside then. Well, I suppose he was killed by someone he ripped off in a real estate deal." Frowning, she added, "I can't help wishing the killer had waited until *after* this weekend to do him in. Or, better yet, had murdered him somewhere else entirely. Neither the Highland Games nor this town needs the kind of bad publicity murder generates."

"I'm sure Jason Graye would have preferred not to be murdered at all."

Margaret winced at Dan's sarcasm. "Oh, my dears! I'm so sorry. I don't know what's the matter with me. I'm overtired, I guess. And appallingly insensitive!" She abandoned her mug on the end table. "You've had a terrible experience, and here I go saying thoughtless things right and left."

"You're only saying what lots of other folks in town will be thinking," Liss assured her. "Jason Graye never went out of his way to make friends, not even when he was running for selectman."

Rising from the sofa, Margaret briefly rested one hand on Liss's shoulder. "We'll just have to make the best of a bad situation. Fortunately, there are one or two little things I can do to spin the story in a more favorable direction. You get a good night's sleep and leave everything to me."

Liss regarded her aunt through wary eyes. "What are you up to now?"

Margaret ignored her question. She was already halfway

to the front door. "I really need to get going. Dandy and Dondi will be wondering what's keeping me. I'm rarely this late getting home."

Liss didn't move from the sofa. Her legs felt as if they were made of lead. It took all the energy she had left to set aside her untouched mug. The hot chocolate had stopped working its magic after the first infusion.

Dan followed Margaret to the front door and locked it behind her. He returned to stand in front of Liss, both hands extended toward her. "Up you go. Your aunt is right about one thing. We can do with some rest."

"Do you really think I'm going to be able to sleep?" The image of Jason Graye's body popped into her head, and she shuddered.

"I'll find some way to take your mind off things," Dan promised.

She let him pull her to her feet. "What do you suppose Margaret is up to?"

"I have no idea, but there's no sense worrying about it tonight." He slung an arm around her shoulders to get her moving. "Come to bed, love."

Despite all that had happened, Liss felt the ghost of a smile flit across her face. It was good to be cherished. Poor Jason Graye had never had that comfort.

But an hour later, with Dan sound asleep beside her, Liss's restless thoughts refused to settle. She stared at the ceiling until her eyes itched, listening to the steady, over-loud beat of her own heart. She felt as if she was on the verge of a panic attack. Stupid, but there it was!

Calm down, she ordered herself. *You have to be up and at 'em bright and early to open the Moosetookalook Scottish Emporium booth at the Highland Games.*

She tried running inventory in her head as an alternative to counting sheep. Two dozen ties in assorted tartans. A dozen ceramic mugs decorated with thistles, the symbol of Scotland. An assortment of imported cashmere scarves. Two pewter figurines of bagpipers. She'd ordered more, but they hadn't come in. Miscellaneous kilt pins and ceramic figurines—pipers, drummers, and soldiers in Highland dress, each six and a half inches tall. Somewhere around the half dozen tins of canned haggis, she finally drifted into sleep.

On Lowe Street, seated in the Moosetookalook police cruiser with the windows down and the engine off, Sherri Campbell struggled to keep her eyes open. Everything was quiet, just as it should be. The neighbors had all gone to bed. No dogs barked. Ten minutes earlier she'd heard what she thought was an owl. A half hour before that, a white cat had crossed Jason Graye's front lawn, bound on some important nocturnal errand. Sherri had already been so bored that she'd wasted a few minutes debating whether the feline's quarry was a juicy field mouse or a female of its own species.

Nothing, however, could distract her for long from her most pressing concern. There had been three serious crimes in her jurisdiction in less than a week—arson, vandalism, and now murder. What if they were connected? She couldn't see how, but the possibility nagged at her. So did the fact that she had no leads to go on in any of the cases.

Was she dealing with one criminal? Two? Three? She found it hard to believe that there could be more than one major villain in a town the size of Moosetookalook, but neither could she spot any common thread. When she added in the missing persons, things got even more complicated.

Strictly speaking, Angie and her kids were not "missing persons" at all. Angie had every right to leave town without a word to anyone and take her children with her. Even with kids involved, an Amber Alert wasn't warranted. Only the fact that the fire marshal wanted to talk to Angie about the arson gave Sherri grounds to go as far as she had in her search. She felt as if she was wandering in circles, asking the same questions over and over and getting the same non-answers.

Abandoning the cruiser, she circled Jason Graye's house, as she had every hour since she'd taken up her post. Nothing had changed. The doors were locked. There was no sign of another living soul anywhere in the vicinity.

When had her limbs grown so heavy? It was an effort just to keep moving. She stopped at the passenger side of the cruiser to stretch and indulge in a huge yawn.

She yelped when the car door opened.

"Sorry, babe. Didn't mean to scare you."

The apologetic note in her husband's voice did little to steady Sherri's nerves. She wanted to blast him for sneaking up on her like that. At the same time, she was very glad to see him. He had eight inches and seventy-five pounds on her, packed into the solid shape of a linebacker—a comforting presence on a dark night, as long as he was on *her* side.

"Pete Campbell, I ought to whack you upside the head with this flashlight. What are you doing here?"

"Bringing you coffee." He had a go-cup in each hand.

As peace offerings, it was right up there with flowers and candy. She took one of the insulated cups, opened the top, and inhaled. "Who's with the kids?"

"My mom. She insisted."

Sherri's eyebrows rose at that. Thea Campbell, the same Thea Campbell who sat on the town's board of selectmen, was not known for her altruism. On the other hand, she relished the role of doting grandmother. She didn't even mind changing diapers.

Coffee in hand, Sherri circled the cruiser and got in on the driver's side. "I guess Thea heard about Jason Graye."

She already knew that Pete had. She'd called him herself to let him know she'd be working all night. Even if she hadn't explained why, he'd have heard enough on the scanner to figure it out since he was a deputy with the Carrabassett County Sheriff's Department. Two of his colleagues had been on the scene to assist the state police. It was likely at least one of them had swung by Sherri and Pete's house after leaving Lowe Street.

Pete took a sip of his coffee and leaned back against the headrest. "It's been hours since his body was found. I expect most of the town knows by now."

"I suppose so. What the *hell* is going on?"

"Don't tell me you're surprised that Graye ticked someone off enough to kill him?"

"But I am. He was a sleaze. I know that. But—"

"Sometimes it doesn't take much."

They sat in silence for a few minutes, sipping coffee and staring out into the night.

"The state police will handle the homicide," she said after a while. "The fire marshal takes the lead on the arson. The vandalism was probably kids, which means one of them will brag about it eventually and we'll round them up. That leaves it to me to figure out where Angie is."

"Any ideas?" Pete asked. "PLS is the bookstore two days before the fire, right?"

PLS—point last seen. Sherri sighed. "Right." Another acronym summed up the area still to be searched: ROW—rest of world.

"No luck tracing her under another name?"

"Not so far. You know what really bugs me? With all the friends Angie made during the last twelve years, not one of them has come up with a single helpful suggestion."

"Do you think someone knows more than she's saying?"

"Someone must. Someone left that anniversary card at Liss and Dan's."

"Angie herself?"

"Doubtful. But if she gave it to a friend to deliver, that suggests she meant to disappear. Planned ahead. But why? And where is she now?"

"What about Beth's friends? Any luck there?"

"None, and I've talked to at least a dozen of them. And Bradley's teacher gave me the names of his best buddies. Nothing. Nada. Zip." She took another sip of the coffee, brooding. "I wonder if Boxer knows more than he's saying."

Pete was shaking his head even before she finished asking the question. "That kid is really broken up over this whole mess. If he had any idea where they are, he'd have headed there like a shot."

"Maybe. Maybe not. Don't forget, I took off when I was around Beth's age. No one bothered to look for me."

Pete shifted in his seat. "Are you kidding? Your dad was frantic. When there was a report that you'd been seen in New York City, he went down there to look for you. He searched for over a week before your mother finally persuaded him to give up and come home."

Stunned, Sherri stared at him. The hand holding the go-cup started shaking so hard that she had to put it down in the cup holder. "I . . . I never knew. I figured they didn't care. After the things I said before I left, I wouldn't have blamed them if they'd written me off."

"Not that easy to do."

It wasn't until Pete reached across to wipe moisture off her cheek that she realized she'd been crying. God! She was a mess over this!

Get a grip, she ordered herself.

She fumbled for a tissue, blew her nose, and took another long swallow of the coffee. Feeling more in control, she forced her thoughts away from her own checkered past to focus on the present.

"It's stupid to compare myself to Beth. We're apples and oranges. Beth is with her mother and brother. If she wants to contact Boxer, what is there to stop her?"

"That's the real question, isn't it? What's to stop any of them from letting their friends know they're okay?"

On Saturday morning, Liss had consumed three cups of coffee before she remembered that this wasn't just the first full day of the Western Maine Highland Games. It was also her sixth wedding anniversary.

Seeing Dan walk into the kitchen carrying a humongous, heart-shaped box of chocolates was her first clue.

"I know," he said when she started to laugh. "It's hokey. But I have it on good authority that the sixth anniversary is supposed to be celebrated with candy."

"Or with wood." Suddenly the dull headache she'd had when she woke up was gone.

Liss ducked into the combination pantry and laundry room and came back with a small box topped with a big red bow. "Mine's not at all romantic, but I wanted to give you something I was sure you'd like."

Grinning like a little kid at Christmas, Dan ripped open his present. He gave a whoop and pumped one hand in the air when he saw what was written on the slip of paper inside.

After listening to her husband grumble for the last few months about how the orbital sander in his woodworking shop kept breaking down and needed to be replaced, Liss hadn't had any trouble deciding what to give him for their anniversary. "You'll have to pick it out for yourself," she told him. "I'm not qualified to select specialty woodworking tools."

"Well, now I feel like a cheapskate," Dan said when he'd given her a thank-you kiss. "This will cost a lot more than a lousy box of chocolates."

"Don't worry about it." She was already biting into a chocolate-covered cherry. Who cared if it was eight o'clock in the morning? "It's the thought that counts, and it *is* the candy anniversary."

"And wood, you said." He brightened. "Just to clear my conscience, pick an item of furniture you'd like to have and I'll make it for you."

"Deal," Liss said with a laugh. "I want a new dresser for the bedroom. One with big, deep drawers. Those little narrow ones on the one we've been using drive me crazy. Put away two folded T-shirts and they barely close."

"You got it," Dan promised, and sealed the agreement with another kiss.

One thing led to another, with the result that Liss was almost late setting out for The Spruces. She was feeling much more chipper as she drove the short distance to the hotel.

Chapter Eleven

Margaret was hard at work at her desk when Liss entered her office at The Spruces, but she at once dropped what she was doing. "Coffee? Or would you prefer tea?" She rose and headed for the side table that contained the fixings for both.

"No time, but thanks. I'm just here to collect that box you were keeping for me." It contained the most valuable of the small, easily portable items she offered for sale.

Since Liss's "booth" at the Highland Games was in fact a tent, she had rolled down the sides and tied the sections together after setting up the previous day. The whole structure was anchored to the ground, and the treated canvas did a good job of keeping out the elements, but it didn't offer much protection against a thief with a sharp knife. Although there was a guard patrolling the grounds at night, he couldn't be everywhere at once.

Liss's plan was to grab her box and run, but Margaret was too fast for her. "Nonsense. You can't go off to work without fortification. I have scones."

"Margaret, really, I—"

"And I expect a nice cup of chamomile tea would be

just the thing to go with them. It's only natural you'd be frazzled after everything you went through last night."

"I'm fine," Liss insisted. "And I'm already awash with coffee. I don't need anything else to drink."

Margaret turned away from the side table, a worried expression on her face. "Are you going to be able to manage all right?' "

"Trips to the port-a-potty? I'm pretty sure someone will cover for me if I need to go."

Margaret gave a ladylike snort. "That's not what I meant, and you know it."

Liss hefted her box. "I'm a little short on sleep, but I'll manage. And I have a lovely big box of chocolate to tide me over if I'm feeling hungry."

For a moment, before chagrin replaced that expression, Margaret looked puzzled. "It's your anniversary, isn't it? Sixth is candy? How . . . sweet."

Liss made a face at her. "Thanks for thinking of the scones." They were a particular weakness of hers. "But I've been fed and watered, and if I don't get going I won't be ready by the time the first customers show up. I'll talk to you later, okay?"

"Liss, wait."

Reluctantly, she turned.

"It occurred to me last night after I left your place that I might be considered a suspect in Jason Graye's murder. I did quarrel with him."

"Yes, you did. But you also have an excellent alibi. You were here, surrounded by witnesses."

"Everyone was watching the fireworks, not me."

"You introduced them, didn't you?"

Margaret shook her head. "Joe Ruskin did the honors. I

Liss quickly unpacked the box Margaret had kept for her, rearranged a few more items of stock, and unlocked and removed the lid on the tray that contained money for change. Then she booted up her iPad, silently blessing modern technology for making it possible to accept credit cards using a small swiping device and the hotel's Wi-Fi. Such a simple thing, and yet it made transactions so much easier, as well as much less expensive for a small business-person like herself. It wasn't all that long ago, she reflected, that she'd had to lug two small cash registers with her to this event. Today, once she'd placed a battery-powered hand calculator within easy reach and made sure she had plenty of pens and receipt pads, she was ready for business.

All around her, other vendors were making similar preparations. The hotel's vast green back lawn, the approximate size of a football field, was jam-packed with tents and awnings. Moosetookalook Scottish Emporium had a prime location between a seller of Scottish-themed books and a T-shirt vendor. Farther along their row, a falconer had set up shop, offering instruction manuals and demonstrations as well as the paraphernalia associated with keeping hunting birds in a society that no longer rode out with hawks and hounds. Beyond his booth was another perennial favorite—a demonstration by two women who still practiced the ancient arts of spinning and weaving. They also sold the results of their labor.

Dozens of Scottish clans had booths, as well as several Scottish societies. Beyond them, nearer to the "gate," there was a cluster of registration centers—one for dancers, one for pipers, and another for athletics.

There were food vendors, too. Liss could already smell

stayed in the background—so far in the background th: was probably invisible. There's nothing to say I coulc have zipped into town and killed Jason Graye. Do y think I should talk to Gordon Tandy before he comes lo ing for me?"

Not for a moment did Liss believe her aunt was a m derer, but she was right in thinking that Gordon wo want to interview her. "It couldn't hurt. I, uh, didn't thi to mention you to him. I only ratted on Dolores."

"Oh, yes. The crisis over the library. Well, I can't im: ine Dolores taking such drastic measures when she ha perfectly good plan in place to force a recall election a boot Graye out of office."

Liss wondered if Margaret had heard about the sho ing incident at the Mayfield house. She hadn't been at tl meeting. Instead of asking, she made a production out looking at the clock on the wall. Exclaiming over the tin she fled before Margaret could say any more about l: night's horrific discovery or, worse, launch into an accou of her plans to mitigate the bad publicity that was sure come out of it.

On her way to her booth, Liss gave herself a stern lectu She would not even think about Jason Graye for the rest the day. Her sole focus would be on selling all things Sco tish.

In short order, she had turned the tent back into a awning, rolling up and securing the side panels to reve four long display tables arranged in a square. She'd left narrow aisle at the end of one of them to allow custome: access to racks of ready-made kilts, tartan skirts, and oth clothing.

the delightful aroma of baking scones. Janice Eccles, known far and wide as "the Scone Lady," had brought her portable ovens. Knowing Janice, she'd also been the one who had supplied Margaret MacCrimmon Boyd with an assortment of the uniquely British treats.

By the official opening time, there were at least a hundred people lined up to get in. Liss had to smile as she watched them surge through the banner-draped entrance to the grounds and descend on the venue. Small children tugged their parents' hands, urging them to hurry. Girls dressed for the dance competitions rushed toward the registration tents. A stage had been set up for them at one side of the grounds, on the way to the open field at the side of the hotel that was the designated site for the sports competitions. Liss picked out one or two people she felt certain would be among the athletes—strong, burly men wearing T-shirts with their kilts.

The lawn at the other side of the hotel had been earmarked for performances by pipe bands. The day would end with that most stirring of events, the massed bands, when every pipe and drum corps in attendance would join together to play some of the most enduring bagpipe music. Dan always covered his ears for that portion of the program or left the area entirely, but Liss loved every minute of it.

A smaller field had been roped off for animal events. Sheepdog trials were standard fare at Scottish festivals. This being Maine, there would also be a performance by the local llama drill team.

Liss shared the sense of anticipation that flowed in with the crowd, and not just because she expected to make a profit on the day. Her buoyant mood lasted until she caught sight of Angus Grant at the forefront of the horde. The bright smile on her face faltered.

Go somewhere else, she thought, looking at him. *Get yourself a scone. Buy a book. Find someone new to pick on.*

Janice Eccles's cheerful voice rose above the noise of the crowd. "Fresh-baked scones," she sang out. "Get 'em while they're still warm!"

Being Maine born and bred, Janice rhymed *scone* with *stone*.

Grant veered off just before he reached the Moosetookalook Scottish Emporium booth and headed for the scone-maker's stand. At once, Liss felt guilty for wishing him on anyone else. She watched, appalled, as he marched right up to the counter, cutting ahead of the three people already in line.

"If you are going to bake and sell scones," he said, rhyming *scone* with *con*, "you should know how to pronounce the word correctly."

Janice was not impressed by bluster. "That's a matter of opinion." She leaned around him to address the next paying customer in line. "What can I get for you, hon?"

Grant waited only long enough for her to fill one order before he started in again. "As any true son of Scotland knows—"

"You speak for all of them, do you?" Janice lifted one finely shaped eyebrow. "That surprises me, especially when a recent survey taken in the UK proved that not everyone there agrees with you. In the U. S. of A., of course, we never did pay much attention to pronunciations from across the pond."

Liss stifled a laugh, silently applauding Janice's put-down. She was even more tickled when a woman standing in line chimed in with her two cents.

"I don't see what's wrong with rhyming *scone* with *cone*. I've heard more than one of those television chefs pronounce it that way." That was clearly enough to settle the matter in *her* mind.

"You aren't going to win this debate, mister," Janice said, "and unless you intend to buy something, I suggest you take yourself elsewhere."

The customer at the end of the line backed her up. "Move it along, bub. I don't care how you say it as long as it tastes good. What difference does it make, anyway?"

Face almost purple with suppressed outrage, Grant abandoned the scone stall and headed for Liss's booth. Out of sight behind a display case on the front table, Liss's hands were curled into fists. Only with concentrated effort could she relax her fingers. Angus Grant hadn't yet said a word to her, and she was already fighting the urge to throttle him. Vowing to hold on to her temper, Liss braced herself for yet another unpleasant encounter.

"Still haven't learned to spell *sgian dubh*, I see." Grant jabbed a pudgy finger at the hand-lettered sign next to a small dagger. One of the items Liss had stored in Margaret's office, the little knife had a handle that was silver-mounted and hand-carved, and it came with its own leather sheath.

Liss replied through gritted teeth. "Shall we compromise? I'll go all the way to English and change the sign so it reads BLACK DAGGER."

"Compromise? There is no compromise. What's right is right. What's wrong is wrong."

Liss enjoyed a momentary fantasy in which she reached into the display case, withdrew the knife, and told him what he could do with it. According to one of those traditions he seemed to value so highly, a warrior never returned a black dagger to its scabbard without first spilling blood.

A split second later, this pleasing if unpleasant image was replaced by a vivid memory of Jason Graye as Liss had last seen him, his lifeless body sprawled on the floor just inside his front door. Her imagination added the weapon used to kill him—a *skean dhu* with a hand-carved, silver-mounted handle.

Swallowing bile, she blinked to dispel the image.

Focus on business, she ordered herself. *Be pleasant to the customer. Heck, why not try for a sale?*

Like many of the men at the Highland Games, Grant was wearing Highland dress. Liss recognized his clan's tartan, a pattern that looked a little like Royal Stewart, except that it had no yellow in it. She had just the thing to go with that kilt.

"Have you thought of purchasing a plaid?" she asked. "I know I have one in the Grant tartan."

She also knew that he wouldn't find cause for complaint in her pronunciation of plaid. She was well aware of the difference between a plaid, pronounced "played"—the rectangular woolen cape in a tartan pattern that was worn over one shoulder—and plaid, pronounced "plad"—the pattern. Of course, when it came to Scottish clothing, the proper word was tartan rather than plaid. Each clan had one or more tartans that distinguished their members, just as each clan had a distinctive crest and motto.

Grant scowled. "I own a plaid already."

"A new dress sporran, then?" The one he was wearing was a very plain, black leather pouch decorated with three tassels.

"No."

Grant wore a Balmoral on his head, one of the two most popular styles of hat for men wearing kilts. Liss was debating whether or not to bother suggesting that he try on a Glengarry when he abruptly changed the subject.

"Fireworks do not belong at a Scottish festival!"

Liss blinked at him in surprise. Where had that come from?

"A proper Highland games should have been opened with a *ceilidh*." Grant looked so smug that Liss wanted to smack him.

She wished she knew what his problem was. At a *ceilidh*, the main attractions were folk music and dance. There had been both on the previous evening at the hotel, together with a procession of pipe bands, all offered at no extra charge to hotel guests.

"How odd," she said aloud, her tone of voice carefully neutral. "I was under the impression that, leading up to the fireworks display, there were performances by two of the bagpipe bands, a virtuoso on the Scottish harp, a group of fiddlers, and a team of Highland dancers."

As for pyrotechnics, there was no rule against them. In fact, she could remember seeing a documentary about the famous Edinburgh Tattoo on television and was quite sure there had been fireworks.

Liss's jaw ached from holding her shopkeeper's smile in place as Grant droned on. It didn't help that she could see potential customers, one after another, giving her booth a wide berth. No one wanted to risk catching the attention of someone as obnoxious and belligerent as Angus Grant. Until he decided to move on or someone else was brave enough to challenge him, she was going to keep losing business.

Like an answer to a prayer, such an individual appeared.

He did not wear a kilt, having realized on a previous

visit to the Western Maine Highland Games that he did not have the knees for it. Civilian clothing, however, did not dampen the effect of his arrival.

"Angus Grant, right?" The newcomer grabbed Grant's hand in a death grip. "I'm Murch. Jake Murch. Private investigator extraordinaire. I've been looking for you." Without giving his victim any opportunity to escape, Murch shifted his hold to Grant's elbow and steered him away from Liss's booth.

"What's this all about? What do you want with me?" Grant tried to break free, but Murch was by far the stronger of the two.

The detective's jovial voice drifted back to Liss as they disappeared into the crowd: "Nothing to worry about, Grant. Not unless you have something to hide. I understand you were a witness to that terrible fire last week in the village."

Murch to the rescue, Liss thought.

The last time Jake Murch had attended the Highland Games, she'd been in mortal danger. She'd managed to save herself, but the private detective had provided very welcome backup.

She wondered if he truly suspected Angus Grant of setting the fire. The idea seemed absurd. If Grant was going to torch any of the businesses in Moosetookalook, the Emporium would have been a more likely target.

That horrific thought provoked an involuntary shiver. Liss was glad to have the distraction of a customer. Then, for the next hour or so, she was far too busy to dwell on any of the troubles that had plagued her hometown.

Liss worked on her own until noon, when her young cousin Boxer reported for duty. She had recruited him weeks earlier to help out at the booth. He pitched in with a will, and since business was brisk, it was not until there was a lull that Liss noticed how haggard he looked. She didn't have any trouble figuring out why. He'd been worrying about Beth Hogencamp.

"When did you last get a good night's sleep?" she asked him.

"Do you really need to ask?" He brushed an unruly lock of reddish brown hair out of his eyes and sent her a rueful look.

"I wish there was something I could say that would help, but all I have are more questions."

"Questions for me?"

She nodded.

"Might as well ask them, then. Maybe one of us will come up with something." The hopeful look on his plain, square face broke Liss's heart.

"Did Beth ever talk about any of her mother's friends? Maybe someone from out of town?"

Boxer shook his head. "I've been asking myself that. Beth and I were good buddies long before we started dating, but I never paid all that much attention to her mom." He shrugged. "She never liked me much."

When she'd first met him, Angie had thought Boxer was a wiseass and a troublemaker, and he had been back then. That his mother was a Snipes hadn't helped his reputation. Members of that family tended to be shiftless and hard on their wives. Boxer, however, had turned out to be the exception that proved the rule. He was headed for college in the fall and had a bright future ahead of him.

"They can't have vanished so completely without help." Liss fished a bottle of water out of the cooler Boxer had brought with him and tossed a second one to him.

"Seems to me you're the one Beth's mother was closest to." Boxer opened the bottle and took a long swallow.

It wasn't abnormally hot for summer in Maine, but it was late July. The air was just muggy enough to make Liss sweat if she did more than take in money and rearrange stock. She held the cold bottle against her forehead before she followed Boxer's lead.

"Besides me, who else?"

He shrugged. "I guess that would be Gloria Weird."

"Gloria *Weir*." The correction was automatic, as was Liss's smile. Gloria *was* an odd duck. "I didn't realize she and Angie were particularly friendly."

"She lives right across the street. I guess they see a lot of each other."

Did Gloria know anything? Sherri hadn't seemed to think so after she'd talked to her. Murch, too, had interviewed the owner of Ye Olde Hobbie Shoppe and come up empty.

"Anyone else?"

"Patsy, I guess." Suddenly he grinned. "Hey, all you old fogeys go to Patsy's."

Caught by surprise, Liss had no comeback. Then the arrival of a customer kept her from responding. Where *did* the kids hang out? He was right. It wasn't at Patsy's. Graziano's Pizza, maybe? Deciding that it probably didn't matter, she took another pull on her water.

The more time that passed, the clearer it became that Angie must be staying away deliberately. Was she in hiding? If so, was it because she was a fugitive from the law or because she was afraid to show herself for some other reason? The only other possibility Liss had been able to come up with—that she and her children had been prevented from returning—didn't bear thinking about. What kind of psychopath would kidnap an entire family?

Liss was glad to be pulled from such fruitless speculation by a customer wanting to buy a kilt pin. As she wrapped it in tissue paper and tucked it and the receipt into a small red bag with the Moosetookalook Scottish Emporium logo emblazoned on both sides, she listened to the music filtering through the noise of the crowd. The sound soothed her troubled mind.

There were performances scheduled throughout the day—singers, fiddlers, and harpists as well as pipers. At the moment, somewhere not too distant, a woman with a lovely soprano voice was singing a ballad to the accompaniment of a guitar.

"Liss, do you carry Scottish-themed bumper stickers?" Boxer asked.

A boy of about fifteen stood on the other side of the display table, a look of deviltry in his eyes. "I want one for my dad," he said. "The one that says 'Old Pipers Never Die. Their Bags Just Dry Up.'"

"The gentleman selling T-shirts also has bumper stickers," Liss called back, trying not to grimace at that old chestnut.

"How come you don't stock them?" Boxer asked when their customers had moved on. "You've got all this other Scottish stuff."

"I'm aiming for a slightly more high-class clientele."

"But you do sell T-shirts."

"Only the ones that have thistles or Scottish lions on the front. No risqué slogans. When I first took over the business, I discontinued all the truly tacky items in the inventory." She was careful not to mention the fact that it had been Boxer's father who had ordered most of them in the first place.

"My cousin the prude," Boxer teased her.

"Am not."

"Are too!"

They grinned at each other.

Reminded of their kinship, Liss remembered that she had yet to ask Boxer about Angie's sister-in-law. Murch had not had any luck identifying her, nor had Sherri. Neither Patsy nor Gloria had admitted to knowing Angie *had* a sister-in-law.

Boxer reached into the cooler once more and this time snagged a soda. The crowd around the vendors had thinned out. Cheering from the field where the athletic competitions were under way explained why. There was only one customer at the Emporium's booth, a woman examining the rack of ready-made kilts.

"I don't suppose," Liss said without much hope, "that Beth ever mentioned an aunt. Her father's sister? Or maybe the wife or widow of Angie's brother? A sister-in-law, anyway." She supposed, these days, a sister-in-law could also be the spouse of a sister.

"Nope." Boxer took a long drink.

"She visited at the time of the Maine-ly Cozy Con. You probably don't remember that. You may not even have known Beth back then."

"I knew who she was. And I used to go in the bookstore sometimes. Just looking around. I didn't have the money to buy anything." A rueful expression on his face, he added, "Angie always thought I was going to shoplift stuff. She kept an eagle eye on me."

"Do you remember someone else manning the store while Angie was at the Cozy Con?"

Boxer drank again. Frowning, he considered. "Y'know, I do. A woman. She didn't kick me out."

"Do you remember what she looked like?"

She was unsurprised when he shook his head. It had been more than six years. But then the most peculiar expression came over his face.

"Bumper sticker," Boxer said. "There was a car parked in Angie's driveway that day, and it had a bumper sticker that said 'Virginia Is for Lovers.' I remember thinking that was a pretty stupid slogan, but then I was only, what? Twelve? Does that help?"

"Not much," Liss admitted, "but it's more than we knew before."

Boxer polished off his soda and tossed the empty can into the bag they were using for recyclables. "You want to take a break while it's quiet?"

The same woman was still browsing among the kilts. No one else had shown any interest in their booth for a while now.

"Are you sure you can answer any questions she has?"

"I've only heard your spiel about a gazillion times. All those are tartans anyone can wear, clan or no clan. The red, green, yellow, blue, and white is Royal Stewart. The dark one is Black Watch. The dark green and blue with black and pink worked in is Flower of Scotland and was specifically created for those who don't have Scots roots. The fourth one is called Hunting Stewart."

"Okay. Okay. You pass the test." His sing-song recitation had her smiling again. "Just don't forget to tell her we can also special-order kilts in any tartan."

"Yeah, yeah. Go if you're going."

"And don't count on making a sale," she warned him.

"The cheapest kilt on the rack is priced at over three hundred dollars."

They were labor-intensive to make, requiring at least eight yards of material apiece. Tightly pleated at the back with an apron front, a kilt had to hang just right and be the correct length, just clearing the ground when the wearer knelt. At one time, when Margaret had been sole proprietor of Moosetookalook Scottish Emporium, she had made kilts herself. She'd given up the sideline when she went to work at the hotel.

Liss's first stop was at the row of port-a-potties. Her second was the scone-maker's booth.

"I was so sorry to hear about all the troubles in Moosetookalook," Janice said as she passed over the freshly baked pastry and took Liss's money. She was from Waycross Springs, a good hour away by car, but news traveled fast on the Carrabassett County grapevine.

"It's just been one thing after another," Liss agreed.

"And this latest! I hear you know a little more than most people about what happened."

Liss repressed a groan. She didn't think she'd been identified in any news reports as the one who'd found Jason Graye's body, but the local gossips must all know by now. Neighbors would have recognized her at the scene.

"I'm sorry, Janice, but I can't talk about it."

The Scone Lady looked disappointed but didn't press for details. Whether she thought Liss found the subject too upsetting to discuss or guessed she'd been ordered to keep quiet by the police, Liss couldn't tell.

"You take care of yourself now, Liss," Janice called after her as she turned to wait on her next hungry customer.

A quick glance at the Emporium's booth reassured Liss that Boxer was doing just fine on his own. She fished a copy of the schedule of events out of her pocket. She'd just missed the sheaf toss, an event that involved tossing a sixteen-pound sheaf of hay encased in a burlap bag over a bar using a three-tined pitchfork. The current athletic competition was the hammer throw.

Liss grimaced. The hammer, a metal ball attached to a wooden handle, weighed a little over twenty pounds and had been known to fly more than a hundred yards. She'd come close to being coldcocked with one once and had been a little leery of the sport ever since.

She did enjoy watching the caber toss. The cabers, which most people compared to telephone poles, were nineteen feet long and weighed 120 pounds and took a good deal of skill to lift, let alone throw. That event, however, wouldn't be held until later in the day.

Her timing was off to attend any of the dance competitions, too. No one was currently performing on the stage set up for those events. There were, however, a few people lingering in the area. She walked in that direction, hoping to spot someone she knew from the old days.

Liss did recognize one face, but it was not that of a dancer. It was the gentleman who'd come into Moosetookalook Scottish Emporium looking for postage stamps—Martin Eldridge. Omnipresent walking stick in hand, he was deep in conversation with another man, one who looked vaguely familiar.

The second man was both shorter and younger than Eldridge. His hair was cut so close to his scalp that he very nearly looked bald. Was this the same man she'd seen talking to Eldridge in the town square? She had no idea. On the previous occasion, he'd been too far away for her to see clearly.

Murch would know for certain. He'd been close enough to eavesdrop on that earlier conversation. Although he'd dismissed what he'd heard as harmless, Liss had to wonder if he might have missed something. Watching the two men near the stage, she had a strong sense of something "off" about them.

Try as she might, Liss couldn't quite put her finger on what it was that made her so uneasy. At first she thought it might be the way they were dressed. At the Highland Games, people wore everything from full Highland regalia to cutoffs and T-shirts. Eldridge stood out in dress slacks and a long-sleeved, button-down shirt, an odd choice for a warm July day. The man with him wore a short-sleeved polo shirt and chinos—also a bit dressy for a Scottish festival.

A woman towing two young children passed close to the two men. When she was near enough that she might accidentally overhear what they were saying, they abruptly stopped talking. Eldridge kept an eye on the trio until they were safely out of earshot. Then he glanced around in a manner Liss could only describe as furtive before resuming the discussion with his companion.

No, she decided, it was not what they were wearing. It was the intensity of their conversation that was out of the ordinary. Whatever it was that the two men were talking about, they were anxious—too anxious—to keep it private.

She very much doubted they were critiquing Shakespearean plays.

Before Eldridge could look her way and realize she'd

been watching him, Liss turned in the opposite direction. Instead of returning to the Moosetookalook Scottish Emporium booth, she headed for the lobby of the hotel.

Despite her best efforts, it had proven impossible to avoid thinking about recent events. Now that her curiosity about Martin Eldridge had been piqued, she felt she had to do something to satisfy it.

As she'd hoped, Joe Ruskin manned the front desk.

"Question for you, Joe—what guests have been here more than a week?"

"Why do you want to know?"

Liss didn't think her father-in-law would balk at giving her the information she wanted, but she hesitated over how much to tell him. "It occurs to me that the troubles in the village might be the work of an outsider. If that's the case, any guest who has been here more than a week could be involved."

"You know Sherri already asked me for this same information?"

"Then there's no harm in sharing it with me. Come on, Joe—what's the harm? If I was helping out here today instead of working at my booth, I could look it up for myself."

True, she'd only substituted for a sick employee once or twice, and that had been in the hotel's gift shop, but she was a member of the Ruskin family, and all the Ruskins had a stake in The Spruces. So did Aunt Margaret.

Shaking his head, Joe consulted the computer terminal behind reception. Liss heard the tapping of his fingers on the keyboard.

Although the hotel was completely modern, it had retained its Victorian roots. The rich wood her hand rested upon was polished to a high gloss, and the wall behind reception boasted old-fashioned cubbyholes to hold guests' keys and messages.

"Like I told Sherri," Joe said after a moment, "there are only four people who came in before last Friday and are still here. There's a couple, Angus and Janine Grant, and two individual men, Eliot Underhill and Martin Eldridge."

"What more do you have on them? Where are they from? What business are they in?"

Joe consulted the screen. "The Grants are from New Jersey. Underhill hails from Virginia."

"Virginia?" Coincidence, she told herself. But sometimes coincidences turned out to be important.

Joe sent her a questioning look as he confirmed it. "Says here he's from Roanoke. Eldridge listed Virginia as his residence, too, but he's from a different city. None of them put down a company name. The Grants drove here in their own car. The other two are driving rentals. That's all the information we ask for, other than a valid credit card number. Funny thing, though. Underhill paid cash. Said he didn't believe in buying on credit. Didn't even quibble when I asked for an additional deposit to cover incidentals."

Liss's brows shot up. That was very unusual. "What does he look like?"

Joe shrugged. "Average height. Average build. Short little nose. Real short hair."

As Liss had expected, Joe's description matched the man she had just seen talking to Eldridge. "Thanks, Joe."

She had already started to turn away when he spoke. "Do my son a favor, Liss. Let the cops handle this."

"I'm not going to meddle. I promise. It's just that I can't help thinking about things."

"Things like arson? Missing persons? Murder?"

"Don't forget vandalism," she quipped, although it was hardly a joking matter. She sobered instantly. "Really, Joe. You don't have to worry. My impulsive days are in the past. If I come up with any bright ideas at all, I'll go straight to the police."

Chapter Twelve

Sherri had worked all night and slept till noon, when a phone call from Liss woke her. Now she was back on duty by two in the afternoon on Saturday. She had too much on her plate to take any more time off, even though she was not the one responsible for investigating the murder of Jason Graye. Fortunately, Pete's mother was willing to keep an eye on the children while both their parents worked. Thea, Sherri suspected, was mellowing in her old age. Or maybe she was just shaken by the death of a fellow member of the board of selectmen and wanted the comfort of loving grandchildren around her. Whatever her motivation, Sherri was grateful.

Before Sherri went to the police station, she drove to the scene of the crime. As she'd expected, the state police were still there. She parked and climbed the steps to the porch to rap at the door. Gordon Tandy himself came to open it.

"Do you need any additional help today?" she asked.

Overnight, Sherri's department had taken on the responsibility of making sure no one got inside Jason Graye's empty house. Until the state police were sure they had taken away everything of importance, even the carpet beneath Graye's body, no one wanted to risk potential evidence being contaminated.

"We're covered." Gordon's tone was brusque and slightly impatient. "With the games going on, there's not a lot of traffic in town."

"Any progress you can talk about?" She doubted it, but figured she might as well ask. After all, Moosetookalook was her responsibility. She was the one the board of selectmen held accountable when it came to upholding the law and keeping order.

Gordon unbent a fraction. "I expect we'll be through with Graye's house by the end of the day."

"Excellent." She'd have her officers check the place periodically, but there would no longer be a need to assign someone to stand guard.

She was starting to walk away when Gordon called her back. "There is one thing you can do. Liss didn't know the names of that young couple on the swings. You probably have a better shot at finding out who they are than I do."

"I'll see what I can come up with," Sherri promised.

She'd intended to pursue the matter even if Gordon hadn't brought it up. The odds that one of the young lovers had seen the killer weren't good. Courting couples tended to be completely absorbed in each other. Still, it was worth looking into.

The other item on her day's agenda was tracking down the man calling himself Eliot Underhill. She'd meant to talk to him on Friday, but with one thing and another—a traffic accident, a complaint about cows running loose in the middle of one of the back roads, a domestic dispute over to Lower Mooseside, and a dog complaint in Ripley—she'd never had the chance. And then, of course, there had been the murder. She didn't put much stock in Liss's new information—that Angie's sister-in-law apparently lived in or had visited Virginia—but she certainly intended to show the bookseller's photo to the mysterious Mr. Underhill.

After a brief stop at her office, Sherri left the municipal building and crossed Main Street to the town square. She settled herself on one of the swings, facing into the rest of the square, and pushed off. For a few minutes, she closed her eyes and allowed herself to enjoy the sensation of flying up into the air. Then she got back to work.

From this vantage point, her view took in the municipal building, the remains of the bookstore, the historical society's museum, and the jewelry store. The trees and various other objects in the town square prevented her from seeing any of those buildings in its entirety. She glanced to her left and caught a glimpse of Moosetookalook Scottish Emporium. Had the courting couple seen Liss and Dan leave for the fireworks? Given the distance and the time of day, Sherri didn't suppose that the Ruskins would have been more than shadowy shapes. Someone crossing the square wouldn't have been easy to recognize, either—unless he . . . or she . . . happened to pass directly under one of the street lamps that dotted the paths.

Sherri got up, circled the swings, and sat down again facing the other way. This gave her a fine view of Liss's house and those on either side of it on Birch Street. By turning her head slightly, she could see Patsy's Coffee House.

A few minutes later, Sherri was inside the café, seated in the corner booth Pete always chose when he came to Patsy's. The entire dining area was compact, containing only three booths and two tables, plus the five stools at the counter.

When Patsy brought her coffee, Sherri gestured toward the bench seat opposite. "Got a minute?"

Patsy shot her a suspicious look. "Why?"

"I need to pick your brain."

"Huh! I don't have time to do your work for you, hon." But she eased her tall, skinny frame into the booth and waited, an expectant look in her eyes.

"There were two people sitting on the swings in the town square last night. Probably teenagers. I figure chances are good that wasn't the first time they'd sat there in the dark."

"Amie Fitzwarren and Kent Humphrey," Patsy said. "They come in here sometimes. She likes my ginger cookies."

Pay dirt, Sherri thought. She knew them both. In fact, she'd talked briefly to each of them just the other day, since their names had been on Boxer's list of Beth's friends. "You saw them sitting on the swings last night? You're sure?"

Patsy nodded. "Last night and every night for the past week."

"I don't suppose you know why?"

"I've got ears, don't I? Amie's father doesn't approve of her dating Kent, so she tells her folks she's studying at a friend's house. Then they meet up in the town square."

"Better there than in a motel room, I guess."

Patsy snorted. "If either of them had a feather to fly with, you can bet they'd have moved it indoors. You'd be surprised how steamy things can get just sitting in the dark on a pair of side-by-side swings."

"I do remember being young and stupid," Sherri conceded.

"What do you want to know for anyway?" Patsy leaned across the table. "I hope you're not going to cause trouble for that girl. She's a nice kid, even if she does have stars in her eyes."

"I just need to talk to her, and to Kent. They might have seen something last night."

Patsy reared back, eyes wide, as she caught the significance of what Sherri had just said. "Something? Or someone?"

Sherri was reluctant to tell her more. The last thing she wanted was to add grist to the town's gossip mill. On the other hand, Patsy was more discreet than most people, and if she'd picked up any other useful information, Sherri wanted to hear it.

To give herself time to decide how much to confide, she made a production of checking the rest of the coffee house for potential eavesdroppers. The only other customer was Alex Permutter. He was sitting with his back to them as he drank coffee and polished off one of Patsy's gigantic chocolate chip muffins. He didn't look as if he planned to leave anytime soon. He had a newspaper spread open on the table in front of him.

"Don't worry about Alex," Patsy said. "He can't hear a word you say unless you shout right into his ear."

From firsthand experience, Sherri knew this was true, but she still hesitated.

Patsy plucked a napkin from the nearby dispenser and wiped up a spot of coffee, crumpling the napkin in one hand when the tabletop was clean. "I guess maybe there's something else I should tell you."

Sherri waited, watching in fascination as Patsy smoothed the napkin flat again. "Same time as I saw those kids, I caught sight of someone else in the town square."

Although she was careful not to react outwardly, Sherri felt a jolt of excitement pass through her. "When? What time was this?"

"It was just before the fireworks started." With precise movements, Patsy tore the napkin into long, thin strips.

Disappointment replaced elation. That was too early. But Patsy wasn't done with her revelations.

"I'm thinking I must have seen him when he was on his way to Lowe Street, right before he up and killed Jason Graye."

Sherri stared at her, momentarily at a loss for words. When the ability to speak came back to her, she all but shouted at Patsy. "Do you mean to tell me you've thought all along that you saw the killer?"

"I don't know that I did!" Offended, Patsy left the booth in a rush. "If I was sure, I'd have told you before now. All I saw was a shape. Nothing I can identify."

Calm down, Sherri warned herself. *Honey, not vinegar.*

"I'm sorry, Patsy. Of course you'd have said if you knew who it was. Sit down again. Please?"

Looking grumpy, Patsy complied. She scooped up the napkin shreds and stuffed them into the pocket of her apron.

"Thank you. Now, please, tell me everything. Was there something about this person that made you suspicious of him?"

"I didn't think anything was all that peculiar at the time, although he *was* keeping his head down, like he didn't want to be recognized." She frowned. "Now that I think about it, he must have cut across the grass. There's no path where he was walking."

Hard to see the KEEP OFF signs in the dark, Sherri thought. Was Patsy's information relevant or not? Anyone who lived in the area might have cut through the square.

"When I heard about the murder, I got to wondering if that's where he was headed. You know what they say—hindsight is twenty/twenty." Patsy chuckled, but Sherri heard no amusement in the sound.

Both women fell silent when the bell over the door

sounded and a new customer walked in. Sherri recognized Louie, owner of Graziano's Pizza, and expected Patsy to get up to wait on him. Instead, Louie headed straight for the small alcove where Patsy had installed a couple of coffee grinders and several bins of coffee beans.

"Taking two pounds," Louie called out. "Put it on my tab."

"You got it," Patsy answered.

A moment later, the sound of grinding beans sent a heavenly aroma into air already perfumed with cinnamon and spice from Patsy's baked goods.

"He can't hear us over that racket," Patsy said. "You got more questions?"

"Do you have any suspicion about who it was that you saw?"

"Wish I did. I couldn't even say man or woman for certain, except that I had the impression it was a man." She lifted her bony shoulders in a shrug.

"I don't suppose you'd hazard a guess as to where he came from?"

Patsy shook her head. The look of worry on her face intensified. "Could have parked somewhere east of the town square and walked to Lowe Street. That would account for him coming back the same way, right?"

Although the coffee grinder was still going strong, Sherri lowered her voice and leaned toward Patsy. "As you've already guessed, someone did come this way after the murder. It could well be that he left a car somewhere. It's also possible he lives or works in the neighborhood. He might have ducked inside a building."

Patsy went stiff as a poker. "Are you accusing me of hiding a killer?"

"Of course not! Where did *that* idea come from?"

"Who do *you* suspect, then?" Patsy narrowed her eyes and fixed Sherri with a basilisk stare. "Huh! You think Dolores Mayfield did him in, don't you? Well, you're a damn fool if you think that. She wouldn't kill anybody, not even a lowlife like Jason Graye. She had worse in mind for him."

"Worse?"

"Lawsuits." Patsy's head bobbed up and down on her scrawny neck. "She intended to take him to the cleaners in court. There's nothing Graye would have hated more than being ordered to pay damages."

"Damages for what?"

"Mental anguish, of course, caused by his attempt to shut down the library." Patsy rubbed her hands together, a gleeful look in her eyes. "He'd have been some pissed, let me tell you, when he had to shell out thousands of dollars just to get Dolores off his back."

The noise from the coffee grinder abruptly stopped. Sherri took that as her cue to leave. Patsy wasn't the only one she had to talk to today.

The Fitzwarren house was out past Dr. Sharon's clinic, on Elm Street but a good quarter mile from the town square. Forewarned that Amie's father wouldn't take kindly to the news that his daughter had disobeyed him, Sherri resolved to be careful not to blow the girl's cover—that she'd been studying with a friend. She didn't anticipate any problem getting permission to talk with Amie. The Fitzwarrens already knew the police were looking for information on Beth Hogencamp and that Beth and Amie were BFFs.

As it turned out, no excuse was necessary. Amie was alone at the house.

"We were watching the fireworks," she said in answer to Sherri's question. "I didn't notice anyone else around."

She was a pretty girl, blond and leggy and a few inches taller than Sherri—but then, almost everyone was. That Amie was also skinny as a rail bothered Sherri more than her greater height. She hoped the teenager wasn't starving herself in an effort to look like some emaciated movie star.

"So, no one ran past you while you were sitting there?" she asked.

Amie's blush gave her away. She wouldn't have noticed an earthquake, as long as she and her boyfriend were engrossed in each other.

"Did you notice when I left the municipal building and cut across the northwest corner of the square?"

Amie shook her head.

"But you were facing that way, right?" The fireworks had been set off at The Spruces, and the hotel was northwest of the center of the village. Even if they were more interested in making out than in watching the show, it stood to reason that they'd want a good view of the pyrotechnics.

"I guess so."

Not the brightest bulb, Sherri decided. "Do you think Kent saw anything?"

Her brow furrowed, as if it took a great deal of effort to come up with an answer to this question. "I don't *think* so."

"You sound a little uncertain."

"Well, he did stop . . . I mean . . . he acted kind of funny for a minute there, but then more fireworks went off and everything was fine again."

"Any idea where Kent is today?" The Humphreys lived on the road to Fallstown, near the turnoff to the hotel and close to the gas station and convenience store Sherri's father owned.

"He's probably at work," Amie said.

Sherri waited a beat, then had to prompt the girl. "Where?"

"Willett's Store."

The answer surprised Sherri. Since when did her father hire help? He was the original "I'd rather do it myself" guy.

Thanking Amie for her cooperation, Sherri drove straight to the familiar small, square clapboard building. The bright yellow paint, she noticed as she parked and went in, was sadly in need of a touch-up.

Ernie Willett greeted his daughter with a scowl on his craggy face. In his world, this passed for affection. Sherri gave him a peck on the cheek, told him he needed a shave, and helped herself to a candy bar from the display on the counter.

"That'll be a dollar, missy. I'm not running a charity here."

Sherri fished four quarters out of her pocket and handed them over. "Got a question for you."

He sent her a suspicious look, eyebrows shooting up and dark eyes inquisitive.

"Any idea where I can find Kent Humphrey? I hear he works for you."

"Boy's not in trouble, is he?"

"Not that I know of."

Her father's breath came out in an exasperated huff. "It's that girl he hangs out with, isn't it? I told him to steer clear of her. Thinks he's in love! What does a kid that age know about love?"

She could ask the same question of him, Sherri thought, but she was wise enough not to do so. At Kent and Amie's age, he'd been head over heels for Margaret MacCrimmon. They'd broken up after high school. He'd married Sherri's mother, Ida, and Margaret had become Margaret Boyd. Years later, when she was a widow and he was divorced, it had looked as if things between them might be heating up again, but that fire had apparently sputtered and gone out. They'd stopped keeping company a couple of years ago. Margaret now appeared to be more devoted to her dogs than to Ernie Willett.

"Dad, do you know where Kent is now? I really need to talk to him. I think he may have seen something last night . . . after Jason Graye was killed."

If she'd hoped to shock her father into cooperating, she was doomed to disappointment. A dedicated curmudgeon like Ernie Willett was hard to rattle. He fiddled with the candy display, rearranging the three remaining chocolate bars before he finally offered an answer. "Might be he's at the Highland Games."

"Might be, or is?"

He shrugged. "Said something about going up there if I didn't need him today. I told him to go ahead, as long as he came back before the end. Might be a few folks needing gas for the drive home."

"Thanks, Dad. I'll go see if I can find him."

"You'd do better to wait till he comes back," he called after her.

With a wave, she kept going, but she had reconsidered by the time she reached the police cruiser. Her father was right. For one thing, there was no guarantee Kent was at the games, even though he'd said that was where he was going. Even if he was there, it would be like looking for a needle in a haystack. She'd do better to wait a couple of hours. She could talk to him at the store, or wait until evening and catch him at home.

It was just as well she'd resigned herself to a delay. She'd barely turned the key in the ignition before she was called out to a rollover on Raglan Road, near the old Chadwick mansion.

When Liss took her second break of the day, it was to meet Jake Murch beneath the shade trees at one side of the hotel grounds. The area had been set aside as a venue for performances by the quieter musicians—harpists, fiddlers, and singers. Since it wasn't far from the rows of booths, Liss had caught bits and pieces of the music throughout the day. A soprano she had heard earlier was almost through with her second show when Liss plunked herself down in the chair Murch had saved for her.

He held a finger to his lips. "Let the lady finish this song before we talk."

Liss had no problem with that. She recognized the ballad instantly as "The Bonny Earl of Murray." She was grinning by the time the singer took her bows and left the stage so that the next set of performers—a group of storytellers—could set up for their performance. Most of the audience left. A few newcomers took their places.

"What's so funny?" Murch asked.

"Mondegreens."

"What?"

"Mondegreens are misheard lyrics. The term came about because of the song we were just listening to. The real verse is 'They hae slain the Earl of Murray and laid him on the green,' but the story goes that the woman who coined the word heard that line as 'They hae slain the Earl of Murray and Lady Mondegreen' and imagined the earl and the lady as lovers, dying together on the green. Such things are considered very romantic in some circles."

"Okey-dokey. If you say so."

"Yes. Well, that's the story. And people do it all the time—hear something that just sounds like what was really said or sung. Then they put their own interpretation on it. I've done it myself." She knew she had a sheepish look on her face when she added, "Blood on the cow."

Murch raised his eyebrows in a question.

"I misheard the word *plow* in a song. I don't even remember what one or who sang it, but that image—the cow, not the plow—was stuck in my head for days. Then, of course, there's Richard Stans. He's one of the lesser-known founding fathers, according to a local columnist here in Maine."

Murch looked blank.

"Surely you've heard of him." Liss bit back a giggle. "He's in the Pledge of Allegiance. You know, 'the flag of the United States of America, for Richard Stans?'"

With a groan, Murch indicated that he got it. Then, out of the blue, he said, "Don't call me Shirley."

Now it was Liss's turn to be stumped. She sent him a puzzled look.

"Old joke from a movie. *Surely* heard as *Shirley*? Never mind. That's not what you wanted to talk about."

Liss stared at him, struck by a thought. "I'm not so sure of that. I know this is going to sound crazy, but is it possible you could have misheard what those two men were saying to each other in the town square?"

"The Shakespeare guys? Why?"

"Because I saw them again today and I had the strongest feeling that there was something . . . off about them. I told you it was crazy!"

"I never discount good instincts, and you've got them in spades. Turns out that one of those men is using a phony name. There's no such person as Eliot Underhill, not in Roanoke, Virginia, anyway."

"Then who is he?"

"Don't know yet, but it makes me real suspicious of anything he does."

"Is Martin Eldridge really Martin Eldridge?" Liss asked.

"That's his real name, yes. I didn't do any checking beyond that yet because there didn't seem to be any connection to your missing persons."

Liss told him about the tenuous Virginia connection.

"I'll dig deeper," he promised. "Meanwhile, let's go back to what I heard . . . or what I *thought* I heard," he corrected with a rueful grimace. "The one guy said 'much ado about nothing' and that's the title of a play."

"It's also an expression, meaning someone's making a lot of fuss for no good reason."

"Okey-dokey. What about the reference to Elizabethan tragedy."

Liss had closed her eyes, the better to call up the sound of the words. Her heart began to beat a little faster.

"Jake, could what you heard have been Elizabeth and Bradley? Those are Angie's children's names." She never thought of Beth as Elizabeth, since no one ever called her that, but it stood to reason that Elizabeth was her given name.

"It's a stretch, but maybe. What about the other play, *Julius Caesar*?"

"You only heard them say the second word, right? Seize her?"

"Damn. You could be right."

As soon as he agreed with her, doubts flooded into Liss's

mind. "Or maybe I'm off in left field. Even if there's something fishy about Eliot Underhill, Martin Eldridge is a respectable-looking guy, and he's seventy if he's a day. What on earth could he have to do with the disappearance of my friends?"

"We won't know until I find out more. As for the one calling himself Underhill, I still think there's something familiar about him." He stood up. "I'll—"

A piercing scream cut him off before he could complete his sentence.

Chapter Thirteen

By late afternoon, Sherri had returned to the police station and was wrapping up some of the endless record-keeping that went with the job of chief of police. The Highland Games wouldn't wind down until six, so she didn't see any point in looking for Kent at the Humphrey house until after that. Once she'd talked to him, she was looking forward to a quiet evening at home with her husband and kids. She was 99.9 percent certain that Kent hadn't seen anything more than his girlfriend had.

She sat back in her swivel chair, rotating her neck and shoulders to get rid of the kinks. She was about to get up and pour herself another cup of coffee when Dolores Mayfield came barreling through the waiting room and straight into the office, face flushed and eyes shooting sparks. She was so agitated that her entire hand shook when she pointed one finger at Sherri.

"Good. You're here. Stay right where you are. I want to file a complaint."

Sherri gestured for the librarian to have a seat in the uncomfortable plastic guest chair. She saw no sign of blood. Not a hair on Dolores's head was out of place. Whatever was bothering her, it didn't appear to be a matter of life and death.

"What sort of complaint?"

"Harassment." Dolores dropped into the chair, landing so hard that it gave a creak of protest.

Sherri bobbled the pen she'd just fished out of a drawer. "Harassment," she repeated. "Do you mean sexual harassment?"

"Of course I don't mean sexual harassment. Get your mind out of the gutter, young woman! I want you to do something to keep that man away from me. Get me a restraining order."

Taking a firm grip on the pen, Sherri prepared to take notes. "Are you talking about a stalker?"

"Of course not." Dolores sat up straighter and glared at Sherri, but she did not elucidate.

This is like pulling teeth, Sherri thought. She'd interrogated criminals who were more forthcoming. "Have you been threatened with bodily harm?"

"I have been threatened with incarceration!"

Finally, the penny dropped and Sherri's pen along with it, this time deliberately. "Oh, for heaven's sake, Dolores. Are you talking about Gordon Tandy?"

"Well, of course I am. First that man came to my home. Then he showed up at the library to badger me with the same ridiculous questions. And when I said I didn't have time to waste on such nonsense, he said I could talk to him there or at the county jail. I ask you, is that any way to behave toward a respected member of this community?"

"I can't prevent the state police from talking to you, Dolores. You are a person of interest in Jason Graye's murder. You did quarrel with him. You did threaten him. You were not only mounting a campaign to keep the library open, you started a petition to have him impeached."

"I never threatened to kill him!" Dolores's glare would have turned a weak person to stone.

"That's not the way I heard it."

Dolores said a word Sherri had never expected to hear coming out of the older woman's mouth before she added, enunciating each word with care, "It . . . was . . . a . . . joke."

"Okay. Fine." Even if Dolores's words had been meant in all seriousness, she wouldn't be the first person to say something in the heat of the moment that came back to haunt her. In an effort not to rile the librarian further, Sherri adopted a soothing tone of voice. "The detective has to talk to you, Dolores. That's how he rules you out as a suspect. The more you cooperate, the sooner he'll move on to someone else."

"That's just it. He's not moving on. Roger just phoned me to tell me he came back with a search warrant and confiscated every weapon in the house."

Sherri almost asked who Roger was, before she remembered that Roger was Moose Mayfield's given name. "I'm sure you don't have anything to worry about, Dolores. You'll get everything back as soon as the police run some tests."

Dolores did not look reassured.

Was she worried that her husband might have killed Graye? Sherri tried to imagine big, awkward, boozy Moose Mayfield planning and executing a murder. It didn't compute. Besides, the form Liss had seen running away from the scene couldn't have been Moose. His silhouette was distinctive, and so was his lumbering gait. More to the point, he'd have no reason to flee toward the town square when his house was in another direction entirely.

Dolores heaved a deep sigh. "I suppose you've heard the whole story by now—about what happened the other night?"

"Several times over and in various versions." One of Sherri's sources had Moose Mayfield foaming at the mouth as he emptied his pistol into the wall. She felt certain the account Liss had given her was much closer to the truth. "Fortunately for you, no one made a formal complaint. If they had, I'd have been obliged to charge your husband with discharging a firearm in a populated area." After a moment, curiosity made her add a question. "Was that your gun or your husband's?"

"Roger and I both belong to the Moosetookalook Rod and Gun Club. We shoot at targets. There's nothing wrong with that."

"You mean there's a second handgun in the house?"

"Roger keeps . . . *kept* his in the garage. Your state trooper friend took that one, too."

"I'm sure you have nothing to worry about. The state crime lab will test them both. If they don't find a match to any bullets they found at the scene, then they'll know neither gun was used in the crime."

Dolores seemed a little calmer, but that only meant she was thinking more clearly. She added up what she knew and reached a conclusion that did not compute. "Why did they confiscate my collection of bladed weapons? There was no need to do that if Graye was shot."

"They're just being thorough," Sherri said.

She wasn't prepared to share the truth with Dolores. According to Gordon, Graye appeared to have surprised an intruder. Armed with a gun, he'd likely confronted that person and fired one shot before he himself was fatally stabbed. It was hard to say for certain. A license wasn't required to own a gun in Maine, so they couldn't tell if Graye had kept one in the house. Since neither weapon had been found at the scene, it had to be assumed that the killer had walked off with both.

Dolores's eyes narrowed. "Thorough my left foot! What aren't you telling me, Sherri Campbell?"

Sherri stood up. "I'm not telling you anything, except that if you and your husband are innocent, you have nothing to worry about."

Leaning forward, Dolores pounded her fist on Sherri's desk for emphasis. "Roger did not kill Jason Graye, and neither did I."

"Then go home, Dolores. Let the police do their job."

"Hah! What if they try to frame one of us?"

"Why on earth would they?" Sherri's astonishment was genuine. She had complete faith in Gordon Tandy's integrity.

"Everyone expects the police to solve crimes quickly. Nobody cares if they arrest the wrong person."

"Now, Dolores, you know that's not true."

When Dolores stood up in a rush, Sherri quickly circled the desk. The other woman's increased agitation made her nervous. Once again, Dolores's color was high, and her breathing had become erratic.

"Settle down, Dolores. You're going to work yourself into a heart attack if you keep this up."

"Well! Aren't you the one for plain speaking!" Dolores pressed her fingertips to the pulse in her neck. After a moment, she closed her eyes and took a series of long, deep breaths.

Sherri watched her, both concerned and suspicious. It wasn't like the town librarian to be so irrational. She went off on tangents, yes, but there was usually a modicum of common sense behind them.

Was it possible she *had* killed Jason Graye? Liss's description of the shadowy figure she'd seen had ruled out Moose Mayfield, but it might fit a tall, sturdily built woman. Dolores was in good physical condition, and she seemed more upset than was reasonable about the police confiscation of her bladed weapons.

Dolores's eyes popped open again.

"Better?" Sherri asked.

"No thanks to you. If you're not going to do anything to stop that detective from hounding me, then I may as well go home."

"There's nothing I *can* do. If you truly feel threatened by the investigation, then I suggest you hire a lawyer."

"Have you lost your mind? I can't afford some fancy lawyer's fees."

Sherri fought the urge to roll her eyes. "Then go home and do whatever it is you usually do to calm frazzled nerves. Tea? Meditation?"

"Vigorous exercise." Dolores snapped out the words. "I'll have you know I work out on both a treadmill and a stationary bicycle."

The mental image of Dolores training for an ironman competition left Sherri at a loss for words. She was saved from having to say anything by the ringing of her phone. By the time she pressed the receiver to her ear, Dolores had gone, slamming the door to the waiting room behind her.

"Moosetookalook Police Department," Sherri answered. "How may I help you?"

Thirty seconds later, she was on her way to The Spruces. There had been another stabbing.

* * *

Mike Jennings met Sherri at the scene. He'd already secured it and called for the state police. "The victim is unconscious but still alive, although he may not be for much longer. The local EMTs are with him. The ambulance is on its way from Fallstown."

"ID?" she asked as Mike lifted the police tape so she could enter a wooded area to the side of the field used for athletic competitions.

"Kent Humphrey."

Sherri stopped short as she felt herself blanch. "Oh, damn," she whispered.

"You know him?"

"He's the kid I was going to talk to, to ask if he'd seen anything last night after Graye was killed."

Sherri knew it was foolish to feel responsible for what had happened to Kent. It wasn't a sure thing that he could identify Graye's murderer. Even if he had been able to provide her with useful information, there was nothing to say he wouldn't have stayed on at the games afterward and ended up exactly the same way.

He lay on the ground, tended by two Moosetookalook volunteer firemen who'd qualified as emergency medical technicians. Sherri couldn't tell what they were doing for him and wasn't sure she wanted to. The wail of the ambulance siren was the most welcome sound she'd heard all day.

"Who found him?" she asked Mike.

"A couple of spectators." With a jerk of his head, he indicated a man and woman waiting a little apart. The man had his back braced against a tree. The woman sat on the ground, her face ashen.

Sherri glanced toward the athletic field, where competitions had resumed. There was a lot of noise—crowd chatter, cheering. "Was there something going on at the time?"

"The tug-of-war," Mike said.

"Then how—"

"Call of nature. Guy was too lazy to walk over to the port-a-potties. He told his lady friend to stand guard while he ducked in among these trees to take a leak. She thought she heard something while he was watering the grass, so she went to take a look."

"Fools rush in," Sherri murmured, "and thank God for it. Did she see anyone else around?"

Mike shook his head.

Since there was nothing she could do for Kent Humphrey, Sherri went to talk to the woman who had, hopefully, saved a young man's life. As she approached the couple, she read herself a lecture. She was a professional. The near-paralyzing mixture of emotions she was feeling had to go on the back burner while she did her job.

Ten minutes after the ambulance showed up, Kent was on his way to Fallstown General Hospital. Sherri sent Mike along with him with orders not to let anyone near him who wasn't family. It stood to reason that Kent must have seen Graye's killer and that the killer had seen Kent. Coming across him at the Highland Games, that same person had then stabbed Kent, just as he'd stabbed Jason Graye, intending to silence him forever. If he realized Kent was still alive, he'd try again.

Five minutes later, Gordon Tandy arrived on the scene. Sherri gave him a clear, concise report, including the fact that Kent Humphrey, age seventeen, was a friend of Liss's cousin Boxer and of the missing girl, Beth Hogencamp.

The thought that those kids were only a few years older than her own son, Adam, left Sherri choking out the rest of what she had to say around a humongous lump in her throat: "Kent is the boy who was on the swings with his girlfriend in the town square last night."

Gordon's "cop face" was replaced by an expression of alarm. "Where is she?"

"Home with her parents. Safe. I've already phoned the Fitzwarren house. I spoke to Amie's mother. I didn't give her any details, but I convinced her she needs to keep her daughter at home until someone from my department or from the state police can get there."

"Had you interviewed either Amie or her boyfriend?" Gordon asked.

"I talked to her earlier today. She didn't see anything last night and didn't think Kent had either. I hadn't yet connected with him."

"Either he saw something or someone thinks he did."

"Looks that way. And that someone was here. Why? What was he . . . or she . . . doing attending a festival the day after killing a man?"

Gordon had been surveying the area. Now he turned his sharp-eyed gaze on her. "Are you okay? You look shaky."

"I *feel* shaky. He's just a kid." Her voice broke, but she shook her head when Gordon touched her shoulder in a gesture of comfort. "Don't worry. I'll hold it together. It's just that I knew Kent was here. I should have come looking for him right after I saw his girlfriend. Instead, I figured it would be easier to wait and catch him at home. I should have—"

"Stop beating yourself up. You can't know that things would have turned out any differently. No one can."

Sherri said nothing. Despite Gordon's words, guilt weighed heavily on her.

"Snap out of it, Chief Campbell." The command was issued in such a sharp and authoritarian voice that she came to attention. "You've got a job to do, and so do I. I don't have time to pamper you."

As he no doubt intended, Sherri felt a bracing flash of anger at his words.

"I want you to go stay with the girl. Make sure she doesn't take it into her head to go off on her own, especially if she hears that the boyfriend is in the hospital."

"How much do you want me to tell her and her parents?"

"Whatever it takes to keep her safe."

Sherri sent him a curt nod and headed for the parking lot where she'd left her cruiser. The girl's father was going to react badly to the news that his daughter had been sneaking out to meet a boy he didn't approve of, but that secret wasn't worth keeping if it meant an innocent sixteen-year-old girl might become the killer's next target.

She left the wooded area and had gone barely a dozen yards beyond the athletic field when she ran into Liss MacCrimmon and Jake Murch.

"This isn't just an accident, is it?" Liss asked. "Not with Gordon Tandy here."

Sherri shook her head. Belatedly, it occurred to her that Liss had caught a glimpse of Graye's murderer, too. Amie wasn't the only one who needed to be warned of potential danger.

"Someone stabbed Kent Humphrey, the boy on the swings. It looks like whoever killed Jason Graye is trying to cover his tracks."

Liss's eyes widened as she absorbed the implications of Sherri's words. "Oh, no," she whispered. "What about the girl who was with him?"

"Amie Fitzwarren. So far, she's okay. But you saw him, too."

"I don't think he saw me. He, or she, was heading away from me."

"If there's the slightest chance you were recognized, you need to be on your guard."

Sherri was already moving again, but Liss trotted along beside her with Murch lagging a little behind. "Sherri, wait. There's something peculiar about a couple of the guests at The Spruces. I don't know if it connects to the murder, but it may to Angie."

That stopped her in her tracks. "Which guests?"

"Underhill and Eldridge, only Eldridge isn't his real name. Jake overheard some things they said to each other, and we think they may have been talking about Angie and her kids."

Sherri gave the private investigator a sharp look. "Let me know what you find out."

"What?" Outrage underscored Liss's words. "Sherri, you need to follow up on this."

"Much as I like Angie and Beth and Bradley, finding three people who appear to have disappeared of their own volition is not at the top of my current to-do list, nor is figuring out why a guest at the hotel is registered under a pseudonym. Right now, priority number one is to make sure a teenaged girl stays safe."

Certain she had made the right decision, Sherri hurried on her way without so much as a backward glance.

Liss returned to the Moosetookalook Scottish Emporium booth in an unsettled state of mind. Although it was already close to the six o'clock closing time for the Highland Games, the grounds were still crowded with people, both festival-goers and vendors. No one who had been in the area when Kent was discovered could leave without first speaking to an officer. Liss didn't envy the state troopers that job. They'd have to take hundreds of statements. Worse, chances were good that no one had seen anything useful. From what she could gather, Kent Humphrey had been found in a wooded area that was not being used for any part of the Highland Games.

Boxer had loyally remained on the job, but he was bursting with curiosity. "What's going on, Liss? Why are the cops swarming all over the place?"

"You haven't heard anything?"

He shrugged. "I know better than to listen to wild speculation. Is there really a body?"

"No, thank goodness. At this point it's a case of attempted murder. A young man who may have seen the person who killed Jason Graye was just taken to the hospital in the Fallstown ambulance."

Boxer's frown deepened. "Who?"

Liss caught herself before she could blurt out the name. She didn't know Kent Humphrey, but it seemed likely Boxer did. The two boys were about the same age. "You'd better sit down."

"Hey, I—"

"Sit down, Boxer." She waited until he'd grudgingly settled himself in one of the folding chairs behind the display tables. She took the other. "The boy who was attacked is Kent Humphrey, Boxer. Do you know him?"

He started to laugh, then stared at her in disbelief. "You're kidding me, right?"

"I'm sorry. I'm not. He and his girlfriend were in the town square last night."

"Amie—is she okay?"

"Yes. Sherri's taking care of her." She put a hand on

Boxer's shoulder and was not surprised to discover that it was shaking.

"I don't fu—I don't bleeping believe this!"

"You know, if there were ever an occasion when bad language was acceptable, I think this is it."

He almost cracked a smile. "My grandmother would wash my mouth out with soap. But damn, Liss, if Kent really saw something, he'd already have told the cops, so what was the point of trying to kill him?"

"Maybe he didn't realize what he saw." She wished she had more to offer, but anything she could think of to say seemed inadequate.

Whether Kent had seen anything or not, if the killer had run into him, he might have recognized Kent and decided to take no chances. And if Kent had seemed to recognize *him*?

"We double-date," Liss's cousin said, interrupting her thoughts. "Me and Beth and Kent and Amie. Movies. A concert once. He's a good guy."

A soft voice called Liss's name. She looked up to find Margaret Boyd standing on the other side of the display table. By the stricken expression on her face, she'd already heard the bad news.

"I could use your help," Margaret said.

"Boxer—"

He waved her away. "I'm okay. Just give me a minute."

Margaret sent her grandson a sympathetic look, but she had too much on her plate to do more than that. "We have to cancel the rest of the Highland Games."

With a sick feeling in the pit of her stomach, Liss realized she should have seen that decision coming. The police would need time to process the crime scene, which included the area surrounding the scene of the crime.

"I'll start packing up."

"I wish it were that simple," Margaret said. "I've been asked to gather all the vendors together inside the hotel. We can cover the merchandise and remove the cash and receipts, but everything else needs to be left as is. It will all have to be searched. I need a hand to spread the word."

"Can you take care of the money and receipts for me?" Liss asked Boxer.

"Yeah. Sure." But he didn't move.

"I know it's crass to fuss over the day's profits when you're worried about a friend. I'm sorry."

"It's okay." He shook his head, as if to clear his thoughts. "Go. Tell the rest of the vendors."

Margaret sent Liss off in one direction while she went in the other, taking the majority of the booths. She'd barely gotten started when the PA system, installed to announce the start of various events and reunite lost children with their parents, blared out a request for everyone to proceed to the ballroom of the hotel. She heard grumbling as well as excited chatter from those who had no idea what was going on. Piercing through those sounds were the wails of overtired children.

"Vendors, too?" Janice Eccles asked as Liss reached the scone-maker's booth.

"I'm afraid so, and the police want us to leave everything and head inside. I suppose they're searching for a weapon."

Janice reached over and turned off her portable oven, then scooped up her cash box and tucked it under one arm. Then she paused.

Although they rarely saw each other outside of this annual gathering of the clans, Liss had known Janice Eccles for years. She could see at once that something was bothering the other woman, and that she was hesitant to speak. More than that, she was avoiding Liss's eyes.

"Is there a problem?" Liss hoped the answer would be no.

Janice looked up, but only to turn slightly, so that she was staring at the section of woods where Kent Humphrey had been attacked. "Someone said it was a teenaged boy who was killed."

Liss didn't correct her assumption that Kent was dead. "Go on."

"Earlier, I saw a man stroll up to a teenaged boy and talk to him. After a couple of minutes, they walked away together."

"That's a pretty common sight. It might have nothing to do with what happened later."

"Even if they were headed that way?" She gestured toward the trees.

"You need to tell the state police. They're in charge of catching the guy who stabbed Kent Humphrey."

But Janice was shaking her head. "I'm probably making a mountain out of a molehill. Like you said, two people talking together at a Scottish festival is hardly unusual."

"Can you describe them? The teenager? The man?"

"Not really. They weren't all that close." She was getting antsy just talking to Liss. In another minute, she'd convince herself to keep mum about what she'd seen.

Liss caught her forearm. "Was the man talking to the boy young or old?"

"An older gentleman." Janice frowned. "I'm not sure why, but at first glance I thought he must be the young man's grandfather."

Liss's heart began to race. Was it possible? "Was the older gentleman carrying a cane?"

Janice's face lit up. "Did you see him, too?"

"No, but I may know who he is. Janice, you have to talk to the state police right away and tell them what you saw."

When she'd seen her on her way into the hotel, Liss hurried through the task Margaret had set for her and then rushed back to the Moosetookalook Scottish Emporium booth. Seeing Martin Eldridge, if it was him, with Kent, didn't prove anything, and it certainly didn't explain why Eldridge would have killed Jason Graye, but it was all connected somehow. It had to be.

Chapter Fourteen

"We've got to go." Liss collected her iPad, cash box, and calculator, slipping all three into the tote bag she'd used to transport them to the grounds that morning.

Boxer was still sitting behind the display, looking lost and miserable. "Who would *do* something like this, Liss?"

"The police will find out," she said with more assurance than she felt.

"He rubbed his forehead, as if he was trying to force his thoughts to come together in a coherent fashion. "Was it the same person who torched the bookstore?"

She stopped in her tracks. "Why would you think that?"

"If they'd been there, they might not have made it out. What if that was an attempt to kill Beth and her mother and brother?"

Although the very thought made her ill, Liss had to admit that this was a possibility that had occurred to her, too—that one person was behind all of Moosetookalook's troubles. Martin Eldridge? He'd seemed like such a nice gentleman at first, until she had begun to suspect what he and that other man had been talking about in the town square.

She blinked rapidly as a piece that had been missing from the puzzle suddenly fell into place. That other man—he'd been in Patsy's the day she'd gotten all teary-eyed over the fact that Angie always sent her an anniversary card. He'd been in the booth behind her, perfectly able to overhear every word she said.

A crazy idea began to form as she and Boxer walked toward the hotel, part of a crowd of others obeying the command to go and be questioned. The post office had been vandalized right after that conversation. What if the arsonist *had* tried to kill Angie and her children? What if he'd still been looking for them? If he'd suspected that Angie would write to someone in Moosetookalook, would he have searched the mail in the hope of finding a return address or a postmark?

Liss felt a chill go through her. The more she thought about the stranger in the café, the more certain she became that he was the man she'd twice seen with Martin Eldridge. Eliot Underhill. Were they working together? And if Eldridge was the man Janice had seen talking to Kent, had Eldridge lured Kent into a remote area so Underhill could kill him?

"Crazy," she muttered to herself. "Far-fetched."

Maybe there was a link between the fire and the vandalism, but what possible connection could those two events have to Jason Graye's murder?

Silent, his expression grim, Boxer accompanied her across the lawn, around the hotel to the front entrance, and into the lobby. A uniformed state trooper had been stationed just inside the door to direct everyone up to the mezzanine level. Liss heard him assure each new arrival that they wouldn't be kept long. He was less charming to Liss when she tried to slip away from the herd.

"Hold it right there, miss."

"I just want a quick word with my father-in-law." Liss flashed her most ingratiating smile at him as she indicated Joe Ruskin, who had been watching the proceedings from behind the reception desk. He lifted one hand to acknowledge that he knew her.

"Make it quick," the trooper said, and turned to give his prepared spiel to the tartan-clad members of one of the clan societies.

Despite orders to the contrary, Liss deliberately moved at a snail's pace, pretending to admire her surroundings. In keeping with the hotel's origins, the entire lobby was done up in Victorian splendor. The floors were highly polished wood, uncarpeted except for a spattering of plush area rugs to delineate cozy seating areas. A huge fireplace with an ornate marble mantel dominated one wall. At this time of year, the tile-lined hearth was filled with fragrant herbs.

"You're getting dirty looks from the cop," Joe said when she finally reached him.

She could almost feel the heat of the officer's glare burning a hole in her back, but she kept her eyes on Dan's father. "I need a favor, Joe. You remember two of those guests I asked you about? Underhill and Eldridge? When Gordon Tandy shows up, will you tell him that I found out something important about them?"

"I'll give him the message," Joe promised, "but whatever you think he needs to know, he's not going to be able to talk to either one. They've both checked out."

"What? When?" Before he could answer, she added another question. "Together?"

"Maybe a half hour apart. It was after I talked to you earlier but before all hell broke loose. Sometime in mid-afternoon."

Feeling shaky, Liss gripped the desk with both hands. The sudden departure of the two men struck her as extremely suspicious and seemed to lend credence to her theory. She felt sure now that one of them was guilty of both arson and murder. The other was likely his accomplice.

Had they been quarreling when she saw them? Or plotting? And—worse thought yet!—had they left the hotel after attempting to kill Kent Humphrey because they'd finally figured out where Angie was?

Liss shook her head to clear her thoughts. She was stringing suppositions together without any beading wire. Was it any wonder they kept falling to the floor and scattering? *Focus,* she ordered herself.

After taking several deep breaths, she lobbed another question at Joe. "Was either of them *planning* to leave today?"

He shook his head. "Both were booked through Monday. Eldridge said he'd had a change of plans. Underhill didn't offer any reason for taking off early. Didn't gripe about not getting a refund for tonight, either."

"That's right. He paid cash in advance."

Joe nodded. "He's lucky I had enough money on hand to reimburse him for Sunday night's stay. There's not much call to keep the jingly around when anybody with any sense pays with a credit or debit card." He sent a morose look toward the stairs that led to the mezzanine. The last of the potential witnesses was just disappearing in the direction of the ballroom. "Once the police get done with their questioning, I've got a feeling there will be a lot more folks wanting to check out early."

Liss shared his pain. The whole weekend was turning into a disaster for Moosetookalook businesses. That serious crimes like arson and murder had been committed was terrible enough, but now repercussions had begun to ripple out in an ever-widening circle. Lost revenue couldn't compare to loss of life, but that didn't make the hit any easier to take. The shops around the square, the vendors at the Highland Games, and The Spruces would all suffer. For some, barely making ends meet as it was, this might well be the straw that broke the camel's back.

The phone behind the reception desk rang, making Liss jump. She started to turn away, only to be pulled back by Joe's response when he answered.

"She's fine," he said. "She's right here." He offered Liss the receiver.

She was not surprised to find her husband on the other end of the line.

"What the hell is going on up there?" Dan demanded. "There's a state police cruiser blocking the entrance to the hotel. He won't let me onto the grounds."

"I love you, Dan."

He swore. "Now you're really scaring me."

She clutched the phone tighter. "There's so much I want to tell you and so little time. Any minute now, another trooper is going to insist that I join everyone else in the ballroom. Someone stabbed that poor boy who was on the swings, and now everyone has to be questioned before anyone can leave. I'll be home as soon as I can. I promise."

"I'll wait for you by the entrance."

Hearing the stubbornness in his voice, Liss didn't argue. "Then I'll look for you there." She handed the phone back to Joe. "He worries."

"Sounds to me like he has cause. You're sticking your nose in, Liss. You know that's dangerous."

"I'm not meddling. Well, only a little. And as soon as I talk to Gordon and tell him everything I suspect, then I'm out of it. The last thing I want is to come face to face with a murderer."

"Tell *him,*" Joe suggested, indicating the state trooper heading their way.

"I need to talk to *Gordon,*" Liss insisted. No one else would take her seriously.

With a little wave for Joe, she hurried past the approaching officer and scurried up the stairs.

She spent the next two hours twiddling her thumbs in the ballroom. One person after another was called out, questioned, and sent home. Janice. Murch. Boxer. And still she waited.

Frustrating as the delay was, it did give her plenty of time to think. About a half hour in, another idea occurred to her. She turned it over in her mind, weighing the logic. Preposterous as the scenario seemed at first glance, it was possible.

Jason Graye had been a real estate agent. That meant he had lists of all the empty houses in the area—places where someone could hide out. What if the arsonist, having failed to find an address for Angie when he vandalized the post office, decided to break into Graye's house to take a look at the listings. He went during the fireworks, on the assumption that Graye would attend. Instead, he'd heard the man open his door, taken the gun from wherever it was he kept it, and fired at the intruder when he came at him with a knife.

Liss shuddered. Martin Eldridge? Or the other man, Eliot Underhill? Whichever one it had been, he'd seen Kent and Amie on the swings and been afraid Kent would be able to identify him. Was that what Eldridge and Underhill had been arguing about earlier in the day? How to deal with the threat?

Shaking her head, Liss tried to envision what had happened next. Eldridge had met with Kent. The man with the cane *had* to have been Eldridge. But from what Janice had said, it didn't sound as if Kent recognized him. Maybe he wouldn't have. It had been dark in the town square. Kent had been distracted by Amie and by the fireworks. Still, someone afraid of being arrested for murder might kill again, just to make sure there was no witness.

On the other hand, if Underhill was the killer, Eldridge could have been sent to lure Kent into the woods so Underhill could kill him.

She was beginning to get a headache. She had no proof of anything, just speculation. But what if she was right? If she was, and if Angie was the killer's original target, then a murderer was still looking for her and her children.

Angie Hogencamp wasn't her real name. Sherri thought she'd changed it when she came to Moosetookalook. That had to be the key—someone from her past was after her, and he didn't care who got hurt so long as he found her.

She looked up to discover that she was the last "witness" left. One by one, everyone else had been called into one of the smaller rooms for questioning. Another five minutes passed. Then Gordon opened the door to the ballroom. For a long moment, he just looked in at her, an enigmatic expression on his face. Then he stepped inside. "You can go now, Liss."

"Just like that? No questions?" The long wait had frayed both her nerves and her temper. She propelled herself out of the chair. Grabbing her tote, she stalked toward him.

"I've already verified that you were nowhere near the scene of the crime."

"That doesn't mean I didn't see anything. If you talked to Jake Murch—he would be my alibi, I presume—then you know that we are suspicious of two guests at the hotel. And then Janice Eccles—"

"Yes, I talked to her, too."

"So you know that Martin Eldridge fits the description of the man she saw with Kent."

He nodded. "We're checking into it."

"I'm sure you are, but you'd better make it a priority." By now they were nose to nose, so close that Liss could pick out the golden flecks in Gordon's dark brown eyes. "There's more you don't know."

"Of course there is."

With an effort, she managed not to yell at him. She kept her voice level and not too much louder than usual. "Take out that notebook of yours, Gordon. Like it or not, you're going to listen while I tell you everything I've deduced."

He might have smiled—just a tiny twitch of the lips that caused her to narrow her eyes—but he complied. Gesturing for her to sit down again, he took the chair next to her and held his pencil poised. "Go ahead."

Her theories burst out of her, the words tumbling together until she was breathless. Gordon dutifully wrote everything down, but she could tell he was not convinced.

"You do have a talent for coming up with far-fetched explanations," he said when she finally wound down.

"Some of them have turned out to be right."

"Yes, they have. Which is why we'll check into all these possibilities and talk to Eldridge and Underhill, even though apparently they both left the grounds well before Kent Humphrey was stabbed."

"There are ways to get back onto the property and away again without using the main entrance. You know that, Gordon."

There was a path from the road through the woods—town property—that adjoined the hotel grounds on the east. There were probably other ways in as well. It wasn't as if The Spruces was trying to keep people out. Now that she thought about it, Liss was surprised Dan hadn't taken an alternate route, rushing in to reassure himself that she was okay.

"Think what you're saying, Liss. How would a stranger to the area know—?"

"Those two strangers have been here for over a week. They've had plenty of time to explore."

"From what I understand, Eldridge is a senior citizen who uses a cane. He hardly seems the type to go traipsing along rough woodland paths."

"He's spry for his age. I noticed the first time I met him that he didn't really need the cane. It seemed to be an affectation, not a necessity."

"You and Janice have both referred to him as an older gentleman. How old is he?"

"At a guess, in his seventies."

"Then he's not likely to be the person you saw running away from Graye's house."

"That person wasn't exactly moving at warp speed. And what about Underhill? Sherri says that's not even his real name!"

"Liss—people check into hotels under assumed names all the time."

"He wasn't here to have an illicit affair—unless you think he and Eldridge were lovers. You're just being pigheaded about this." She didn't doubt that Gordon would try to locate and question both Eliot Underhill and Martin Eldridge, but every moment's delay gave them more time to escape.

His eyebrows lifted nearly to his hairline. "*I'm* being stubborn?"

"Don't you dare laugh at me, Gordon Tandy! I demand to be taken seriously."

He ran one hand through his short, reddish brown hair. "I do listen, Liss, and I take your ideas into account, even the ones that sound completely bonkers. You're going to have to trust me when I tell you that we're pursuing *every* lead. There is no need—and I can't emphasize this enough—*no need* for you to involve yourself further in this investigation."

"I won't fire Murch."

"So long as all he's doing is looking for Angie and her children, that's fine."

Liss thought better of reminding him that she thought Angie's disappearance was directly responsible for everything else that had happened.

She hadn't been lying when she'd said, repeatedly, that she did not want to get involved in police matters. But what else could she do if Gordon didn't see the urgency in following up the lead she'd given him?

Aloud, she said only, "May I go home now?"

"With my blessing."

More than ready to leave, Liss hefted her tote bag. The clink of coins from the cash box she'd stuffed inside it reminded her that she had one more question to ask Gordon. "When can I pack up my booth?"

"You can do it now if you like. The booths were searched at the same time we were questioning people. Once they gave statements, they were free to collect their stock."

"Did you find a weapon?"

"No."

"Was it the same kind of knife that was used to kill Jason Graye?"

"Liss, you know I can't tell you that." He held a hand up, palm out, to stop her automatic protest. "Literally, I can't. The medical examiner will have to determine if they were the same. It's possible," he conceded. "Looked to me like a long, thin blade of some kind was used in both instances."

Knowing that he shouldn't have confided that much, Liss didn't badger Gordon for more information, but she was still in an unhappy frame of mind when she left the ballroom. She cheered up, if only slightly, when she discovered that the police had allowed Dan through their barrier. He was waiting for her in the lobby.

As Dan drove his wife home, he kept stealing glances at her, alarmed by her pallor and wary of the way she kept clenching and unclenching her fists.

The first thing she did when she walked into the house was scoop up Glenora and cuddle the little black cat in her arms. Glenora, having no idea what had been going on at the Highland Games, objected to being rudely awakened from a nap on the back of Dan's recliner, her favorite spot in the living room. She made her feelings known with a set of claws that were in dire need of clipping.

Liss yelped and released her. With a flash of bushy tail, Glenora disappeared into the dining room.

"Let me see that." Dan reached for her forearm, where a thin line of blood was welling up, stretching nearly all the way from wrist to elbow.

"I'm okay." She jerked away from him and reached for a tissue to dab ineffectively at the injury.

Dan wanted to steer her toward the bathroom medicine cabinet and doctor her arm, but he knew his wife well enough to realize that he'd do better to wait a bit. If she didn't take care of the scratch herself, he'd use brute force to sit her down and slap disinfectant on it.

Lumpkin poked his head around the corner of the pocket doors that separated living room from dining room. When he realized Liss was looking at him, he sent her a superior glare. She grabbed a pillow from the sofa and hurled it at him.

"You're never appreciated in your own home," Dan quipped.

His offhand remark, intended to break the tension, instead pushed Liss over the edge of reason. She whirled on him, fist raised, and thumped him on the shoulder hard enough to make him wince.

In the next instant, her eyes widened, aghast at what she'd done. She tried to back away, but Dan caught her by the shoulders. He could feel his own temper rising. An answering spark of anger flashed in her eyes.

Was she *trying* to taunt him into fighting back?

Dan Ruskin had never hit a woman in his life, and he wasn't about to start with his own wife. With an effort, he dialed back his emotions until he had control of himself. "What the hell was that for?"

Well, maybe not 100 percent in control, Dan thought as he heard the outrage underlying the question.

"The devil made me do it!"

Dan blinked at her. Now she was trying to diffuse the situation with humor. Her quip was only partly successful.

He pulled in a deep breath and stooped until his forehead rested against hers.

"What are we doing, Liss?"

"I don't know about you, but I am seriously losing it. You know it's not you I'm mad at. I'm just frustrated by this whole situation—the fire, then finding Graye's body, and now this . . . this . . ."

He eased his grip on her shoulders, sliding his hands down her arms until he could catch hold of her hands. "We both need to chill. And you need to accept that you can't solve all the problems of the universe. Not even close."

"I know." Her voice sounded choked, as if tears threatened. "I can't even figure out where Angie is."

"Maybe, just maybe, since she's made it so hard to find her, she needs to *stay* hidden, even from her friends."

"But—"

Dan released her right hand and lifted his fingers to her lips to stop her protest. "No buts. I know it's not possible to forget everything that's happened over the last week, but you have to stop driving yourself nuts over it. Things will sort themselves out eventually. You'll see."

He'd been terrified when he'd found out, thanks to a summons on the brand-new pager he'd been issued—only that morning—as a Moosetookalook volunteer fireman, that there was a stabbing victim at the Highland Games. His first thought was that Liss had gotten too close to finding Jason Graye's murderer and paid the ultimate price.

He didn't know what he'd do if he lost her. She could be exasperating, but she was the other half of himself. They were supposed to be a *team,* damn it!

"I need you to promise me something," he whispered as

Liss—finally!—collapsed against his chest and let him wrap his arms around her.

"I—"

"Shhh. I won't ask the impossible. Just try to keep me in the loop, okay? No running off on your own. No risking your neck on a hunch."

Her hunches were just too damned accurate.

"Okay," Liss whispered back. "Next time I have a brilliant idea, you'll be the first to know."

Unable to sleep, Liss tossed and turned for hours and finally gave up, got up, and went downstairs to the kitchen. A cup of hot chocolate beside her, she reached for her iPad. She had a name—Martin Eldridge. She had the city in Virginia he supposedly lived in. It was probably a futile effort to type both into a search engine, but doing something felt better than doing nothing.

She tried various combinations, with quotation marks and without. Nothing seemed relevant until she switched to a search for images. She was clicking through them, growing more and more discouraged, when something caught her eye.

The photograph showed an accident scene. There were police cars and an ambulance. Gawkers stood around rubbernecking. But off to the side was a figure that seemed vaguely familiar—a woman. A very pregnant woman.

A few keystrokes enlarged the image. They also blurred the woman's features, but not enough to keep Liss from recognizing Angie Hogencamp's dark wavy hair and the way she held herself.

There was a story to go with the photo. A young woman named Marianna Eldridge had dashed in front of a car and been killed. The pregnant woman wasn't identified, but the accident had happened in the Virginia city Martin Eldridge called home. The clincher was the caption—a date just over twelve years earlier.

The source of the photo was a blog entry posted only five years back. The author was writing about ambulance chasers, having apparently been one for some time. He'd taken the picture but provided no additional details about what had happened.

To Liss's immense frustration, no related articles showed up, no matter what combination of words she used to search. Because of the early hour, she e-mailed Murch rather than phoning him and passed on what little she had found. Then she sent the same information to Gordon and to Sherri.

By the time the sun rose, Liss felt the need for a hard physical workout. Fortunately, the best place in town to get one was right next door at Dance Central.

Zara Kalishnakof was already in the studio, warming up with a series of pliés at the barre. She glanced at Liss and did a double take. "You look like hell."

"Just what a girl wants to hear!"

Slipping off the shoes she'd put on for the short walk across her driveway and Zara's side yard, Liss plunked herself down on the floor to begin her regular stretching routine. She avoided looking into the mirror that covered all of one wall by turning her back to it. Instead, she faced Zara and the barre. Her friend lifted one leg onto the wooden rail and bent over it, touching her forehead to her knee. Zara's long red hair was scooped back into a neat ballerina's bun.

For a short time, neither woman spoke. Then Zara, inevitably, raised the subject of the missing family.

"I'm worried about Beth." She switched legs. "She lost interest in taking dance lessons once she was in high school and had so many more exciting extracurricular activities to choose from, but she used to stop by every once in a while just to talk."

Liss paused with one arm curved over her head and her body stretched sideways until her fingertips touched the floor. "No one seems to have a clue where her mother could have taken them."

"Have you talked to Beth's friends? Did any of them have a suggestion as to where she might be?"

"Boxer says not, and he'd know. He gave Sherri a list, and I'm pretty sure she talked to everyone on it. If she'd gotten a lead, she'd have told me."

Thinking of Beth's friends took Liss's thoughts straight to the attack on Kent Humphrey. The latest report from the hospital, passed on from Kent's mother to Amie, Amie to Boxer, Boxer to Margaret, and Margaret to Liss by e-mail, had the boy holding his own but still listed in critical condition.

"Angie always struck me as having lots of friends."

Liss sat up and stayed upright to stare at the other woman. Zara might look like a flake, with her bright, carrot-colored hair and her penchant for dressing in short skirts and high boots long after both went out of fashion, but she had a good head on her shoulders.

"Who would you say Angie was closest to?"

Zara slung a towel around her neck and came over to squat beside Liss on the floor. Her expression was thoughtful. "She's an outgoing person, the kind who makes you feel like you're a personal friend when, in fact, you're only an acquaintance. Off the top of my head, I'd say you, Margaret, and Patsy. Was she really close to any of you? She was busy running her bookstore and raising her kids. Maybe she didn't have a lot of time for friendships."

"You're right about that, but maybe keeping herself to herself was deliberate, too. I certainly don't have a clue where she could have gone, and both Margaret and Patsy have said they don't know, either. "

Zara stood. "Speaking of Patsy, did she catch up with you the other day?" Without waiting for an answer, she started a series of pirouettes that took her to the far side of the dance studio.

"I didn't know she was looking for me."

"She must have been." Running leaps brought Zara back to where Liss sat, exercises forgotten. "I saw her circle around your house, heading toward the door to the kitchen."

Liss frowned. It wasn't at all odd for a neighbor to visit by way of a back or side entrance. Some Mainers never used their front doors at all and left them covered with insulating plastic all year round. But Patsy wasn't a regular visitor to Liss and Dan's house. As far as Liss could remember, the only time she'd come over had been to attend a meeting of the MSBA.

"When was this?" she asked.

"Let me think." Zara stopped to stand flat-footed with her hands on her hips. "I'm pretty sure it was Wednesday afternoon. Yes. I'd just put the kids down for a nap, and Sandy was finishing up that break-dancing class he teaches. Yes, I'm sure that's right. My session with the group learning to belly dance hadn't started yet."

On Wednesday afternoon, Liss had been at the Emporium. Why would Patsy have expected to find her at home? Had she stopped by to talk to Dan? That seemed unlikely. She'd have picked up the phone and called him or waited until the next time he stopped by for coffee. Besides, it wasn't like Patsy to leave the café unattended.

Then she remembered. Wednesday was the day someone had stepped up onto her back stoop and tucked an anniversary card into the screen door. That could mean no more than that Angie had left the card with Patsy, to be delivered when it got close to the twenty-fifth of July.

Or it could mean Patsy knew where Angie was and had been protecting her, even from Angie's other friends.

Chapter Fifteen

When Dan and Liss arrived at The Spruces, it was with every intention of taking down the booth and packing up the contents as quickly as possible. Liss was anxious to get back to town and talk to Patsy, who had been busy with the Sunday morning rush at the café and put her off until later in the morning.

The majority of the vendors had taken away their stock the previous evening, once they'd been questioned and their booths had been searched for the knife used in the attack on Kent Humphrey. Liss had been in no mood to pack delicate figurines or cart boxes around. She'd made do with rolling down the sides and left everything else for today. With all the police around, she hadn't been worried about theft.

"Is Boxer showing up to help?" Dan asked.

Liss shook her head. "When he called, he said he plans to spend most of the morning at Amie Fitzwarren's house. Then he'll give the Scotties a run for his grandmother and go home. If he's as short on sleep as he sounded, I hope he plans to take a long nap once he gets there."

They didn't talk much after that, and in short order Dan

had both tent and stock stashed in the back of his truck. "Give me a minute to check with Dad?"

There was a good deal of cleaning up to be done on the grounds. The hotel gardeners had already started work to repair the damage to the lawn.

Liss went with him into the hotel, but they never made it to Joe Ruskin's office. Teacup in hand, Margaret poked her head out into the corridor at the sound of their approaching footsteps.

"Oh, good. There you are. I have someone here who wants to talk to you two."

Dan gestured for Liss to enter ahead of him. He stopped just inside the door, taken aback by the sight of his wife's aunt serving tea to Jake Murch. The PI handled the delicate little cup with extreme caution. The look on his face made it plain he had no idea how he'd ended up sitting on the love seat that faced Margaret's desk, as out of place as the proverbial bull in the china shop.

Liss waved away Margaret's offer of a calming herbal brew. "I'd just as soon keep every nerve on alert."

"Suit yourself." Margaret cocked her head in Dan's direction and accepted his shake of the head as a negative answer to the same question. Pouring herself a cup, she carried the tea to her desk and sat.

"Have you found something new?" Liss asked Murch after joining him on the love seat. She tucked one leg beneath her and turned so that she was facing him.

The detective looked relieved to have an excuse to abandon his cup on the glass-topped coffee table in front of him. "Remember how I said Eliot Underhill looked familiar?"

"You figured out where you've seen him before!" Liss's

whole demeanor changed. For all her denials, she loved solving puzzles.

Dan perched on the front corner of Margaret's desk, right foot on the floor and left leg bent at the knee. He listened closely for Murch's answer, determined not to be left out of the loop. If he had any say in the matter, he and Liss would be joined at the hip until Kent Humphrey's attacker was behind bars.

"Turns out I was remembering something I saw online not too long ago," Murch said. "Underhill—well, his real name is Arbuthnot—lost his private investigator's license for some shady dealings. The case was written up in a professional journal I subscribe to."

"Is he connected to our other suspect?" Liss asked. "You were going to do background checks on both men."

"I'd like to hear that answer, too," Joe Ruskin said from the doorway. "Margaret has been keeping me up to date on what's been going on, but it sounds like there have been some new developments." He propped his back against the wall, arms crossed in front of his chest, and looked expectantly at Murch.

"First off," Murch began, "you should know that I already passed all this information on to the state police."

Dan didn't know whether to be relieved or worried. Private detectives were no more fond of sharing information than the cops were.

"If you remember, the hotel register listed addresses."

"Two towns in Virginia," Joe agreed.

"Right. Edgar Arbuthnot lied about where he was from, but Eldridge didn't. Truth is, they're both from the same small city. It wasn't much of a stretch to figure out that these two guys knew each other before they came here. My take is that Eldridge hired Arbuthnot. Since Arbuthnot's license was revoked more than six months ago, it isn't much of a stretch to place Eldridge among the not exactly law abiding."

Impatience had Liss interrupting again. "But *why* did Eldridge hire him?"

"I'm still working on that, but the information you found may be the key. Marianna Eldridge was Martin Eldridge's daughter, an only child. She stepped out in front of a car and got herself killed. There was nothing the driver of the car could have done to avoid hitting her."

"And?" Liss asked.

"And that's it so far. No charges seem to have been filed, so records are scarce. But if your friend Angie is the woman in that photo you found online, then there's your connection. Looks to me," Murch said, "that Eldridge hired Arbuthnot to help find your friend."

"As if he blames her for his daughter's death?"

Murch shrugged.

Dan thought they were jumping to conclusions, but if this theory was all they had to go on, he supposed they had to pursue it. "If Angie spotted him in town before the fire, and he was the reason she changed her identity, then it was a smart move on her part to take off."

Liss turned so she could meet his eyes. "Not so smart if she didn't go far and Eldridge and Arbuthnot managed to track her down."

Sherri leaned back in her swivel chair, certain her skepticism was obvious. Liss had arrived at her office a short time earlier to spin an incredible yarn. So much for a quiet Sunday afternoon!

"Let me get this straight. You think that Martin Eldridge, or Eliot Underhill acting for him—"

"Edgar Arbuthnot, according to Jake Murch."

"That Edgar Arbuthnot broke into the Moosetookalook Post Office in the faint hope that Angie sent you an anniversary card and was stupid enough to include a return address?"

"I know it sounds unlikely, but what are the odds that all these incidents *aren't* connected? You don't believe in coincidence any more than I do!"

Sherri had to admit, if only to herself, that she'd already considered the possibility that the arson, vandalism, and murder might be connected. At the time, the idea had seemed too preposterous to pursue, but only because she couldn't come up with any logical reason to link the three crimes together.

"And you think that one of them broke into Graye's house because, as the local real estate agent, he had lists of all the empty houses in the area?"

"Right. He was looking for places where Angie and the kids might be hiding. It makes sense, Sherri. And then, when you factor in what Janice Eccles saw—"

"She saw a man with a cane and a teenaged boy talking together at the Highland Games. That's a long way from being a witness to Martin Eldridge attempting to kill Kent Humphrey."

"Have you heard anything from the hospital?"

"Kent had surgery. They're hopeful, but they're keeping him sedated."

"So no one has been able to question him?"

Sherri shook her head. "Even if he regains consciousness—which we all hope and pray he will, and soon—he may not remember much. And from what you've said, Janice didn't get that good a look at the man with the cane."

Liss huffed out an exasperated breath. "If Gordon shows her Eldridge's photo, she might be able to make a positive identification."

Sherri knew better than to count on that happening, even if Gordon had come up with a good recent likeness of Martin Eldridge. Most people made lousy witnesses. Ask five individuals to watch the same incident and then describe what they saw and you'd get five wildly different accounts. If there was a car involved, no one would agree on what color it was, let alone the make or model.

"Maybe when they bring him in . . ."

"Don't pin any hopes on it."

"But, Sherri, it all makes perfect sense, especially when you add in that accident twelve years ago."

"That's a long time to hold a grudge. And you don't know why Angie was in the picture. She could have been an innocent bystander."

"If Adam or Amber or Christina had been killed crossing the street and you thought the person responsible had gotten off scot-free, would you still be wanting revenge a dozen years later?"

The question made sweat break out on Sherri's brow at the same time her insides turned to ice. She had to swallow convulsively before she could speak. "Not if the authorities had cleared that person. And, again, we don't know that *Angie* was involved."

Liss waited a beat.

"Okay. She might have been the one driving the car that struck and killed Eldridge's daughter. And yes, I'd be pissed if it was one of my kids and the driver got off with a slap on the wrist. I might even be tempted to take matters into my own hands. But I wouldn't. Not that week or the next month and certainly not twelve years later."

She willed herself to calm down and think rationally. She wasn't wearing her mother hat right now. She was functioning as the chief of police of Moosetookalook, Maine. A glance at Liss showed her that her friend's jaw jutted out at a stubborn angle. She was convinced her theory was right. The last thing Sherri wanted was for Liss to go off half-cocked and get herself into trouble, but short of locking her in the police station's one tiny cell, there wasn't much Sherri could do to stop her.

She tried reasoning with her. "What has Martin Eldridge done with his life since his daughter died? For all you know, he may have founded a charitable institution and channeled his loss into good deeds."

"Murch is trying to find that out."

"Good. I hope he succeeds. Soon. Meanwhile, I can tell you that a BOLO has gone out for both Eldridge and Underhill—"

"Arbuthnot."

"Arbuthnot. They're wanted for questioning as potential witnesses to yesterday's attack on Kent Humphrey. Right now, that's the best anyone can do. There isn't a shred of hard evidence to tie either man to the attack on Kent, let alone to Jason Graye's murder."

The expression on Liss's face—ruefulness combined with frustration—had Sherri narrowing her eyes.

"Gordon already told you the same thing, didn't he?"

Liss's grimace was answer enough.

"Then take my advice, and his, and let the state police handle this."

"I wish I had your confidence in them."

Sherri toyed with the pen on her desk, avoiding Liss's too-perceptive gaze. She had nowhere near as much faith in Gordon and his colleagues as she wanted her friend to believe.

"Look on the bright side," she said after a moment. "Since it appears that Angie voluntarily went into hiding, then she and the kids will come home as soon as Eldridge is out of the picture."

"Home?" There was incredulity in Liss's voice. "Home to what? He burned down her business and her apartment. I'm sure she had insurance, but just putting up a new building couldn't replace what was lost in the fire. Photographs. Mementos." She gave a choked laugh. "Angie's collection of designer teddy bears. She loved those stupid stuffed bears. She never let her kids touch them, let alone play with them."

"But she still has her kids, wherever they are," Sherri reminded her. "That's what's truly important." She leaned across her desk, as earnest as she'd ever been. "Martin Eldridge and Edgar Arbuthnot will be found and questioned. If the evidence is there, they will be punished for their crimes. You've passed on the information you found, and Murch did the same. That's all you can do. That and trust Gordon to make an arrest. Go home, Liss. Let him do his job."

Chapter Sixteen

Liss left the police station and headed for Patsy's Coffee House. She should have gone there first, for all the good talking to Sherri had done!

As soon as she stepped inside, the wonderful bakery smells began to work their calming magic. They also reminded her that she'd never gotten around to having lunch. Her stomach growled so loudly that she was sure even Alex Permutter, seated at his favorite table and engrossed in a newspaper, was able to hear it.

Since he was the only customer in the café, Liss had her choice of seating. Instead of choosing one of the booths or grabbing the other table, she slid onto a stool at the counter. Patsy automatically reached for the coffeepot, but Liss shook her head. She was far too wired already.

Wet cloth in hand—she'd been wiping down the food-prep surfaces behind the counter—Patsy brought the smell of bleach with her. "What can I do you for?"

"Information," Liss said.

With a practiced swipe, Patsy ran her cloth over the Formica countertop. She didn't look directly at Liss until Liss's stomach gave a second loud growl. At that sound, she stalked to the pastry case, removed a chocolate chip muffin, plunked it on a plate, and passed it to Liss.

"Eat," she commanded.

Liss ate. She knew how good Patsy's muffins were, and given what she intended to ask her, she wasn't at all sure she'd ever have the chance to sample another. Patsy was perfectly capable of banning a customer from her coffee house for life.

"That's better," Patsy said after the last crumb disappeared. "Now what is it that has you in such a tizzy?"

"I heard you were looking for me on Wednesday."

Whatever Patsy had expected her to say, that wasn't it. She frowned, considered, and finally asked, "Who told you?"

"Zara. She saw you."

"Huh."

"Look, Patsy, let's not beat around the bush. Are you the one who left the anniversary card from Angie?"

"Why would I do that?"

"Because she asked you to. The real question is when? Have you seen her since she disappeared?"

A stubborn expression on her thin face, Patsy said nothing. Industriously wielding the cleaning cloth, she went over the same surface she'd just wiped, scrubbing at an imaginary spot with intense concentration.

"You aren't doing her any favors by staying silent," Liss said.

Ignoring her, Patsy started to turn away.

"Wait a second. I need to ask you something else."

"I can't tell you where Angie is."

Can't? Liss wondered. *Or won't?*

"It's not that. Not exactly. Do you remember when I was in here the other day? We sat in one of the booths, and I was talking about how Angie always sends me an anniversary card? There was a man in the next booth. A guest at the hotel."

"I get a lot of those in here." Although she was willing to admit that much, Patsy had a wary look in her eyes, as though she suspected a trap.

"Well, this one was apparently working for Martin Eldridge."

Patsy tried to hide it, but it was obvious that she recognized the name. She gave an involuntary start.

"That's right, Patsy. Martin Eldridge—the man Angie is afraid of. He's been here all week, and he's still on the loose. He's not going to stop looking for her. Please, Patsy. You've got to tell me everything you know. Angie's life—and Beth's and Bradley's—may depend on it."

Whether out of misguided friendship or pure pigheadedness, Patsy continued to deny that she knew where Angie was hiding out.

"You . . . you're withholding information in a murder investigation."

Patsy snorted. "Going to take me in and use the brass knuckles to beat the information out of me? Our police department doesn't even own a taser. Go home, Liss. You're wasting your time here."

Discouraged, Liss left the café. She paused on the sidewalk to look toward her house, two doors away along Birch Street. She'd left Dan at home, planning to watch a baseball game on TV. There had been no need for both of them to be there when she talked to Sherri, or to Patsy. She supposed she might as well join him. There didn't seem to be anything more she could do to find Angie.

Behind her, a door opened and closed. She glanced over her shoulder, wondering if Patsy had changed her mind about confiding in her, but it was only Alex Permutter. She sent him a vague smile and started to step off the curb.

"Liss?" he called, arresting the movement. "A moment of your time?"

"Of course." She'd been brought up to be polite to her elders. She accompanied her words with a nod, since she knew he was extremely hard of hearing.

Taking hold of her elbow, Alex steered her across the street and into the town square, heading for the octagonal gazebo, at present unoccupied. Once they were seated on the bench that circled the interior of the structure, Liss studied the old man. She couldn't imagine what he wanted with her.

The first thing that struck her was the twinkle in his faded blue eyes. The second was that, contrary to everything she'd heard about him, he was sporting a pair of hearing aids.

"I thought you claimed you aren't deaf?"

He chuckled. "Suits me not to hear some things, especially when the wife is nagging. I got these babies a year ago. I stick them in when I'm out and about. You'd be amazed the things people say around me, thinking I can't hear them."

Liss did a quick memory search, trying to recall what *she* might have let slip in his presence. Lately he always seemed to be hanging around Patsy's place when she was there. Aside from anything he might have heard on earlier occasions, he'd just listened in on what she and Patsy had said to each other.

"Mr. Permutter, do you know where Angie is?"

"I might know. Sounds to me like she needs to stay put. Out of sight so that Eldridge fella can't find her."

"Maybe so, but her friends are looking for her, too. Now

that the police have some notion of what's going on, they can protect her, but they can't do that if they don't know where she is."

"Convoluted logic, young lady." He wagged a gnarled finger at her. "Still, you may have a point."

"So—do you know where she is?"

"It's not so much me knowing as having a hunch." His gaze strayed to the coffee house. Patsy stood in the window, watching them.

"Something you overheard?"

He nodded. "Angie was in there the day before the fire. I heard some of what she and Patsy were saying to each other. Didn't make a lick of sense then, but later . . ." He fingered his close-shaved chin, as if that would somehow aid his memory. "The thing is, Patsy was talking about taking groceries somewhere for Angie. She said no one would think it was odd if she went out there."

"Out where?" Liss asked. Then she remembered. "Patsy owns a camp."

"That's what I'm thinking," Permutter agreed.

"Do you know where it is?"

He sent her a beatific smile. "In fact, I do. Kate's brother used to have a place out that way."

After Alex Permutter had given Liss precise driving directions, he headed home to his wife. Liss was sorely tempted to jump in her car and drive straight to Patsy's camp, but common sense took her from the gazebo to her own front porch instead.

It was possible Martin Eldridge and his tame PI were still around. If so, they might be keeping an eye on Angie's friends, hoping that one of them would lead them to her. Liss had no intention of making it easy to find Angie and her children. Then, too, she'd made a promise to Dan. As long as there was a murderer on the loose, she wasn't going any farther from home than the police station or Patsy's unless someone was with her, preferably her big, strong husband.

From the porch, she took a long, careful look around. She couldn't spot anyone watching her, not even Patsy, but she knew a murderer was still out there somewhere. In spite of the warmth of the July afternoon, she shivered.

Inside the house, Dan was not camped out in front of the television in the living room, as she'd expected. Liss called his name. She didn't spot the note on the refrigerator until she was about to go out to his workshop to look for him.

"Sam needed me at the construction site," he'd written. "This shouldn't take more than an hour. Love you."

The time he'd written below his name indicated that he'd left the house only ten minutes after she'd set out to talk to Sherri. That had been well over an hour ago.

Telling herself she was foolish to worry, Liss tried his cell phone.

It rang . . . right there in their kitchen.

"Figures," she muttered, belatedly remembering that she'd watched him plug it into the charger when they returned from The Spruces.

Dan's brother Sam, now sole proprietor of Ruskin Construction, often called on his younger brother for a second opinion. That this was Sunday didn't matter. And yet, if she was in danger, maybe Dan was, too.

Liss phoned her sister-in-law. Once she'd confirmed that Sam had gone to deal with a minor problem at the house he was remodeling and that he had planned to ask Dan's advice, Liss relaxed. Dan was safe. She was safe. No worries.

Lumpkin chose that moment to pad into the kitchen. He sent Liss a baleful look.

"You are not starving," she informed the big Maine coon cat.

She checked his food and water dishes. Both were half full. That settled, she fidgeted, unable to settle. In the end, she left Dan a note and went over to the Emporium. She and Dan had unloaded her unsold merchandise as soon as they got back to town, but they'd left it in the stockroom, still boxed up. She managed to kill several hours putting everything back on shelves and racks, preparatory to opening on Monday morning.

She'd barely returned to the house when the landline rang. She expected to hear Dan's voice, since he still wasn't home, but it was Sherri. She sounded a trifle breathless.

"Can't talk, but I thought you'd want to know. I just got a report that the car our friend Arbuthnot rented as Underhill has been in a traffic accident out on Academy Hill Road. I'm headed there now."

"Was Eldridge with him?"

"Sounds like it. Gotta go. I'll call you when I know more."

Liss hung up slowly, lost in thought. If Eldridge and Underhill/Arbuthnot were both accounted for, it should be safe for her to go out to Patsy's camp. Yes, she'd be on her own, but she'd leave a note for Dan so he wouldn't worry.

She didn't waste time arguing with herself. She scribbled her message on a Post-it and used a refrigerator magnet to hold it in place. Dan would find it as soon as he got home. Then she used her cell phone to call her aunt and leave a message on Margaret's answering machine. As she pulled out of her driveway, she congratulated herself on taking sensible precautions. If there were any problems, two people would know where she'd gone. With any luck, though, she'd be back before either of them realized she'd left. If things went really well, she'd have Angie, Beth, and Bradley with her.

At the crash site, Sherri had no trouble recognizing the driver of the car that had slammed into a telephone pole. Edgar Arbuthnot, aka Eliot Underhill, sat on a boulder at the side of the road. From the look of things, he had suffered only bumps and bruises in the accident.

Unfortunately, the man with him was not Martin Eldridge.

"He picked up a hitchhiker," Mike Jennings said, indicating a scruffy-looking fellow with a backpack.

"He know anything?"

Mike shook his head. "Said they'd barely got up to speed when a deer leapt in front of the car and the driver lost control."

"Let him go." She turned her attention to Arbuthnot

He frowned when he saw a second uniformed officer approaching him.

Officially, the police were only looking for him to question him about what he might have seen at the Highland Games. Given Liss's suspicions, however, Sherri had no intention of letting this man out of her sight. She stopped a foot away from him to study his face. He had a long scratch across his forehead, but it wasn't deep and had already stopped bleeding.

"How are you feeling, Mr. Arbuthnot? Ready to answer some questions?"

His eyes widened at her use of his real name. "Hey, what's going on here?"

Mike Jennings came up behind him to catch hold of his arm and haul him to his feet. "Just a few routine—"

"Like hell!" Jerking free, he tried to flee.

Big mistake, Sherri thought.

Mike brought Arbuthnot down with a flying tackle. Arbuthnot reacted by trying to punch the officer in the face. Within seconds, he was in handcuffs and being read his rights.

"Assaulting a police officer is a serious offense," Sherri informed him. "Let's go back to the police station and talk about it."

During the short drive to the municipal building, she indulged in a pleasant fantasy wherein Underhill/Arbuthnot realized it was to his advantage to tell her everything he knew about Eldridge and Angie *before* Gordon Tandy showed up to take over the interrogation.

There was still plenty of daylight left as Liss drove out along Owl Road toward the turnoff to Patsy's camp on Ledge Lake. The sun wouldn't set until nearly a quarter past eight. Evenings in late July were long and pleasant. This one would be even better than most if she found what she hoped to at the end of her journey.

Her destination was about eight miles from the center of town. Another turn, at the seven-mile mark, put her on a camp road. The shocks on her car didn't appreciate the rut-filled dirt surface, but the condition of the access road provided an extra layer of privacy for residents.

A small, hand-painted sign containing only Patsy's last name identified the property. Her driveway plunged toward the lakeshore at a precipitous grade and ended at the closed door of a single-car garage. Rather than attempt that slope or have to back out again, Liss parked on a flat section of grass at the top of the drive and walked down.

She couldn't help but think how quiet it was when it was still relatively early on a Sunday evening in summer. Weren't there any people at nearby camps? This was prime swimming, boating, and cookout weather. Kids should still be splashing around in the lake. Families might have to head back to their real homes for the workweek ahead, but surely they'd stretch out the weekend as long as humanly possible. She knew she would.

The distant hum of a boat motor reached her, but other than that she heard only the faint stirrings of leaves above her head and the soft crunch of gravel as she walked down the driveway. No voices. No windows opening or doors slamming. No crying babies or children shouting.

Eerie, she thought, before deciding that the silence had a simple and obvious explanation. Patsy's neighbors probably rented their camps to people from far away. In that case, it made sense that those folks would leave early on Sunday evening to make the drive back to Boston or New York or wherever.

She reached the detached garage and peered through the small windows in the door. She was so certain she'd see Angie's car inside that it took her a moment to accept that the bay was empty. No car. No vehicle at all. She spotted shelving at the back and a few boxes piled up to one side, but nothing that would indicate anyone had recently left a vehicle there.

Puzzled, she headed for the steps to the porch, alert for any sign of habitation. If Angie was hiding out because she was afraid of Martin Eldridge, then she wouldn't dare leave herself without a means of escape. She'd want to keep her car handy in case he found them again and they had to make a quick getaway. So where was it? She supposed it was possible to hide a vehicle in the nearby woods. The trees were thick enough to conceal a Sherman tank, but access would be tricky.

Doubts began to creep in. Had she guessed wrong? Had they never been here at all?

Maybe they'd been here and gone away again. If so, they might have left some clue behind. Liss was not about to leave without checking things out. If she was wrong, she'd apologize to Patsy later.

The rustic building was built of logs, but it was far from being a cabin. It was a generously proportioned house. From the porch, Liss looked through a large, square window into the dining area. Beyond that, she could see the kitchen and on into the living room. The floor plan was open . . . and the camp appeared to be completely uninhabited. Discouraged but not yet ready to give up, she hopped back off the porch and circled the house, heading for the side that faced the lake.

Getting there required her to clamber down a steep set of stone steps. Given the lay of the land, the basement was below ground at the front of the house but above at the back. That level had no windows. Liss presumed it was used for storage. Her guess seemed confirmed by the heavy padlock on the basement door.

A freshly mown lawn ran down to a dock. Beyond, the still, blue water glistened invitingly as the sun sank closer to the horizon. *What a great place to take the kids,* Liss thought. *And how cruel to bring them here and not let them enjoy themselves.* If they *had* been hiding out at Patsy's camp, Angie would not have been so foolish as to let Beth and Bradley out of the house. She'd have been too afraid that someone would recognize them.

Turning her head to the right and then to the left, Liss considered what she could see of Patsy's neighbors, and what they could see of her property. Not a darned thing, she concluded. Trees grew thick on both sides of the camp, so densely packed together that she didn't catch so much as a glimpse of another building.

Squinting, she spotted what appeared to be a narrow path through the trees to her left, but it wound in among them in such a way that anyone approaching Patsy's place would have to be right on top of the house before it was visible.

All in all, Patsy's camp was a fine and private place. By rights, Angie and her kids *should* be staying here. So where were they?

Turning to study the building once more, Liss contemplated the flight of stairs that ran up the outside of the building and ended at a small covered deck. From the ground, she could see that it was equipped with a grill and several chairs.

Might as well be thorough, she decided, and went up. She had no great hope of success when she grasped the handle of the sliding glass door that led into the house. The front door had been locked when she'd tried it.

To her astonishment, this one silently slid open.

For a moment, Liss just stood there, unable to believe her luck. It took a few more seconds to convince herself that she wouldn't *really* be doing anything wrong if she went inside and took a look around. It wasn't as if she was planning to steal anything, and she'd do Patsy a favor by making sure no one else had burgled the place, either.

A stickler for the rules could easily demolish this logic. Liss freely admitted to being a flawed human being, although in this instance she preferred to think of her behavior as "flexible."

Inside, she found herself standing at the point where the kitchen turned into the living area. What she had not been able to see through the window on the porch was that the living area continued on around a corner and took up the entire back of the camp. Comfortable-looking sofas and chairs were grouped so that some faced the large windows with their spectacular view of Ledge Lake and others were aimed toward a flat-screen TV.

Liss's spirits plummeted. The room was impossibly neat—much too pristine for anyone to have been living at the camp. Despite that, she continued to explore. Halfway across the living area, a door opened into what appeared to be the master bedroom. There were clothes in the closet, but Liss could tell at a glance that they belonged to Patsy. None of them would come close to fitting Angie.

Another door, on the far side of the bedroom, took her through to a bathroom. Again, Liss saw no signs of recent use. Toiletries were all neatly put away. The sink, bathtub, and shower were bone dry, as were the towels.

Discouraged, she very nearly left without checking the remaining rooms, but she was nothing if not thorough. She climbed up a steep staircase and there, under the eaves, discovered two more bedrooms, one on each side. Passing through the right-hand room, she entered a third. It was much smaller, more walk-in closet than extra bedroom, and it appeared to be used for storage. Several stacks of cardboard boxes were piled on the floor. The flaps were tucked in to keep them closed, but none of them were sealed, and there were no labels on any of them. All the while telling herself she shouldn't snoop, Liss opened the nearest carton.

What she saw made her gasp in surprise. Fumbling, she reached inside. Her fingers touched soft mohair as she lifted a teddy bear free of its wrappings.

Liss couldn't swear the bear belonged to Angie Hogencamp, but Angie was the only person she knew who collected designer teddy bears. The odds that Patsy shared the same hobby, without ever mentioning it to anyone, were slim to none.

A quick check of nearby boxes confirmed that several of them also contained teddy bears. Her mind whirling, Liss carefully repacked them. This discovery made no sense. All of Angie's bears were supposed to have been destroyed in the fire.

There was only one way they could have ended up at Patsy's camp—if Angie had brought them to this location before the fire. But if she'd done that, why weren't she and her children hidden here, too?

Still pondering this new wrinkle, Liss headed back downstairs. She had reached the bottom step before she simultaneously realized two things. One was that the sun was sinking fast, leaving the once-bright room in twilight shadow. The other was that she was no longer alone in the house.

Someone stood just inside the door to the deck. His back was to her as he closed it. The latch engaged with an ominous click.

Her heart in her throat, one hand fumbling for the cell phone in her pocket, Liss held her breath. She nearly collapsed with relief when the intruder turned to face her. "Boxer! What are you doing here?"

"Is she here? Did you find Beth?"

"No sign of her. And we both need to leave. Now."

Liss was painfully aware that she'd set a very bad example for her young cousin. It had been wrong of her to waltz into Patsy's camp and snoop around without permission. That was not behavior she wanted Boxer to imitate.

But Boxer wasn't moving. "Nothing? You sounded so sure on the phone."

It took a moment for the penny to drop. "Ah," she said. "I take it you listened to the message I left for Margaret?"

"I was in her apartment when you called. I agreed to feed and walk the dogs this afternoon. I got outside as fast as I could, but I was too late to catch you before you drove away." Sounding aggrieved, he added, "I had to go all the way home to get my car before I could follow you out here."

Liss knew that Boxer's fears for Beth's safety were as great as, if not greater than, hers for Angie's. He'd probably run the whole way home, at least a mile, and then he'd have had to coax that old clunker of his into starting.

"How did you know how to find this place?" she asked, remembering that although she'd said where she was going, she hadn't bothered to leave directions. She'd assumed that Margaret would already know where Patsy's camp was located.

"Beth pointed it out to me once. She said she'd come along a time or two when her mother was visiting Patsy. I'd forgotten all about it until you left word that this was where you were headed and that you thought Angie was here."

While they talked, they made their way back to the grassy area where Liss had parked. Boxer had pulled in right next to her. Liss looked around, noting that here, too, the trees formed a nearly impenetrable barrier. They weren't all that far from civilization. In fact, she was pretty sure they were still in the town, if not the village, of Moosetookalook. But their surroundings made the location seem far more remote than it really was. It would be easy to believe that there wasn't another human being within the sound of their voices.

She was about to say something to that effect to Boxer when she caught sight of the look of astonishment on his face. He was staring at something behind her. Liss closed her mouth with an audible snap as her cousin pushed past her. She turned to find him running full tilt toward a slender figure standing at the tree line.

"Beth," Liss whispered.

Then she was running, too.

Chapter Seventeen

"We've been staying at the camp next door, just in case someone came looking for us at Patsy's place," Beth explained. "Her neighbor isn't using his camp until mid-August and asked Patsy to look after it for him until then."

Liss followed the two young people along another of the winding, narrow paths through the trees. This one led to Angie's real hiding place. Scarcely able to believe that her hunch had been right—well, almost right—Liss murmured, "You had time to plan."

Beth looked over her shoulder, not an easy trick when Boxer had his arm slung over them both and didn't seem inclined to loosen his grip. "Mom spotted Martin Eldridge the minute he set foot in Moosetookalook." She sounded proud of that fact.

That explained, Liss supposed, how they'd been able to take along a few prized personal possessions when they went into hiding. She wondered what else Angie had stored at Patsy's besides the teddy bear collection. Photo albums, she supposed. Things that were irreplaceable. Had she expected Eldridge to destroy her home?

A sudden thought stopped her in her tracks. She was almost afraid to ask. "Uh, Beth?"

Both Beth and Boxer turned to face her.

"Do you know . . . that is . . . did someone tell you about the fire?"

There was still enough daylight to see the expectant look on Beth's face morph into a mask of sadness. "I know. It's all gone." Her grip on Boxer's arm tightened enough to make him wince. "I know about Kent, too." She looked up into Boxer's face, her eyes pleading with him to give her some good news. "Is he doing better?"

"I guess so," Boxer mumbled. "I can call Amie."

"No," Liss cautioned him. "Not yet."

He glared at her. "I'm not going to give anything away."

"Not intentionally, but it's best you don't take any chances. Wait until you've settled a bit."

Acknowledging her point, he gave her a curt nod, oddly mature for a young man who was only seventeen. He and Beth started walking again, their feet making soft shushing noises on the pine needles and mulch that carpeted the path.

"Has Patsy been here?" Liss asked.

Beth shook her head but didn't look behind her again. "Too dangerous, she said. She made sure we had enough groceries for a couple of weeks and then left us on our own. If we have to stay longer, she'll bring stuff to her place for us to pick up."

"Then how is it you're up on the news from town?"

"We have Wi-Fi. Plus Patsy's been phoning with regular updates. She bought one of those cheap cell phones, the ones where you buy as many minutes as you need in advance, and gave it to Mom so we could stay in touch."

The path ended abruptly in a clearing that contained a

camp that was very nearly the twin of Patsy's place. The biggest difference was the worried-looking woman standing on the deck, her eyes fixed on the three people who had just emerged from the trees.

Angie's troubled expression remained in place even after she recognized Liss and Boxer. "Come inside," she called, gesturing for them to hurry. She stared past them at the trees, as if she expected Martin Eldridge to pop up at any moment.

Liss understood her concern. If they could find her, she must fear that someone else might, too.

"It's all right," Liss reassured her friend, giving her an impulsive hug. "We'd never have known where you were if Beth hadn't come out of hiding. Boxer and I would have left, convinced that you were long gone."

"Oh, Beth," Angie whispered, sending her daughter an exasperated look.

"I'm sorry, Mom," Beth said, "but you know we can trust Boxer and Liss to keep our secret." She was still wrapped tight in Boxer's arms.

Angie sighed. "It's been hard on you, sweetheart. I know."

"I'm the one who insisted on looking for her," Boxer said. "I'm sorry if that upsets you."

Angie sent a rueful glance in Liss's direction. "I doubt you deserve *all* the blame."

"Let's call it credit," Liss said in a dry voice. "Anyway, I came to bring you good news. When I talked to Sherri a little while ago, she was on her way to arrest Martin Eldridge and the PI he hired to find you."

The elation Liss had expected to see was conspicuously absent. Angie said only, "You'd better come in and sit down."

The living area was almost identical to the one in Patsy's camp. Young Bradley Hogencamp sat on the floor in front of the TV, so engrossed in a video game that he didn't even look up when they entered.

"Scenic vista," Angie said, gesturing toward the windows. "At least it is by daylight. If we were renting this place, we'd be paying a premium for the lakefront property and the view."

"Whereas you're probably ready to throw a rock through that window in sheer frustration. Let me guess—you've barely dared step outside, let alone swim or sunbathe, since you got here?"

"That about sums it up, and I'm sick to death of being cooped up, not to mention being damned tired of feeling scared all the time." Angie turned on a lamp and sat on the sofa, gesturing for Liss to sit beside her.

"You'll be safe once Martin Eldridge is in jail. With any luck, he already is."

"How did you find out about him?" Angie asked.

"And what does he have to do with you being in hiding?" Boxer asked from the love seat where he and Beth had settled. "He's a guest at the hotel, right? The one with the cane?"

Liss had forgotten that she hadn't brought Boxer up to speed. When all the bits and pieces of information began to come together, her cousin had been elsewhere, preoccupied with his friend's injuries and with trying to comfort Kent's girlfriend.

"I'm betting it was Martin Eldridge who was responsible for everything that's happened." She turned back to Angie. "Did he come to Moosetookalook looking for you?"

Angie's bleak expression confirmed her guess even before she spoke. "He's been after me for twelve years, ever since I killed his daughter. She ran out into traffic, right in front of my car. She was roaring drunk at the time, but her father blamed me. After the police told him no charges would be filed against me, he threatened to kill my daughter in revenge for his. A few days later, Beth was almost run down in the street in front of our house."

"Eldridge?"

Angie nodded. "The police couldn't prove he was the one driving. In fact, he came up with an alibi for the time of the incident. He has money. It wouldn't have been hard for him to find somebody to lie for him." She sighed. "There was nothing more anyone could do until he tried again. I couldn't take the chance he'd succeed on a second attempt. I took Beth and left town, even though Bradley was due any day."

"You changed your name," Liss said.

"Yes. My real name is Anne. Anne Howard."

"What about your husband?"

"We'd just been divorced. I was granted full custody of Beth and our unborn child. I found out later that he remarried. He has no idea what happened to me or his kids. He doesn't much care, either."

"So there *was* a visit from a sister-in-law."

Angie looked even sadder. "Yes. She was the only one who knew where I was. She died two years ago. Cancer."

Was that how Arbuthnot had traced Anne Howard? Liss suspected it was, especially if Angie's ex had inherited his sister's effects.

"Beth was just a little bit of a thing when we settled in Moosetookalook, but she was old enough to know her real last name wasn't Hogencamp. I've never hidden the truth from her, but I didn't tell Bradley until this past week."

Liss spared a glance for the boy, who was still busily killing space aliens.

"You probably wonder how I was able to create a new identity," Angie said. "Let's just say that my ex-husband isn't the squeaky-clean businessman he pretended to be. I'd met a few of his associates, and I knew one of them could help me become someone else . . . for a price. Thanks to the divorce settlement, I was able to get hold of a healthy amount of cash." Her lips twisted into a rueful grimace. "I meant to invest it in college funds for the kids, but it wouldn't have helped them much if they weren't alive to enjoy it."

"Oh, Angie!" Liss's heart broke for her.

Angie waved off the expression of sympathy. "Water under the bridge, and the bridge burned down long ago." She heaved a sigh that told Liss, more clearly than words, that she was thinking of another, more recent fire. "I'd do anything to protect my kids. It didn't matter that I couldn't prove it was Martin Eldridge in that car. I *knew* it was him. When he threatened Beth, he meant it. I heard it in his voice. I didn't dare take the risk that he'd try again and succeed."

"So you disappeared." It seemed an extreme solution to Liss, but she'd never been in Angie's situation. Afraid for her child's life. No husband. Pregnant. Liss could see how she might have felt she had no alternative.

"So I disappeared," Angie agreed. "I picked a name out of a phonebook—opened the page to the Hs, closed my eyes, and jabbed it with my finger. After I had the necessary papers, identifying me as Angela Hogencamp and Beth as Elizabeth Hogencamp, and had given birth to Bradley in a hospital in upstate New York, I got hold of a map of the United States and used the same method to decide where to go next."

"Your finger landed on Moosetookalook?" Boxer sounded skeptical.

Liss's lips quirked. "Uh, Angie, I hate to tell you this, but Moosetookalook is way too small to show up on a map of the whole country. Heck, even Carrabassett County is too small for that."

Angie shrugged. "I came to this general *area* and drove around, exploring. When I got to Moosetookalook, I spotted a building on the town square that was for sale. The price was right, so I bought it and opened up the bookstore. It seemed like a good idea at the time." She shook her head. "No, it *was* a good decision. All the years I've lived here, I was never afraid of being found. Maybe I should have been."

"When did Martin Eldridge turn up?"

"It was the day before the fire." Angie stared off into space, seeing nothing. "I recognized him the moment I saw him. That face is burned in my memory. He was sitting on a bench in the town square, looking straight at the bookstore. He saw me clearly when I stepped out to get a breath of fresh air. Even at that distance, I saw the look in his eyes. The hatred. The rage. It was as if the last twelve years never happened. I was filled with the worst kind of panic. For a minute, I thought I might be having a heart attack."

Liss squeezed her hand, silently offering her understanding and support.

"Well, I wasn't. Obviously. But I was so afraid of what Eldridge might be planning to do that I told the kids to pack up what was most important to them and did the same myself. I went around the back way to Patsy's to ask if we could hide out at her camp. It was the only place I could think of off the top of my head."

"Did she already know your story?"

Angie shook her head. "Not then. I've told her most of it since, but that day I just said that someone from my past was after me and I needed to get out of sight. She was the one who suggested using the camp next door instead of hers. She took care of stocking it with groceries."

That was the part Alex Permutter had overheard, Liss thought. A pity he hadn't caught more of the conversation. He'd never have let anything slip to a stranger, but he might have told Sherri what he knew. Then they'd have been able to find Angie and her kids sooner and get them proper protection.

"We left as soon as it got dark," Angie continued. "It's a good thing we did. A few hours later, Eldridge torched the building."

The sound of Beth's quiet weeping reached Liss when Angie, overcome by emotion, abruptly stopped speaking. Hearing her story had quite a different effect on Liss—it engendered a slow-burning anger against the man with the cane. He'd hurt her friends. He, or the PI he'd hired, had killed an innocent bystander and nearly killed a second. There were no words adequate to describe what she thought of him.

Beside her, Angie stared out at the lake. Moonbeams played across the surface, but Liss doubted her friend noticed.

"After the fire proved I was right to be scared," Angie continued in a low voice, "I was too frightened to talk to anyone, let alone make any accusations. Only Patsy knew where we were, and she agreed it made sense to stay put until we were sure Eldridge had left town. At first I thought

I'd be able to return—maybe pretend I'd gone away for a few days and hadn't heard about the fire—but the longer he stayed, the less chance there was that my fake identity would hold up."

"It's not illegal to call yourself by any name you like," Liss said. "I read that somewhere."

"True. And I've paid income taxes under my own name, but I'm pretty sure I've broken a few laws along the way."

"There were extenuating circumstances," Liss insisted. "Even if you end up being charged with something, I bet you'll only get probation, or maybe community service."

"That's so unfair," Beth said.

Boxer, who had more than one relative who'd served time, stayed silent.

"No matter the consequences, Angie, you have to go to the police."

"I can't trust them. I had no proof Martin Eldridge tried to run Beth down all those years ago, and I have no proof now that he burned down my bookstore."

"Maybe not, but that's not all he's done."

"He tried to kill Kent Humphrey, Mom." Beth's voice was anguished. "Just because Kent might have seen him right after he killed Jason Graye."

Angie looked to Liss for confirmation.

"It looks as if Eldridge, or the defrocked private investigator he hired, did a lot more than burn down your building."

She listed all the crimes she suspected one or the other of them had committed, ending with the stabbing of Beth and Boxer's friend Kent. By the time she was done, Angie's face, already pale, had lost every vestige of color.

"He was looking for us. That's why all the rest happened. Maybe if we hadn't gone into hiding—"

"If you hadn't hidden, you'd be dead."

Liss's blunt words snapped Angie out of her guilt trip. More than that, they finally convinced her that she had to talk to the police.

Edgar Arbuthnot, aka Eliot Underhill, was not impressed by the charges thrown at him by a rural chief of police. He held onto his cocky attitude even when faced with a state police detective. With a laugh, he waived his right to have an attorney present during questioning.

"An innocent man doesn't need a lawyer," he insisted.

Stupid, Sherri thought. He had to know Gordon Tandy was investigating a homicide. She felt certain that the prisoner was not as innocent as he claimed, but if he could be persuaded to give evidence against the man who'd employed him, both Eldridge and Arbuthnot would get what they deserved.

She kept her thoughts to herself. She was also careful to stay out of Gordon Tandy's line of sight. He could order her out of the interview room at the county jail if he chose. She did not intend to give him any reason to do so.

"You were hired by one Martin Eldridge?" Gordon asked.

"That's right. He wanted me to find a woman named Anne Howard. I traced her to Moosetookalook." He didn't say how. Sherri doubted his methods had been entirely within the law.

"I'm surprised you accompanied Eldridge here. Wasn't your job done when you found her?"

"I came at my client's request. Hey—free vacation at a luxury resort hotel. Who's going to pass that up?"

"Where's Eldridge now?"

"No idea. My job for him was finished, and I was on my way home when I was unfortunate enough to be in a traffic accident."

"You attacked Officer Jennings."

"Just defending myself."

Gordon shuffled some papers on the table between them and glanced at a report. "It appears that your registration as a private investigator was revoked some time ago. In fact, you are currently facing prosecution for falsifying information on that registration and the business license that went with it." Gordon waited a beat, long enough for Arbuthnot's overconfidence to start to slip. "Even if you had been legally licensed in Virginia, there is no reciprocity with the state of Maine."

Arbuthnot/Underhill answered this with a defiant stare.

"So," Gordon said, "who set the fire at the bookstore in Moosetookalook? You or Eldridge?"

"Hey, I'm no firebug."

"Eldridge, then?"

"I didn't *see* him do it, but yeah. Who else would want to torch the place?"

"And yet you stayed on after that incident."

"Look, here's the thing. I was supposed to be done with the job when I located the woman and her two kids. Eldridge insisted I come with him until he could verify their identities. He wouldn't pay me otherwise. Then, when they turned up missing after the fire, he said he wouldn't shell out the cash unless I found out where they were hiding."

"I'll bet he was fit to be tied when he heard there were no fatalities."

Arbuthnot clammed up, too smart to admit that he knew

Eldridge had intended for Angie and her children to die in the fire. Confessing to that knowledge would definitely have made his subsequent search for them the act of an accomplice rather than an "innocent" employee.

"Who broke into the post office?" Gordon asked.

"Eldridge." This time his answer was prompt, if not necessarily truthful.

"Why?"

The prisoner shrugged. "It was because of something I overheard at the coffee house. The Howard woman was in the habit of mailing anniversary cards to this friend of hers. These two women were talking, making it sound like the card was probably already in the mail. It was a long shot, but I . . . that is, *Eldridge* figured that if there was a card, there might also be a return address or postmark. Turned out to be a waste of time to go looking for it. Letters. Bills. Catalogs. Flyers. Not a single envelope the size of a greeting card in the whole damned post office."

Liss had been right, Sherri thought. Sometimes her guesses were uncannily accurate.

"But you weren't the one who broke in?" Gordon sounded skeptical, as well he should.

Arbuthnot spread his hands wide and tried for a "who, me?" expression on his snub-nosed face. "I'm just telling you what Eldridge told me. He did all the dirty work himself. I just provided him with information."

"Why did you register at the hotel under an assumed name?"

"Common practice." His sudden interest in studying his own long, thin fingers gave away the lie in that claim.

"Whose idea was it to break into Jason Graye's house?"

In the long silence that followed Gordon's question,

Sherri sat forward in her chair. Arbuthnot had started to sweat. His hair was cut so short that his scalp showed through. She could see the tiny beads of moisture there and on his neck.

"Were you there?" Gordon asked.

"No! Don't go accusing me of murder. You've got no grounds."

"Oh?"

"I didn't know anything about it until it was all over. I swear it. Eldridge got this wild hair about empty houses in the area. He was sure the Howard woman had to be close by. I don't know why he was so convinced of that. If I'd been her, I'd have been long gone."

"So Eldridge broke into Graye's house because he was a real estate agent?"

Arbuthnot nodded. "Right. Right. Broke in. Meant to go through the listings. I don't know what happened. I wasn't there."

"You didn't get rid of the gun?"

"I didn't even know Eldridge *had* a gun."

"What about a knife?"

"I don't know anything about any weapon."

"But you knew someone had been murdered. You just said so."

At the least, he was an accessory after the fact, Sherri thought. *Maybe before the fact, too.*

Arbuthnot was well aware of how shaky his position was. Perspiration dotted his upper lip. "You can't pin that guy's death on me. Or what happened to that kid at the Highland Games, either. I had no idea what Eldridge was up to."

"You weren't the one who told him he might have been

seen leaving the scene of the crime? You were deep in conversation about something at the games. You were seen."

"He already . . . I mean I was just trying to get my pay. For finding the Howard woman in the first place."

Gordon's voice was so cold that it made Sherri shiver just to hear it. "Here's what I think happened, Mr. Arbuthnot. You knew your employer had killed Jason Graye. You knew he'd spotted someone who might have seen him that night. Maybe you tried to talk him out of a second murder. Maybe not."

"I don't know anything about that kid that got stabbed. I'd already checked out of the hotel."

Gordon shook his head. "You'd paid for two more nights. You and Eldridge both cut your stays short. Nothing to say when you actually left the grounds, though."

And how, Sherri wondered, had he known Kent was stabbed if he hadn't been there?

The suspect lapsed into sullen silence. Sherri had a hard time containing her disgust for him. He hadn't been bothered by Eldridge's crimes, not even murder. Only now that he'd been caught and implicated was he attempting to distance himself from his client's actions.

"Do you know where Martin Eldridge is now?" Gordon asked for the second time.

The shady PI from Virginia swallowed convulsively and used his sleeve to swipe at his sweaty face. "If I knew, I'd tell you."

This time Sherri believed him.

Then he lawyered up.

It was full dark by the time Liss and Angie set out for the Moosetookalook police station. With the aid of flashlights, they followed the path through the trees to Patsy's camp to retrieve Liss's car. The plan was for Boxer to stay with Beth and Bradley while their mother met with Sherri Campbell.

"I don't know about this, Liss," Angie protested as she opened the passenger-side door. She looked spooked as she swiveled her head, peering into the shadows as if she expected an ax-wielding maniac to leap out at them. "Are you sure it's safe?"

"You need to talk to Sherri in person. What you can tell her will add weight to the case against Eldridge and his flunky. It could mean the difference between keeping them in jail and letting them get out on bail."

Bail was next to impossible in Maine if the charge was murder, but Liss wasn't sure the police had enough evidence to make that one stick. If they didn't, the crime of arson would have to be enough to keep Eldridge behind bars. Once he was safely locked up, Angie and her children would be out of danger.

Reluctantly, Angie eased herself into the car. "Let's make it quick, then. I don't like leaving Beth and Bradley alone."

"Trust me. No one is going to figure out where they are. If Beth hadn't shown herself, even Boxer and I wouldn't have found you."

"Just go," Angie said.

Liss started the engine and backed carefully off the grassy verge onto the dirt road. At first her headlights were the only illumination. There were no streetlights, and the thick growth of trees reduced to a glimmer the signs of life from other summer camps. The paved road, when they reached it, was almost as deserted. She made good time getting home, but instead of pulling into her own driveway, she parked in the lot behind the municipal building and got out of the car.

The back door led directly into the hallway outside the police station. Unfortunately, it was locked.

"There are no lights on." Angie, coming up beside her, indicated the window of Sherri's office.

Liss was already pulling out her cell phone. She tried the number for the police department first. There was rarely more than one officer on duty at a time. The usual practice, when that officer was out of the office, was to set the office phone to forward calls to his or her cell. Emergency calls, which went through the county dispatch center, were rerouted the same way.

Sherri picked up on the fourth ring. Liss started talking before her friend had finished identifying herself.

"I'm outside the municipal building with Angie. She's ready to make a statement. Where are you?"

"At the moment? Pulled over to the side of the road so I could answer the phone." Sherri's voice was dry. "Can you wait for me there? I'm about halfway back from Fallstown. I just sat in on an interview with Edgar Arbuthnot, otherwise known as Eliot Underhill."

"What about Eldridge?"

"Still out there."

Liss's heart sank. Damn! She'd been hoping Sherri had both men in custody. Hadn't she said there were two men in Arbuthnot's car?

"Disconnect, Liss," Sherri said into her ear. "I need to get back on the road."

"Yes. Okay. Hanging up."

It was a twenty-minute drive from Fallstown to Moosetookalook. If Sherri was halfway back, they didn't have long to wait. Liss tucked the cell phone away and turned to Angie. "Ten minutes, max. Do you want to sit in the car while we wait?"

Before the other woman could answer, or ask a question Liss didn't want to answer about Martin Eldridge's whereabouts, the back door swung open, nearly slamming into her. Dolores Mayfield barreled through it.

"I thought I heard voices."

Liss frowned at her. "What are you doing here so late?"

"Just finishing up some paperwork in the library."

"Without any lights on?"

"The exit signs are enough to keep me from falling down the stairs. I was already on my way out when I heard someone trying the door. Hello, Angie. Long time no see."

"Dolores."

An awkward silence fell. Dolores showed no sign of leaving. Given how nosy she was, Liss wasn't surprised.

How much, she wondered, had she overheard from the other side of the door before she made her presence known?

Liss had intended to phone Dan after she talked to Sherri, but her reluctance to say anything in front of the librarian stopped her from doing so. She was a little surprised that he hadn't tried to call her. That note she'd left for him would not have stopped him from worrying about her for long.

Angie broke first, unnerved by the fact that the other two said nothing. "We're waiting for Sherri."

"Is that right?" The light beside the door revealed a thoughtful expression on Dolores's face. "I wouldn't mind talking to her myself. I want my guns and knives returned to me."

That was a conversation-stopper.

Liss felt a rush of relief when her cell phone rang. "That's probably Dan," she said as she moved a little apart to answer it.

But the voice on the other end was that of Jake Murch, and what he said drove the breath right out of her. Liss's fingers clenched hard around the phone. "Say that again," she whispered.

"I spotted Martin Eldridge out on Owl Road a couple of hours ago," he repeated.

His words sounded no better the second time. This was *so* not good.

"I lost sight of him before I could do anything," Murch continued. "I've been driving around ever since, keeping my eyes peeled, but no luck."

"Did he have a car?"

"He was on foot when I saw him, but he must have one stashed somewhere. He had a rental at the hotel."

"Exactly *where* on Owl Road?"

Murch's description confirmed Liss's worst fear and had her running for her car, fumbling with her keys as she went. Angie trotted after her, alarmed by the way Liss had suddenly bolted. Dolores followed, too, her ears stretched so she wouldn't miss of a word of Liss's end of the conversation.

"That's where Boxer lives, Jake. If Eldridge was there when my cousin picked up his car, it's possible he followed him straight to where Angie and the kids have been staying." She rattled off directions as she slid in behind the wheel and stuck her key in the ignition.

She could hear Jake cussing on the other end of the line.

He'd been heading home for supper when he called and wasn't much closer to Moosetookalook than Sherri was.

Breaking the connection, Liss tossed the cell phone to Angie. "Hit three on the speed dial and tell Sherri we're headed back to Ledge Lake. I need both hands free for driving."

Chapter Eighteen

"It will be okay," Liss said for the hundredth time since leaving the parking lot. "We're worried for nothing."

She didn't believe it any more this time than she had the first, and Angie, keeping a white-knuckled grip on the passenger-side armrest, wasn't buying her logic, either. If Martin Eldridge had followed Boxer as far as Patsy's camp and then trailed Liss and Boxer through the woods, they might already be too late.

It was no good trying to phone and warn the young people. Boxer kept his "stupid phone" turned off when he wasn't using it. Beth didn't have a cell phone, and there was no landline at Patsy's neighbor's camp.

Moments after Liss turned onto the camp road and accelerated again, her car hit a pothole. In spite of her seat belt, she was bounced high enough to smack her head on the underside of the roof. She took that as a warning to slow down. She and Angie weren't going to do anyone any good if Liss knocked herself out or ran off the side of the road and into a ditch.

They couldn't go in with tires squealing, either. If Eldridge was there but hadn't yet harmed anyone, the last thing they wanted was to give him warning of their arrival. When she reached the top of Patsy's driveway, she pulled onto the grass, parking next to Boxer's car. It was still the only vehicle there, but somehow that didn't reassure her as much as it should have.

"What are you doing?" Angie shrieked. "Go on to the next driveway."

Although Liss's every instinct cried out to do exactly that, she shut off the engine and killed the headlights. "Listen to me, Angie. You can't go charging in like the cavalry. We need to creep up quietly and stay out of sight. That way, we should be able to see Eldridge, if he's there, before he realizes we're back."

Her face set in hard, determined lines, Angie got out of the car. "Let's go, then. I have to get my children out of there."

As Liss fumbled for the flashlight she kept under the driver's-side seat, her common sense, somewhat belatedly, reasserted itself. Acting on impulse could end disastrously for them all. She was convinced that Martin Eldridge was a cold-blooded killer who had stabbed two people, one of them fatally, and if what she'd gathered from Gordon and Sherri was accurate, he'd walked off with Jason Graye's gun. He was armed, dangerous, and desperate enough to attack anyone who tried to stop him from taking his revenge.

One horrifying scenario after another unfolding in her mind, Liss scrambled to catch up with Angie. She'd had to stop at the tree line in order to look for the all-but-invisible opening that was their end of the path. When Liss joined her there, Angie grabbed the flashlight out of her hand. The beam moved erratically, but it took only a moment for her to pick out the break between two towering pines. Angie set off at a trot.

Liss caught her arm. "We can't afford to do anything stupid."

Angie shook her off and increased her speed. "You do whatever you want. I'm going after Beth and Bradley."

Fearful that their voices would carry and alert Eldridge to their presence, Liss spoke in a whisper. "We've got back-up coming. You need to wait for them."

Sherri was on her way. So was Murch.

Angie made a strangled sound that Liss belatedly recognized as a laugh. "There's the pot calling the kettle black."

Liss knew she deserved the rebuke. She'd been known to rush in when she shouldn't . . . in the past. She hoped she'd matured since then. At least she had sense enough to know that this situation was fraught with peril. As Angie plowed forward, moving ever deeper into the trees, Liss hurried after her.

"Angie, think! If he's in there with a gun, you don't want to do anything to make *him* act impulsively."

"Shut up, Liss."

Liss opened her mouth and then closed it again. Angie was only throwing her own advice back at her. They needed to be quiet as little field mice. In the still night air, every sound was magnified.

The flashlight might also give away their presence, but without it they couldn't find their way along the narrow, twisting path. Angie must have had the same thought, because she shifted the direction of the beam until it was aimed at the ground. Silently, walking single file, Liss followed her as she stepped over gnarled roots and protruding rocks. Every step brought them closer to the camp where they'd left Boxer, Beth, and Bradley.

Angie turned the flashlight off just before they rounded

the last twist in the path. Still sheltered by the trees, she stopped at the edge of the clearing. Liss came silently up beside her. She had a clear view of the side of the camp with the stairs leading up to the deck and the sliding glass door. The interior was well lit, making it possible to see part of the living room.

Someone moved in front of a lamp, causing Liss's breath to catch. His size and shape, even in silhouette—and the fact that he had a cane tucked under one arm—gave away his identity.

"Eldridge." Angie's voice shook as she spoke his name.

Liss caught her arm, preventing her from rushing out into the open. "Wait."

"I don't dare. Look."

Eldridge had turned, one hand raised. What he held in it was unmistakable—a gun.

Sherri turned the Moosetookalook police cruiser onto the dirt road, squinting to see better. Her headlights didn't add much to the visibility when trees grew close to the shoulder on both sides.

At one time or another, as Moosetookalook's chief of police, she had patrolled every rut-filled, one-lane cow path in her jurisdiction. She knew exactly where Patsy's camp was located and where Angie and her kids had been hiding out. What she didn't know going into this situation was how volatile it was. She'd heard nothing more from Angie and Liss since the frantic phone call Angie had made en route.

Sherri had already alerted both the sheriff's department and the state police, but for the moment she was on her own. She'd wait for backup if she could. If Eldridge was already at the camp, the best-case scenario was a hostage situation. She didn't even want to think about what the worst-case scenario would be.

The cruiser's lights picked out the back of Liss's car parked next to Boxer's old clunker and instantly showed her that no one was sitting inside either of them. So much for the vain hope that Liss and Angie would wait for her!

The presence on the scene of two emotionally involved civilians was a complication Sherri did not need. The odds that either Angie or Liss would do something stupid were way too high for her peace of mind.

It was only after she'd slowed to a stop that she spotted two more vehicles. Both pickup trucks, they had been parked haphazardly partway down the driveway that led to Patsy's lakeside camp. One, clearly the first to arrive, since the other now blocked it in, was light-colored but angled so that Sherri couldn't get a good look at it. She had no such difficulty identifying the other one. Red and dilapidated-looking, it sported a vanity plate reading MURCH PI.

Murch himself emerged from the surrounding darkness the moment she stepped out of the cruiser. "I don't know where to go from here. I've been looking around, but there's no one in the camp."

"Wrong camp," Sherri said. "Looks like we'd best approach the other one through the woods." Clearly, that was what everyone else had done.

She set off at a trot, flashlight in one hand and the other resting on the firearm holstered on her utility belt. Murch was right behind her.

"There's something you should know," he said as they ran. "Eldridge has been in a mental institution for most of the last twelve years. Word is that he's obsessed with revenge."

Since she already had an inkling of how dangerous Martin Eldridge was, Sherri wasn't entirely surprised by this news. Still, Murch's words sent a chill straight to the marrow of her bones. She had dealt before with people who were off their meds. There was no way to predict how they'd react. At any moment, she expected to hear a volley of gunshots blast through the stillness of the evening.

She lobbed a question over her shoulder, careful to keep her voice low. "Did you see anyone else around when you got here?"

"Not a soul."

Driven by a renewed sense of urgency, Sherri ran on.

This is crazy.

Against her better judgment, Liss followed Angie as she circled the camp to the entrance that faced the road. She breathed a sigh of relief when she saw that there were no lights on in the kitchen. She was less sure how she felt when Angie turned the knob and the door silently swung open. It didn't matter. She was committed. A moment later, both women slipped inside.

Angie froze at the sound of Martin Eldridge's smooth, polished voice.

Standing just behind her, Liss started to sweat. The sense of what Eldridge was saying was lost to the roaring in her ears. The hammering of her heart was nearly as loud. She swallowed convulsively, willing her legs, which had gone rubbery, to carry her to their right, into the shelter of the camp's bathroom.

Angie's plan was simple, and she was determined to carry it out, with Liss or without her. The bath in this camp, as in Patsy's, had a second door that led into the downstairs bedroom. That room also had two doors. The other one opened into the living room at the opposite end from where Eldridge was standing. When they got that far, they should be able to see Boxer, Beth, and Bradley.

If all three young people were unharmed, Liss prayed she could persuade Angie to pull back and wait for reinforcements. At the least, they needed to take enough time to assess the situation.

Angie eased the bathroom door closed as soon as Liss was safely inside, leaving them in inky blackness. Only the soft swishing sound her sandals made on the tiled floor allowed Liss to track her friend's progress toward the door to the bedroom.

It creaked when she opened it, a noise loud enough to send new waves of panic shuddering through Liss's body. She held her breath, but nothing happened. No one at the front of the house had heard the sound.

The door on the other side of the bedroom was already ajar. The light of a table lamp seeped inside, spreading its golden glow far enough to reveal a treacherous obstacle course. Angie, who had been sleeping in this room for more than a week, had never been a paragon of neatness, but she knew where to step to avoid discarded shoes, piles of dirty clothing, and a paperback book she'd apparently tossed aside. Liss, trailing after her, narrowly avoided cracking her shin on the edge of the hope chest positioned at the foot of the bed.

They both stopped short when they saw what lay beyond the door. Only a small section of the living room was visible, but it included the back half of one of the chairs. Liss recognized the person sitting in it by her dark hair, even though she couldn't see Beth's face. She felt her stomach clench and her mouth go dry. Eldridge had used a clothesline to tie Angie's daughter to the chair.

Angie backed up a step, her fist going to her mouth to prevent any sound from escaping. In the dim glow from the lamp, her eyes looked haunted.

Motioning for her friend to stay back, Liss leaned to one side, hoping to see farther into the living room. Beth didn't appear to be hurt. There was no blood. And as Liss stared at her bound hands, she saw Beth's fingers twitch.

Eldridge's soft voice had not paused once since Liss and Angie had entered the house. It was only now, however, that Liss was able to make out what he was saying. He was describing, in graphic detail, how he intended to kill the three young people he held prisoner.

He wasn't going to shoot them. Oh, no. He intended to make them suffer, especially Beth. A shudder of revulsion passed through her as he listed the torments he had in mind for his victims.

Hearing what he planned to do to her children cost Angie what little self-control she had left. With a cry of mingled anguish and rage, she charged past Liss, making a beeline for her daughter.

Eldridge's gun went off a second before Liss could follow her.

Still hidden from view, she froze, terrified of running straight into the path of a bullet. Moving only her eyes, she searched for Angie.

By some miracle, the bullet had scored a gash in the wall but missed her friend. Angie had thrown herself to the floor behind Beth's chair. Now, working with frantic, clumsy fingers, she struggled to undo the knots in the clothesline.

"Come out to where I can see you!" Eldridge bellowed.

With rapid but cautious steps, praying a man who killed with a knife was a novice when it came to handling firearms, Liss retreated. While Eldridge was distracted, she might have a chance to get behind him. She wasn't certain how much good that would do. She doubted she was strong enough to tackle and disarm him, but she had to do something to prevent him from slaughtering everyone in the living room.

She only stumbled once, tripping over a pair of running shoes, before she made it back to the bath. Then she was in the kitchen, and Eldridge was still unaware of her presence. She could hear him yelling at Angie to stand up and show herself, but at least he was not shooting at her.

Was it too much to hope that he might be out of ammunition?

There was enough light from the living area to reveal the countertop between the sink and the refrigerator. Liss looked around for a weapon. A knife. A cast-iron frying pan. Anything. But in contrast to the bedroom Angie had been using, the kitchen was as neat as a pin. There was not a single useful object in sight.

Liss didn't waste time searching through cabinets and drawers. Taking a deep breath, she headed into the living room. If she was going to get the jump on Eldridge, she had to do it now.

A half dozen steps brought her level with the door to the deck. Just as she passed it, she heard it slide open. She gasped as two people rushed inside.

One headed straight for Martin Eldridge.

The other grabbed her and hauled her back into the relative safety of the kitchen.

The gun went off for the second time just as Liss realized it was Dan who held her and stopped struggling.

"Stay here," he ordered, and ran toward the sound.

Ignoring the command, she followed close at his heels. As she rounded the corner into the living area, the gun skidded past her to slide beneath an end table. Liss had to go up on her toes to avoid being hit by it. Perched like that, she gaped at the scene before her eyes.

Eldridge lay sprawled on his back on the floor. The sharp blade that had been concealed in his cane was pressed against his throat, poised to slice into him if he so much as twitched.

"I ought to gut you like a fish," Dolores Mayfield said. "Do you have any idea how much trouble you've caused me?"

Dolores?

Liss had barely grasped the fact of the librarian's presence when the sliding glass door opened again. This time Sherri Campbell and Jake Murch came through the opening.

Sherri's shock at seeing Dolores appeared to be as great as Liss's had been, but that didn't prevent her from holstering her service revolver and taking out her handcuffs. While she read her prisoner his rights, Murch relieved Dolores of her weapon. Dan retrieved the gun. Liss came down off her toes and went to help Angie untie the hostages.

All three young people were unharmed, although Boxer was mad as a wet hen that he hadn't been able to do a better job of protecting Beth and her little brother. As soon as they'd been freed, Liss returned to Dan's side. When he took her into his arms once more, she could feel how badly his hands were shaking. He buried his face in her neck, squeezing her so tightly that she had to push gently at his shoulders to give herself room to breathe.

"How did you get here?" she whispered when he loosened his hold. "And with Dolores, of all people?"

He had to clear his throat before he could answer. "I was just pulling into our driveway after giving Sam a hand when Dolores came barreling across the street from the municipal building. She climbed right into the passenger seat of my truck and told me to get a move on. She said we had to get out to Ledge Lake pronto because my wife was headed for disaster."

"So you *went*? I thought you were the sensible one in the family." With the danger safely avoided, Liss suddenly felt euphoric enough to tease him about his actions.

A wry smile tugged at the corner of Dan's mouth. "I hoped she was exaggerating. Besides, Dolores said Sherri was already on her way. Then she repeated everything she'd heard in the parking lot. To tell you the truth, I wasn't sure how much of it to believe, but I wasn't about to take any chances, not where your safety was concerned."

"I don't get it," Murch interrupted. "Why was Ms. Mayfield so ticked off at Eldridge?"

"I can answer for myself, thank you very much," Dolores said, coming up beside them and snatching the sword stick back from Murch.

"Well?"

"It's his fault Roger and I were suspected of murder."

"That's it?" Murch's face wore an incredulous look.

"Isn't that enough? I wonder if the police will let me have this for my collection." With a twist of the wrist she engaged the mechanism that exposed the blade hidden in Eldridge's cane, once again turning it into the deadly weapon that had been used to kill Jason Graye and wound Kent Humphrey.

Murch took a prudent step away from her.

"He *shot* at you, Dolores," Liss said, struggling to reconstruct what had taken place during those few seconds when Dan had prevented her from seeing what was happening. "You could have been killed."

The complacent smile on Dolores's face was very nearly a smirk. "On the contrary. It only took me a moment to spot this cane for what it really is and grab it from under his arm. When he swung around to face me, I used it to smack his wrist. The gun went off as it flew out of his hand." She shrugged. "No big deal. The bullet didn't come close to hitting me. By the time I kicked the gun out of reach, he was already off balance. All it took was a good shove to send him to the floor. Then I popped the blade out to convince him to *stay* down. Easy peasy."

Liss couldn't help herself. She started to laugh.

On Monday morning, even though she had been up late the night before to answer questions for the state police, Liss opened Moosetookalook Scottish Emporium at the usual time. If their little town was going to be subjected to reporters, curiosity seekers, and other vultures, she reasoned that she might as well make a few bucks out of the deal. That would go a long way toward making up for the inconvenience of answering their rude and intrusive questions.

All in all, Liss was in a very good mood. Angie had already announced that she planned to rebuild the bookstore when the insurance cleared. The library was on track to stay open, thanks to all the new fund-raising ideas people had come up with and Dolores's decision to run for the empty seat on the board of selectmen. Most important of all, both Martin Eldridge and his shady PI were behind bars and destined to stay there.

When the bell over the door jangled, Liss looked up with a welcoming smile on her face. It took a concentrated effort to keep it there when she recognized Angus Grant and his wife.

Grant was his usual unpleasant self. This time his complaint had to do with how many *sasunnach* had attended the Highland Games. The Gaelic word, meaning anyone who was not Scottish, was traditionally applied in a derogatory way to those of English descent. Liss wasn't quite certain what Grant meant by it and did not feel inclined to ask.

His wife, however, had come to the Emporium with her own agenda. She purchased several pieces of Grant clan crest jewelry, a shawl in the Grant tartan, and a pewter figurine of a piper.

"Why don't you wait for me outside, dear," she suggested as Liss began to ring up the sale. "Turn the air on in the car so it won't be so stuffy."

As soon as the door closed behind him, she leaned across the sales counter and said, in a sympathetic voice, "I hope you haven't let Angus's carping bother you."

"Everyone has a right to his or her opinions."

"How diplomatic." Mrs. Grant smiled, making a dimple pop out in her cheek. "Shall I let you in on a little secret?"

"If you like." Liss returned her credit card and tucked her receipt into the bright red bag that contained her purchases.

"Angus doesn't know this, you understand. It would hurt him terribly if he ever found out."

It took a moment for Liss to realize what Mrs. Grant was waiting for. "I swear I won't repeat anything you tell me," she promised.

Grant's wife nodded. Her expression was serene, her voice amused. "I have done considerable research on every branch of my husband's family tree. Because of his surname, he believes with all his heart that his people came to this country from Scotland. The truth is somewhat different."

She picked up the red bag and moved toward the exit. At the door, her hand on the knob, she stopped and looked back over her shoulder.

"Not a single one of his ancestors ever traveled north of Yorkshire. Yes, my dear, you heard me correctly. Angus Grant is pure *sasunnach*."